Cells of Knowledge

Cells of Knowledge

Sian Hayton

NEW AMSTERDAM
New York

Copyright © by Sian Hayton 1989
All rights reserved.

First published in the United States of America in 1990 by
NEW AMSTERDAM BOOKS
171 Madison Avenue
New York, NY 10016
by arrangement with Polygon, Edinburgh.

The author would like to acknowledge
the assistance of Mr. Patrick Parsons, M. A.

The Library of Congress Cataloging-in-Publication Data is available.

ISBN 0-56131-000-X

This book is printed on acid-free paper.

Printed in the United States of America.

SCENE

An icy blast from the hide-covered door blew across his back as he squatted on the floor and a stone drove into his left buttock. Inwardly the youth cursed these yokels who could not even produce a chair for an honoured guest, and waited, as he had been taught, for the old man to speak first. From the far dim corner of the tent where the old woman was sitting came a sound that could have been laughter, but he could not be certain. He could not even be sure there was anyone in the huddle of sheepskins, blankets and cloaks heaped round the sides of the tent. Only the twirling of a spindle betrayed the presence of the woman. He found his eyes drawn toward the movement but controlled himself hastily. His father had told him these people venerated their women so much that a stranger staring at them invited death. It was said that they kept their faces hidden even from their husbands, and from the glimpse he had had of a mass of dull brown hair, he could believe it.

'They're probably all as ugly as ogres,' he thought. He fixed the manly scowl deeper into his brow and attended to the old man, who had at last started to speak.

'We have been living like this for nine generations, now, and the curse of our ancestors has ripened.' His voice was faint and shrill like the wind in moorland grass, and Kilidh had to lean forward to hear him. The old man whispered,'We should never have listened to the strangers, the men from the north with the bracken-red hair, the men from the south with the flax-white hair, the men from the west with hair like ravens, black. It was always the same. Wherever they came from they told us the same lies. That if we would give up our wandering ways and sit at peace they would protect us from our enemies, and bring us salt and grains in exchange for our tribute and service. Life would be so much better, they said, if we called them king. They even sent one of their magicians with the cross of the tortured god who told us the same thing. So we sat still, and we built houses by cutting the earth that had given us safe passage, we paid tribute, and we sent our young men to stranger's wars, but life got no better.

'And our ancestors deserted us, and come no more to the holy places.'

He closed his eyes and started to sing. Kilidh's blood ran cold in his veins at the sound for it was well known that the singing of this old man had great magic and could leave you weak for days. He started to look

1

at the woman for help, but lowered his eyes before they fell on the great cone of hair hanging round her.

Feigning tiredness Kilidh rested his arms on his knees, put his head down on them and stared at the beaten earth floor until the old man started to speak again.

'Now it comes at last that we need the protection of our Lord and he can do nothing for us. He sends us a boy and a few men at arms to save us from a whole nation.' Kilidh's patience snapped.

'I told your man we knew nothing about this. Your messengers, if you sent any, never reached us.'

From across the floor he heard a hissing intake of breath and the spindle stopped moving. He clamped his lips shut, and knew himself for a fool. His first diplomatic mission and he was losing his temper at a tribal chief and shaman!

'It's as well they're only a crowd of savages,' he thought.

The old man had closed his eyes at the offence and now sat silent. A thumb nail like deer horn scratched at the edge of his lumpy fur cloak. Kilidh realised with a mixture of amusement and disgust that the cloak was made of hundreds of mouse skins sewn together. He started to calculate the work involved in producing such a garment but gave it up to stare at the rest of the tent. Now that his eyes had got used to the gloom he could see that the hide walls were hung with dried plants and bones which had been bleached and strange marks drawn on them. In the corner, behind the woman, stood a stone-weighted loom. Leaning against it was a short iron spear with a blackened shaft. He realised now that the clothes stuffed into the corners of the tent were to keep draughts out. The floor was covered with rubbish in varying stages of decomposition, and that, together with the greasy smoke from the lamp, composed the stench which had nearly unmanned him when he walked in. The chief took up his theme again. The spindle resumed its motion.

'It comes to this — our oldest enemy, the Fir Falbh, never surrendered their lives to foreigners, and still wander the high land as free men. But last winter their ancient road through the glen Shuileach was flooded and has become a quagmire. I have taken the signs and find beyond doubt that it was the word of an avenging ancestor of theirs. Now they must travel by another road, that takes them through our grazing land, and we must fight them for it, or our name will be filth in the mouths of those who come after. And who shall fight for us when all our champions have been taken for the king's warband? We are a cursed people!'

The singing began again, and the youth ground his teeth in impatience. He had heard all this from the chieftain's man who had met them on the way. His training at his uncle's house had been adequate, however, and he kept silent in the presence of an elder. Fortunately the chief was anxious to make his point, and he began again after only two verses.

'Tomorrow I must take the field myself, as champion of my people. Alone I will stand on the sacred hide and alone I will meet the strength of our enemy. If I fail, and it is likely that I will, my tribe will stand without a chief. Three sons I had and three sons I lost at Dun Brynan when Owain called on us.'

The old man stood, and for all his years the movement was as lithe and swift as a fox. The spindle stopped. The hair on Kilidh's neck crawled as the old man looked at him for the first time, and his eyes shone like black sloes.

'Now I put this geas on you and all your family to the ninth generation.'

Suddenly the old man's voice was clear and rang like a bell. It carried through the walls of the tent to every hut in the settlement.

'If tomorrow my spirit should leave this body and never return you will take my tribe, and you will treat them as your own, as free men, not as slaves. You will take them as your family; you will give them your name and your countenance, and their troubles will be yours from now until the ninth generation stands in your hall. If you fail in this your name will be a stink in the nostrils of every people in Alban. Now leave us. You will see me tomorrow at the field of battle.'

Kilidh backed out of the tent into the blinding sunshine of high morning. His father's thegn helped him upright. Down the hill the under-steward was inspecting bundles of hides laid out on benches. Some of the tribesmen were looking eagerly at the bags of salt and grain Kilidh and his men had brought with them, and more locals were approaching from the east with baskets of berries. The soldier watched them warily out of habit.

'Did you hear what he said?' asked Kilidh.

'I think they heard it in the next valley,' replied the other, 'and that's just what he wanted.'

'It's not fair. I shall complain to the king at the next court. We weren't back in this country until two years ago. What's it got to do with me that his sons were killed at Dun Brynan? I was still in my mother's hall then.'

'I was fighting for Athelstan in that campaign,' replied the warrior drily, 'I may have done the deed myself.'

Kilidh sighed.

'I wish we had never left Gwynedd. Just because Maelcolum is a distant kinsman and wanted his men on the ground we had to pack up and run back north.'

'I think I see a couple of fine wolf-skins down there.' said the Dane suddenly, 'I don't know how these people do it.' He started down the hill to the booth, and Kilidh followed him.

'Before you start grumbling to king or under-king,' said the soldier quietly, 'there is something you should consider. A small tribe whose loyalty is to yourself alone might not be the bother you think. Bear in mind the fact that you have two brothers, younger than yourself, but not by much and as strong and generous as you. These tribesmen might not be great warriors in a pitched battle, but for blood-feud, they're hard to beat. Those bare feet of theirs are like rocks. And though the boys are small, in a couple of years they'll toughen up nicely.'

'My brothers are being fostered back in Gwynedd,' muttered Kilidh, 'and will probably elect to stay there. And suppose I do take the people under my protection? I will still have to find them land and food and maintain them. I'll have to settle disputes and go hunting for them, and find husbands for the women. And they're as greedy as any for plunder. No. I'm not in any position to do all that.'

'Only think about it, little father,' said the Dane, and Kilidh scowled.

'The old man's not dead yet.'

The next morning dawned cloudy, and before long the tops of the hills were covered in curtains of rain. The handful of tribesmen appeared with spears and set off to a flat place up the glen with a bundle of hides and twigs. Some time passed while Kilidh and his men packed up their tribute goods and checked their horses. Then a cry went up from the chief's tent and women and children came running from the little turf huts. Kilidh looked up to see what the noise was about and saw a knot of men coming over the pass to the north.

'Is that the ancient enemy?' he asked the Dane.

'Undoubtedly,' replied the other. As if to prove it the chief appeared from the tent naked but for his mouse-skin cloak, a small round shield in one hand and a club in the other.

'Why has he no sword?' asked Kilidh quietly.

'These people won't use metal for some things,' said the Dane and shrugged.

The chief's woman followed him out of the tent and began a war chant which was taken up by the others. Kilidh shivered and some of his men made warding signs.

The chief stood watching the approach of his enemy, his lips moving silently. Just then the rain stopped, and the sun shone brightly on the hillside where the battlefield had been prepared. The women fell silent; from the approaching enemy there came a faint cheering.

'Let's go to the guest house,' said the Dane. 'This is nothing to do with us.'

'I hate that hole,' said Kilidh, 'and besides, this may have a great deal to do with me.'

'As you wish,' said the Dane, and led the other men over to the long hut.

At last the enemy arrived at the battlefield, but the chief did not move. Both groups of tribesmen squatted talking noisily to each other for a long time. The sun came and went and raindrops sparkled in the grass. The chief and the women watched. Then, just as Kilidh grew weary and thought of joining his men in the guest house, all the men stood up and separated, and the chief started up the hill.

The women resumed their war chant, but some of them were weeping.

'They've had their sign,' thought Kilidh. 'They know the old man is going to die.'

He was surprised to find himself weeping also, and wiped his face covertly with his hands.

After that things happened swiftly. When the chief arrived at the battle-field another man stepped forward from the enemy as champion. He too carried a club and was naked but for a cloak which shimmered in the sunlight. They exchanged brief challenges and Kilidh saw that the other man was much younger than the chief. Then the chief bowed his head, the other raised his club and smashed his skull completely with one blow.

Kilidh ran to the guest house, and the keening of the women followed him.

The old man's stone coffin had been carved for him many years before. The tribesmen lugged it to the battlefield on a wooden sled and the body was loaded into it to the wailing of the women. The enemy tribesmen lent a hand to carry it to the top of the nearby hill, where it was tucked in among the stones there. Then all except a few women returned to the settlement and joined in the wake.

'I wonder if I should pay our respects to the mourners?'

'Leave it till they come down from the hillside,' said the Dane. 'I doubt if they will like a stranger and a man around at such a time. Come and have a drink. They've unearthed some wicked stuff for this occasion.'

Some hours and several drinks later Kilidh realised that the wild-haired figures had left the top of the hill.

'I have to see about this,' he muttered to himself, and made for the tent. The chief's woman was sitting in the doorway alone, her hair gathered round her. With confidence bestowed by the mead Kilidh was sure she was waiting to speak to him. He squatted down in front of her.

'I'm sorry for your trouble, lady,' he said. She made no reply.

'I know everyone must die, and for a warrior to die in battle is the best thing that can happen to him. But. . . I'm going to sound like an oaf. . . it all seemed so. . . maybe it's just your way of doing things, but it was . . .very. . . simple. Not enough ceremony. It's a shame for the old man.' And he wept the easy tears of drunkenness, his shoulders shaking with sobs. After a moment he realised he was being foolish, and wiped his face on his sleeve. He drew a long breath and looked at the woman: what he saw added more to his confusion.

The long hair was pushed aside and he was looking clear at darklashed eyes the colour of wood violets; feathery black eyebrows; cheeks brushed with rose; a small, fine-boned nose with gold-dust freckles on the bridge; a mouth of deeper rose, smiling to show white teeth; a neck as long and slender as a peeled willow wand; a white, blue-veined breast, and small, high, conical paps tipped with rose.

Kilidh felt his face burning, then terror ripped through him. He looked all round him for the vengeful man with the knife he was sure was waiting for him to move, but he could see no-one. The whole settlement was indoors. He felt his hand taken and placed over a soft mound of skin. He felt a small hardening under his palm. He was drawn into the tent.

A little time later he said,

'But you're a virgin! I thought the old man was your. . .'

'He was my grandfather.'

And whenever he thought back to those times, those were the only words of hers he could recall.

Kilidh was wakened by the sound of horses stamping and snorting close to his head. He snatched up the first garment he could find and pushed his head out of the tent, where he was embarrassed to see his men with horses saddled and laden, his cloak and arms on one, and beyond them the whole tribe standing with bundles on their backs. The men carried spears and shields, and the women in hooded tunics carried the smaller children. He pulled the cloak around him and stood up. A moan from the tribesmen warned him of something and he looked down. He was wearing the mouse-skin cloak.

'What's going on?' he shouted to the Dane.

'We'd better move off, little father,' he answered mildly. 'We have a long way to go, and we will make poor time with the clan here on foot.' Kilidh marched up to him.

'I haven't agreed to anything,' he hissed.

'Oh, yes, you have. You've seen the nakedness of their queen, and if you turn aside now you are dead. And so, for that matter, are we. So, if you don't mind, we'll take your new tribe, and get started. Or do I have to kill you myself?'

'My father will hear of this,' Kilidh snarled.

'Indeed he will,' was the bland reply.

While they had been talking some of the women had entered the tent and Kilidh heard shouts of joy. Then other women stepped forward and pushed their heads through the doorway and their squeals were added to the growing racket. The men smirked.

'My clothes,' shouted Kilidh, and started for the tent. The Dane's iron grip on his shoulder stopped him.

'Wait!' he snapped. 'They know what's necessary.'

Just then a hooded figure detached itself from the small crowd round the doorway and handed Kilidh his shirt, mail-shirt and drawers. Summoning the remains of his dignity he retired to the guest house, seized the few pieces of food he found there, and dressed. When he emerged, he saw that the tent was down, and strapped to one of his horses. The queen stood waiting by another. Without another word he mounted and lifted her up behind him.

From the clan there came a sigh.

'Your people travel easily,' said the Dane. 'You wouldn't think they gave up being nomads years ago. Tonight we'll stop at the edge of the hills and then it's an easy walk home.'

Kilidh yawned. Three nights in the tent with his young queen were beginning to take a toll on him.

'I hope the weather stays fine,' he said, 'I don't like that last few miles through the swamp.'

'This late in summer it's usually dry.' The Dane looked round the campsite. 'What's happening now?' he said indignantly. 'The tent is still standing. Why are those women standing with their heads together? They should be taking it down.'

Kilidh looked up and saw a cluster of hooded shapes which he had learned to identify as the older women. They were talking to the queen animatedly and with much nodding. By and by they beckoned to one of the tribesmen who approached with bowed head, listened to them then turned and came over to Kilidh. He bowed and said,

'The decision is that we should stay here.'

Kilidh jolted awake.

'What do you mean?'

'We are not going any further. We will not go to your father's stronghold. We will stay here. There is good grazing. There is good water. There is a fine, flat place to build a village. There is even much timber. We are off the road of our enemies. What is the use of going further?'

'I have to get back to my father's hall, and tell him what has happened. We're already late and he will be looking for the goods we're bringing.'

He could hear his father's derision already. 'I send you on a few day's journey and you take over a week. You've done no trading — the tribute's pathetic, and what's more you bring the whole clan traipsing at your back. I knew I shouldn't have sent you. You haven't half the sense of your brother half your age...' and so forth. He flinched.

'Go and tell them to strike camp at once, or the warriors will make sure they do.'

The man said nothing but turned and waved his spear. At the signal the whole tribe ran together and sat down in front of the tent.

'You seem to have a problem,' observed the Dane.

'Tell the men to surround them and draw their swords. I'll show them who's chief.'

'That won't make them move,' said the Dane, 'especially if you threaten the queen. And then what will you do? Have your paid soldiers fight the men and slaughter the women?'

'That could be done,' said Kilidh savagely.

'Don't be a fool. Remember the geas. You can be sure the other clansmen know of it, and if you kill these people while they're under your protection your name will be reviled from here to Vinland. I'd see to it myself.'

'Why are you so keen to see me chief of this tribe? Do you see yourself as my table-companion when we get driven out of Kyil?'

'It could be a pleasant way to spend my last years, it's true. I'll get no more promotion in your father's house. But that's not the point now. You cannot move your people by force; you cannot kill them and hope to salvage your reputation afterwards; you will have to use guile.'

'I've only seen sixteen winters,' said Kilidh, 'and guile has not had time to come to me. Will you help me?'

'Of course I will. Not just because your father pays me. You're a good boy, and one day you'll be a good leader. Let's go and find some fresh meat, and leave the clan to scratch for a while.'

The forest above the camp was dark and dense and unusually silent. Kilidh, the Dane and two of the thegns struggled for an hour and made little distance.

'Odin's cock!' shouted the Dane, and wiped the sweat from his face, 'there's boar here — I can smell it, and I'm not leaving till I find it!'

'Odin's shit,' answered Gwalchmai, his next in command, 'the boar is more likely to find us first!'

'Either way, I intend to eat roast meat tonight! Let's try that thicket over there. Kilidh, you're the lightest, you go round to the far side and beat for us. We'll wait here. Drive him to us!'

Kilidh did as he was told, but with very bad grace. He resented the way the Dane had taken command of everything without blinking. As he ripped at the underbrush he briefly enjoyed imagining it was the Dane whose body he was breaking up till a sound ahead of him froze him to the spot. He stood, taut as a bowstring, turning his head to find the sound again. Then behind him he heard a crashing, shouts and a terrible squeal. 'It's the young ones!' he thought. Then there was laughter, and a yell of triumph.

'Have you caught something?' he shouted. 'What did you get?'

There was no reply and the silence deepened round him. Suddenly it seemed the forest was even darker.

'Answer me!' he cried. Nothing.

Again ahead of him he heard a sound. It was like the rushing of wind or the roaring of water, but faint. And silence fell again.

'Is there anyone there?' he said to hear his own voice.

After a long pause a voice came to him, so deep and loud the ground shook under him. 'What are you doing in my forest?' it said. 'Why are you hunting without my leave?'

Kilidh's mouth seemed sealed shut. He felt his legs turning to water under him, and clung to a low branch for support.

'Sir,' he managed at last, though he could hardly believe this obsequious whine was his. 'Forgive us, sir, we thought this was free hunting ground. That is, we are on the king's business and we thought it our right to take what we needed.'

'The king is nothing to me. This is my forest and has been for time out of mind.'

10

'I apologise, naturally, for myself and for my men. We will of course pay recompense for any animals we have killed. We did what we have done out of ignorance, not insolence.'

'What use would your silver be to me?' said the voice, laughing.

Kilidh began to feel less afraid now he thought he had only an indignant magnate to deal with. 'Who are you? Show yourself,' he said and started to move forward.

'Stay where you are!' commanded the voice, and Kilidh froze again. 'You must know that you are speaking to no ordinary man. My appearance is so terrible that any who look at it know a fear which lives with them to the end of their days. One glimpse of my terrible aspect and your mind may even shatter into madness, and death would be a welcome waking from a nightmare.'

Kilidh found that he had to hold the branch again. 'If you would show me the way back to the valley with the lochan, I will cease to trouble you.'

'You are with the mouse people? I do not recall seeing you before.'

'The old chief died, and I was taken as the queen's husband.'

'I wondered what had brought them to move again. You are the new chief?'

'It was not my decision, believe me.'

'No matter. You must look after them now, though you are a poor choice for them.'

'I'll do my best for them, of course.'

'I can see I must send you back. Turn yourself around and look for an oak tree standing by itself. Do you see it?'

Kilidh turned and saw. 'Only stand beside it and from there you will see the valley and your clan and a track leading to them.'

'Thanks,' said Kilidh, and then a thought struck him. 'I would like to ask you a question. You see, I have a problem with the. . . my people and you may be able to help me.'

'Ask, then, but I warn you, for my help there may be a price you would not like to pay.'

'You seem to know these people,' Kilidh began eagerly, 'and I do not. I am trying to get back to my father's fortress but they sat down and refused to move this morning. They say they like this valley and want to stay here. But I can't have it. I can't abandon them, so I can't get back home. Can you think of some way to get them to move?'

'That will be easy,' said the voice. 'Do you sleep with your men tonight and keep away from the tent. I will visit the queen tonight, and she will be so filled with fear that in the morning nothing will persuade her to stay. You can be on your way tomorrow.'

'God bless you, my Lord,' cried Kilidh. 'I shall be always in your debt.'

'Keep your blessings. And discharge your debt to me as I wish.'
'Tell me your wish, and I shall do it.'

That night they ate roast sucking pigs. Kilidh excused himself from the
queen's tent by pleading tiredness, which was no less than the truth.
The next morning he woke early and watched the door of the tent like
a dog at a rat-hole. He was not disappointed. Very soon he saw the
oldest woman who acted as servant to the queen in some fashion. She
ran from the tent as if Fenris wolf were after her and moved among
the sleeping clan, waking them and wringing her hands over them as
though the end of the world were at hand. So disturbed was she that
she had let her hood fall back and Kilidh saw her face. She was not
very ugly, merely old.

To his delight the tribe at once roused itself and began to prepare
for the road. The elderwomen ran up to the tent and began to take it
down, and one of the men came to speak to him.

'We must go today,' he said, his face curd-white with fear, 'this is a
very bad place.'

'Now that is a pity,' said Kilidh, 'I am starting to like it here. The
hunting is very good.'

'We cannot stay!' said the man and his voice cracked in fear. 'The
queen has had a dream and her dreams are our guide. Last night she
saw a demon, the great demon who lives in the forest. He told her we
cannot stay or he will destroy us all. We will go now.'

And, forgetting his manners, he turned and fled up the hill to his
flustered companions. Kilidh woke his own men who, though surprised
by the turn of events, made ready to leave swiftly.

Kilidh was pleased with himself, and even more pleased to see the
Dane watching him curiously throughout the day's ride. He hugged
his secret to himself until that evening when they pitched camp.
He stood outside the tent for a moment, enjoying the view over
the plains which led to his home and saw with satisfaction the
reddening of the trees and the yellowing of the grass far below
him. He saw the silver line of sea and above it haze hid the land
beyond.

The Dane came to him to report that the camp was ready for the
night and the watches set.

'A fine sight, sir,' he said, nodding at the view.

'Yes, indeed,' smirked Kilidh, 'and one I despaired of seeing yesterday.'

'You must truly have learned Odin's guile to get the people to leave
so promptly, sir.'

'It was not Odin's guile, but Odin himself who helped me.'

'It isn't good to make a sport of such things,' said the Dane, frowning.

'I'm serious enough. While we were out hunting that day I met a demon in the forest who said he owned the land. I told him I was lost and, invoking the Saviour, I compelled him to help me. He resisted of course, but I stood up to him, and asked him also what to do about the mouse people. He promised me he would visit the queen that night and frighten her so that she would be happy to leave, and, as you see, he did.'

'That was not well done,' said the Dane sombrely as the light about them faded. 'Such monsters do nothing for mortals without taking heavy payment.'

'He asked me for payment,' said Kilidh, shrugging, 'but before I pay he will have to find me and I was wise enough not to tell him where I live.'

'Wise you certainly were not. Did you really think you can dupe a demon like that? What was the penalty?'

'He wants me to send my first-born son to be fostered with him. It's not important.'

'Worse and worse,' cried the Dane, 'if the child survives his fostering, and I doubt he will, you will have allied yourself to a demon's family for eternity, and your family will be plagued by him for generations.'

'What if we lose a child? The woman I am to marry is young and healthy, and so am I. We will have plenty of children. And if the child survives and the demon continues to pester us, we will have the support of the Saviour's church to combat him.'

'I have lived too long,' said the Dane, and the last light of the sun carved the shadows deep on his face. 'I do not believe that good can come out of bad. Too many men have died for that. Foolish boy — even the mighty saints of your church knew they took their lives in their hands when they went out to conquer demons.'

'I can take care of myself, and those who depend on me,' said Kilidh, and went into the tent.

'That's good news.' said the other.

It was the cold that woke Kilidh the next morning. He rubbed his eyes to clear them and looked around in bewilderment. The queen, the tent, and all her baggage had gone. Only the loom remained, its threads swinging in the morning air. He was lying naked on the dewy grass, and his clothing in a bundle by his head. Blushing, he dressed rapidly and looked around the campsite.

Heavy mist lay all around, deadening sound. He saw then that the five elder women, who slept apart from the rest, had also disappeared. He ran over to where the spokesman lay sleeping on his thin cloak.

'Where is she?' he shouted, shaking him by the front of his tunic. 'What idiotic tribal practice is she following now? How dare she humiliate me like that? I'll teach her I am the chief now.'

'Speak more slowly,' gasped the man,'I cannot understand you.'

'The queen has gone.' said Kilidh through clenched teeth. 'I woke up to find her and her women gone and her verminous tent stripped from over my head.'

'Where has she gone? It is not one of her travelling times,' said the man, leaping to his feet.

'I don't know where she's gone. I want you to tell me.'

'This cannot be happening to us. This is terrible.' said the man, scanning the campsite. 'She cannot leave us, she is the queen.'

'She has gone, and if you don't know where, you had better ask one of your women.'

'They will not know. How can this have happened to us? We have always been obedient and followed the laws our elders gave us. Why are we being punished?' said the man and tears ran down his face into his scanty beard.

Kilidh was sure the man was as ignorant as himself.

'Don't be alarmed,' he said gently, 'I can look after you all. I've said I will and my word is my bond. Now go and tell the others. Tell them not to worry.'

Discomforted by the man's distress he turned up the hill and wondered what to do next. Just then there was a shout from the rock where the sentry had been keeping watch. He looked up and saw a body lying on its back, one arm raised above its head. A raven sat on its chest and tugged at something. Kilidh began to feel real fear as he ran across. Gwalchmai ran out of the mist to meet him.

'We'll never find the one who did this,' said the warrior, and indicated the body. It was the Dane. There was a ragged hole in his neck and beside it a great pool of clotting blood. One eye stared sightless at the sky; the other was a black and red pit. Since this had been a peaceful mission he had only worn a padded leather jerkin, and beneath his unprotected armpit someone had driven a spear deep into his chest cavity.

'This is no ordinary killing,' said Gwalchmai. 'If death was the object the first wound — the one in the neck — would have been

sufficient. The other wounds were inflicted later, out of revenge perhaps.'

'No one here had a feud with this man,' said Kilidh, sick at
heart.

'A fighting man always has enemies.'

The body was wrapped in its cloak and loaded on to a horse for
burial at home. Kilidh's heartsickness deepened as they made their
way to the coast, and behind him came his mourning clan.

This is a copy of a letter written by Selyf of Rosnat from the monastery of Rintsnoc to him who styles himself Bishop of Alban. There is no one living at the monastery there, since the bishop ordered the seniors to remove themselves to Brychan. I think he was afraid that the wolfish see of Jorvic would claim all the lands which belonged or ever had belonged to the monastery as theirs. I was sent to Orkney many months ago by our Abbot in Athcliath, to serve in the court of Lord Sigurd. While I was there these letters fell into my hands. This, the first one was written to Bishop Cellach two years ago, after I had been sent away. Our beloved Abbot wishes me to prove that there is no heresy among my seniors, so I must study these letters and prepare a case. As the nearest kin to Selyf I would by custom become the Abbot of Rintsnoc myself, but I have no wish to do so. My only wish is to return to Gorze and continue my studies, but that must wait for permission from Athcliath and the denial of these charges against my seniors. I must also find someone to take up the abbacy or I am afraid our rough white robes will not be seen in this country any more, but who among us is fitting?

To the most noble and pious Cellach MacFerdalaig, Bishop of all Alban, father of the christian people of Kyil, of Galwythel, and Alclyth, Selyf, monk and coarb of Nynia sends greetings.

Salutatio.

I humbly pray and beseech that your wisdom will shine like a light in the darkness into which my brothers and I have been plunged. Surely you, who have received the pall from the hands of the Holy Father of Christendom will have more grace than most mortals, and see more clearly than others whose aid I have sought.

Captatio benevolentiae

Pope Benedict IV

Please forgive my writing to you myself, but our holy father Abbot Gwydion has been an anchorite for the last ten years, and it has fallen to me to attend to the administration of our order here.

Petitio. Why must he ask permission? The bishop knows this.

At the beginning of the winter fast Sinnoch, a bishop out of Cathures and Gobhan, came to us here at Rintsnoc. This was a felicitous time for he is the most holy of men and devoted to God's justice. With his loving ministrations to us he showed us our many omissions and impieties, saying that if a dog has not felt the whip for many months he will soon become lacking in devotion to his master. By God's grace I was able to keep to my vow of silence and avoided disputation with him. When he left us last Monday we shed many bitter

Narratio.

15

Bishop Sinnoch has gone to Brychan with his complaint long since.

This is a serious allegation against him considering that he kept the woman who was his wife with him long after he should have sent her to another city. He claimed that she had returned to him for shelter and stayed only for a few days, but this was enough to violate his vows of chastity according to our Rule. Even if, as he claimed, they did not have carnal relations he should have sent her away, with no regard to the weather, or the fact that her city had been destroyed by pirates.

tears at our deserted state and humbly prayed that we will not again slip into the trough of error without his tireless vigilance.

But the source of greatest grief to myself was that visit he made to my cell when he rebuked me and told me that he had heard from many sources that I consorted with demons. He said that it was common knowledge that I had spent many weeks in the company of a succubus, and that I had encouraged my fellow monks in this. We were all, therefore, guilty of heresy and of fornication.

With regard to the charge of fornication I can only offer as witness the large number of my years, and the white hairs on my head, since I know my oath of chastity will not satisfy you. As God will judge us all soon, I declare that the woman, for woman she was, spent many hours with me, but it was always with another in attendance, and this is true of all my fellows. Our only concern in all that time was to prepare her for death and baptism, and she left us as she arrived: a spotless virgin. I can say no more on the matter since the woman is gone from us, but the truth will be revealed on that Day that lies before us all, monk or bishop.

The other allegation I heard with deeper suffering, firstly because it could not have come from the few simple souls who attend the Offering here, but could only have come from a monk of our own rule who heard myself and the woman in conversation. Secondly this intervention has made me examine my conscience and to my pain I find that I have a charge to answer, but only in that I have once more allowed my doubting mind to clamour louder than my faithful heart. I must be grateful to my brother who reported my falling away, since in my eagerness for greater knowlege I would not have paused but plunged headlong into doubt and wickedness. 'He that increases knowlege increases grief.' I would have been like a pig heedlessly rooting for food in muddy ground until I realised too late that I no longer had the solid ground of faith under my feet and wallowed deeper and deeper into fear and sin.

When the woman came to us I saw neither demon nor succubus, but only a troubled soul thirsting for the truth it had glimpsed once in childhood. No one would have turned her away. You will see I am not ashamed of my conduct, for I willingly give you a full account of her stay here so that you can treat this case with justice.

The night she came to the monastery will be remembered for generations for the terror it caused. Men told us of balls of fire that ran through the glens, of shaking ground, of the loch that vanished overnight leaving nothing but slime and worms where it had lain. Here on the seashore we thought that it was only the start of the autumn storms, and when black clouds covered the firth and the wind drove white water onto the shingle we took our books from our cells and gathered in the stone tower. We did not wish to see the roofs of our huts snatched from over our heads in the night, but we were not alarmed.

At the mouth of the night we said the office. We pulled up the ladder at the end of the last psalm and arranged ourselves for sleep around the walls. Our father Gwydion stayed in his dark house; perhaps if he had joined us it might have fallen out differently. I put my satchel under my head and doused the lamp. I saw windblown branches flying past the window, and as the roaring of the wind grew stronger and the twilight turned from blue to black I said a private prayer for any who had no shelter that night.

Some time before the first hour of the night there came a sudden pounding at the door. I awoke in terror from a dream thinking that Leviathan had left the sea and was striking our door with his tail. We looked at each other wondering what monster could reach our door from the ground when we heard a voice which was surely human and in great distress. Ælfrid of Caerluel opened the door and we both looked down to see a human figure lying on the ground. Cadui of Rintsnoc joined us and he frowned and shook his head. Then the figure moved and the cry came again, weak and desperate, and Ælfrid pushed the ladder out. (He is our apothecary and will never refuse to help one in trouble.) The wind nearly took the ladder from his hands so I helped him tie it down and together we descended to the ground.

We found a woman lying almost senseless. We raised her and found that her clothes were soaked and her skin was chilled like death. At once Ælfrid lifted her and took her to our little refectory where he blew up the fire and

I remember this night, even in Orkney the wind blew houses over and two men were lost off the beach.

It was the nones of October. I was finding my exile very hard. The foreigners are barbarous, for all that they have been baptised. It will be years before they can persuaded to moderate their excesses, but that night I put the fear of God into them and told them how they were being punished for their drunkenness and fornication. They were on their knees till Christmas and they got through the feast itself without an orgy for once.

Cadui is in Brychan. He refuses to talk about the woman.

Ælfrid laughed at me when I told him of my errand.

18

*He should not make
so much of the woman's
appearance. Such close study
could lead to unchaste
thoughts. Especially the hair.
If it was not covered she must
be a woman of dubious virtue.
Nevertheless I suppose in
charity we must remember the
Magdalena.*

*One township of poor
pasturage and the cave where
our beloved St Nynia lived for
a while is the support of fifteen
choir monks an abbot and
a presbyter. There is also a
herb garden and a graveyard.
We own a township at Rosnat
where our founder first built
and a stone oratory there. We
also own the fishing.*

*Why does she not name her
father?
This certainly seems very
much like grace, but the
Adversary has many ways to
deceive us.*

started heating water. Then together we removed as many of her clothes as was consistent with our vows of chastity and squeezed the water from them. I saw that her cape and mantle were of a strong, fine wool with much embroidery at the edges, and her shift was of the finest linen, yet her tunic was the coarse, red stuff the poor farm women wear. Her hair also was unusual, being uncovered, even though she was of middle years, and it was knotted into four thick red braids. I saw that there were only three fingers on her left hand.

Ælfrid brought fiery herbs from his cell and we made a warming drink for her. She lay in a swoon all night and we watched over her saying the offices there in the refectory. At the second hour when dawn was lightening the sky the wind dropped and the woman seemed to come to herself. Cienach and Cadui and Eddern retired to the oratory and we heard the ringing of the bell. But when we came to the lines 'Thou rulest the raging of the sea; When the waves thereof arise thou stillest them' the woman stood up and bowed her head and seemed to understand what she was taking part in.

As soon as it was full light we showed the woman our guest house. And since she was still very weak, as soon as clean straw was on the bed she lay down and slept. Before the last hour of the day Ælfrid and I took her food and she asked us if we were a Christian community and we answered in charity that we were. We saw that she was very moved by this for she covered her face with her hands and her body trembled. Then she looked up at us and said,

'My name is Marighal. My father was a great lord, whose hall lies far away in the mountains. He died not long ago and as soon as I could I came to find people of your kind who might receive me into their faith. Many years ago I told my father I wished to be baptised, but he mocked me saying that you were all dreamers and fools; and he forbade me to go. I kept silent, then, for I was sure that one day I would be free to take my own way.'

'We must rejoice,' I said, 'and give thanks for the grace that has been given to you. Many children of pagan families have had to wait for baptism, and few have been able to keep alive the spark which brought them out of darkness. But I must tell you that there is no one here who will perform the rite. There are two who are consecrated priests, but they have taken eremitical vows and will have nothing to do with people of the world. You will see our Abbot and Cienach perform the Offering but they will not even look at you. But in a few weeks we expect to be visited by a bishop of very great holiness and he will save you from everlasting death. We can begin your instruction at once so that you can be received without delay for none who seek relief from their lawless state may be left to languish in darkness.'

I have seen Cienach celebrate the Eucharist. Why will he not perform other rites? Selyf is not a priest since his fornication.

Ælfrid said that she was still a little weak and he sent his student, Josia, to find more herbs for her, but the next day Cadui of Kingaradh and I went to her hut and began to speak to her of the faith. We told her she might choose a soul-friend and she chose myself, but her instruction was always conducted by two of us together. She took her turn preparing the meal and made no complaint about the austerity of our life as might have been expected of one gently raised. The monks all took a part in her instruction and she was provided with a full copy of the Bible and a psalter for her own use. We were astonished to find that she could read most fluently. From the pocket of her golden belt she brought a needle and made herself a veil against her baptismal day, and though sometimes she would look sadly back at the hills she had left she seemed to us to be very happy.

Josia turns up everywhere. Ælfrid has not taught him to control his curiosity. I do not like this system of having personal students — it leads to pride in both the student and the master.

But I must confess I was seized by a desire to discover how one so gently raised knew so little about the church in our country. One day I asked her about her family, and Cadui signed to me to be silent. I reminded him that sin is not purged by learning the word of God alone, but by study in the heart, and he held his peace.

Selyf is most scrupulous but this does not prove there is no lust in his heart.

Where did he learn this or is it a product of his own study? The Benedictines I have spent my time with would have a lot to say on this.

'Did you perhaps learn of our faith from your mother?' I asked her, 'for we have often found that the true faith will grow in a woman's heart before it even takes seed in a man's.'

'Is this, perhaps, because a woman learns sooner what the faith will require of the faithful?' she replied.

Who is her mother?

'Yes, but not from superior understanding,' said Cadui, 'for a woman's understanding is inferior to a man's. It is rather because her life is more lowly and miserable so that she lives closer to the example of our Saviour. The grace of understanding is given to her out of God's loving kindness.'

'This is clear to me,' she said, 'for the women's lives I have seen I would find almost too humiliating to bear. But what if this is not the way of a woman's life? What if she is strong and clever and free? Will God's loving kindness be taken from her?'

'Most certainly,' said Cadui, 'for then she would not be womanly, and God would turn his face from such a creature.'

'Unless she observed the other duty of woman, which is love,' I said, in haste. Cadui can be too severe for the neophyte, and I have often seen a catechumen take fright at his instruction.

It is impossible to be too hard on most of the catechumen. But, 'temper the wind' as St Gregory said.

'I must meditate on this,' she said, 'for it was not explained to me those years ago when I stumbled across your faith. That was the accident that brought me to you.'

'There are no accidents,' said Cadui, 'only the grace of God.'

'So you have told me, but I find it hard to believe that so wicked a creature as myself could have taken up his time.'

Humility can be feigned as who should know better than I?

'Your humility is proper,' I said, 'but you must learn also that nothing is beneath God's notice for all of this is his creation. But who were the people who first showed you His truth? Were they of the true faith or were they back-sliders?'

'Truly I cannot say,' she answered, 'but I will tell you all I can remember about them, and the wicked thing I did against them and you will judge for yourselves.'

The woman Marighal tells about her first meeting with men of God

When I was a child I was sent out to be fostered by an old friend of my father's. When the time came for me to return home my father sent one of his servants to escort me, but to tell the truth I did not wish to go home and I tricked the servant into going on without me. I wandered lost for many hours, but towards evening I found myself near the sea, and following the coast northwards I came upon a low cliff hanging over a settlement. I had no choice but to go and see if they would give me shelter for the night. The village was in two pieces, on either arm of a small bay. Both parts had a wooden palisade around it, and I, knowing nothing, went to the nearest.

A double city? I thought the last one was burnt years ago.

This had several large stone buildings as well as many small wooden ones and I thought the chief would live in a stone house.

As I approached the gate a man in a rough white robe with a hood over it and sandals on his feet came to meet me. He directed me to the other side of the bay saying they were about to say the prayer for nightfall and close the gate, so I could not come in. I walked round the bay and at the other side I was taken to the main house, which was of wood, given food and a place to sleep. I was not used to sleeping in a large hall with others all around me. Yet the bed-platform and the partition around my bed were well made so that there were no trickles of air to break my sleep. Also the straw in my pillow and mattress were sweet and the blankets free of vermin. I hung my cloak over the opening into the hall and slept well.

During the night I was disturbed a little by someone watching me over the top of the partition, but they did not offer me any threat and I slept again to awaken in the late morning. When I left the main house I found that everyone was busy and there was only a small girl child to give me a meal. I sat at the door of the house and watched the work. It was late in the summer and stores were being laid by. Fish were drying, dried fruits being stored in jars, meat was being salted and grain was being taken to a granary out of sight. I started to follow the workers to find out if I could help, but when they saw me coming they stopped and frowned. An older woman came from one of the houses then, and from the glances in my direction I knew they were talking about me. I asked the child who the woman was and she said, 'Bean Ailien.'

To avoid trouble I walked down to the beach and watched the birds fishing. The little girl followed me silently and I envied the birds who needed only a few fish to dive for, and had no need of their own kind to live. I had missed my road, and it seemed I would have to spend the winter with inhospitable strangers. It was not a happy prospect, but I was eager for any kind of experience. I went to Bean Ailien and said,

'Winter is coming fast and there is little chance of finding someone to guide me to my father's hall before the roads are closed. I will have to stay here, but I do not wish to be a burden on you, so please give me work to do. I can spin and weave and sew, and in spite of my gentle rearing I am strong enough to work in the fields and do other things which you might not expect of me.'

'We have all the workers we need,' she answered, frowning, 'nothing you could do would be of use to us, but I will ask the others what they think, for in this city everyone has a voice. In the meantime, you may help any who ask you and you may be sure that if we can find a way to get you home before winter, we will do so.'

Her answer was just, if less than kind, so I tried one more act of friendship. Taking off my neck and arm rings I handed them to the woman and asked her to keep them safe for me, since they would hamper me if I was working in the fields. She took them from me, though her face showed me she had no love of such things, and walked away. All the time the other people had been watching us out of the tail of their eye. I went back to the shore, and the child went with me. I said to her,

Nor should she have.

'Indeed this is going to be a long winter if in all the time I am to find neither companionship nor work. In my father's hall I have learned to love my own company, but there I could always find occupation. I think I might do better to face the unknown passes than die here of loneliness and tedium.'

The child said nothing, and I said, 'Why do you not speak? You have fed me and sheltered me as in guest friendship you must, but I have learned that true courtesy requires more than that. You all treat me as if you hate me, yet I am sure I have done no wrong to you. I do not expect a loving welcome, but I do not deserve to be treated like an enemy hostage.'

At last the child pointed across the bay to the other houses and said, 'When the bell rings for the second time go there and ask to speak to the Holy Father. He understands all things and he will tell you what you need to know.'

About the middle of the day I heard a steady ringing coming across the bay, and I made haste across the curve of the shingle. A white-robed brother met me at the gate and led me through the wooden cells to the centre of the compound. There I saw another monk surrounded by a circle of boys reciting psalms and a tall stone cross. I was led, not to the big stone hall, but to a larger wooden house where the monk bowed and showed me in. Inside, seated at a table, was another dressed the same, but that round his neck he wore a long white girdle. He smiled at me kindly and said,

'Welcome to the city of St Inan and St Thenew. We have great joy in giving you refuge with us. I am father Scoithin.'

'Thank you, sir,' I replied, 'I must admit I had despaired of hearing such a pleasant greeting since I came here.'

'I am sorry to hear you feel unwelcome here, for it is part of our rule that we should succour strangers.'

'Indeed? Then perhaps you can tell me why the people in the other place treat me like an enemy. None of them speak to me except for Bean Ailien, and that has not been warmly. I may have to be here for many weeks, but if I am not treated more as a friend I might well call myself prisoner. What have I done to offend them?'

'It is not what you have done, but what you might do that troubles them. Raiding has started on this coast again after many years and now, when the harvest is in and the cattle are back from the shielings, the seamen are most likely to attack to gain winter provisions. The people are afraid that you have been sent to find out their hidden stores and weaknesses in their defence. Your dress is not of a local style, you speak our language differently, and you cannot tell us where you come from. You may be an enemy.

'But do not be alarmed, for there will be no raiding here. These are a simple people, and they have been loyal to their faith for many years. You may be sure God will protect them. In their simplicity they have never held much gold, which is what the raiders hold dear above all else. The only gold in our city is that which you gave to Bean Ailien for safe keeping.'

'I can see there is little enough to steal,' I said, 'but tell me, who are the people who might come raiding here?'

'You are blessedly ignorant if you do not know that,' said the father. 'I am speaking of the foreigners from Eirinnn. They raided up the coast last year and when they found that the men from Orkney had been many years before and left no plunder, they killed or mutilated the people and took everything they could move. In

A stola? or a pallium? Who is this Abbot and where is this city?

Is it the one that was on the coast beside the river with the belly? Perhaps it is the one that looks out over the island of St Beya. Her followers are generally noted for their habit of severe castigation in her example. I was sure the double city of Thenew and Inan was razed by the men of Innisgall.

I am afraid he has more blessed hope than wisdom.

24

particular they attacked the holy cities and the churches, since they had been told there was much gold to be had there. When they found none they did vile things to the monks to make them tell where it was hidden. There was no gold at all, but they rejoiced in their evil and did not stop torturing them till they gave up their last breath. They are Godless men, truly.'

I saw that he wept as he spoke and I kept silent for a while, then I said, 'Forgive me. I am indeed ignorant. My father's hall is far away and few of us ever leave it except to get married, and then we never return. I am the only one who has ever been fostered, and even so I know little of the world, but I beg you now, give me a chance to learn more about you.'

It is a strange father that will let his daughter go for fostering. It is well known that if a female child is not well supervised by an older relative she will return to her family in a disgraceful condition.

'I will teach you all I can,' he said, 'for it is also part of our rule that we should leave no one in ignorance who seeks enlightenment. To start with what you see here. I am the Abbot, the father of this city, and I have the care of all the souls here. I am also a consecrated bishop and so I must care for all the Christians in this vicinity. It is not usual for an abbot to be consecrated but the times are hard, and we must be prepared to baptise anyone without delay.

It is not so unusual in these days.

'You may have heard from wicked demon worshippers that we eat children and commit fornications in our services but that is a wicked lie. Our simple rites take all their power from the faith and love of the celebrants. Our lives are committed to poverty and we only produce enough food for ourselves. Apart from that our only occupations are teaching and prayer.'

O yes. They said in Lübeck that at Easter we cut a baby boy into pieces and throw the bits into a big chalice. Then we sit around it and eat him piece by piece with the blood still smoking.

'Which is the city of St Inan and which of St Thenew?' I asked, and he laughed a laugh like rain on dusty ground.

'Both cities belong to both saints. Once, many generations ago this was a double city, with the monks dedicated to St Inan in this place and the daughters of St Thenew across the bay. Alas, as the years went by, pestilence and raiding brought our numbers down so that we could no longer spare our women the distress of childbearing. The virgins of the sisterhood and the chaste women who bore only once for the abbey were obliged to forsake their holy vows. Now the other settlement is completely secular and those living there are simple men and women, although some of the boys

are oblates of the monastery. One of them is heir to the
Abbacy of another city, but I am a virgin and will chose
my heir from the brothers here.'

I did not understand clearly everything he said, but I
can recall what I do not understand. Yet there was one
question I wished to have answered at once, so I thanked
the father and said, 'You will have to make good many
gaps in my learning. I know what you mean by teaching,
but please, what is 'prayer'?'

'My dear child,' said the Abbot, 'this is very distress-
ing — although we are a very old foundation, and we
have brought many souls to God from the worship of
demons, I have never met one who did not know how
to pray.

'You must understand it is the most blissful state
which can be enjoyed by man while he is yet clogged
with the flesh. It is the way we come closer to our
Saviour and Creator as long as we are cumbered with
these vile bodies, and often while we pray He will speak
to us and tell us His will.'

'Ah, I know how to do that. I have done it since I was a
child. I fold myself in and forget the world. Then I open
my heart and my father speaks to me.'

'That is indeed very like prayer,' said the Abbot,
laughing, 'someone has taught you well. But tell me,
which demon is it you pray to? In my years as a
missionary I must have heard of them all. Is he of
human or animal form? What foul practices does he
demand of you? Must you placate him with the blood
of animals or men? Must you cut off the heads of
those you kill in battle and range them round his
holy places? Or is he worshipped with lust of the
flesh?'

'We do nothing like that,' I answered, amazed.'He
demands nothing of us but that we should stay faithful
to him and to our family. You would not know of him,
I am sure. But please tell me more about your Creator,
and perhaps he will hear me pray also.'

'He will not hear the prayers of the unbaptised,' he
answered, 'but you may see His image there.' And he
pointed to the wall behind his chair. I studied the thing
and found it was a white bone carving of Him they call
the Saviour, nailed to a wooden cross, and His body was
twisted with pain.

This is a very old rule but not irregular so to speak.

He is asking a great deal from his congregation. Surely not all of them could have found their way to mental prayer?

I think the Abbot is indulging rather in his own curiosity. Prurience.

Is this a godless family then? I have met a few in Iceland.

26

*Obviously she has not been
raised in the worship of Othin.
His followers blasphemously
maintain that he was nailed to
a tree and hung there for nine
days to gain wisdom, and they
say that Christ is no better!*

*That is a pity. But it is the
fate of most women.*

*He is talking about
St Thenew. The child she
bore was the beloved hound
of God — Cunotegernos, the
founder of monasteries all over
Brytain.*

'That is a puny sort of god, surely, that he lets himself
be killed, and in agony too.'

The Abbot was a generous man, for he only laughed
at my discourtesy and said, 'Nevertheless, that is his
finest hour, as you will come to understand when you
join our faith.'

'I may, if I have time enough to learn it, for the practices I learned at home took me many, many years to
master.'

'It will not take you such a long time to learn our
faith, for the most important lessons are to love and
fear God.'

'I am not sure I will have time to learn this. There
is so much to know about the world and I have little
time left in it. I must soon marry the man my father
has chosen for me. In the spring his servants will find
me and I shall be fetched home, and that will be an end
to learning.'

'Do not be dismayed,' said the Abbot, 'one of the
founding saints of our monastery can show you an
example to follow. She had a very great longing to be
a virgin of our faith, but her father had pledged her
since childhood in marriage to a nobleman. She fled
from the man but he found her and forced her and
left her with child. Yet she had a joyful reward for her
sufferings for the child she bore was one of our holiest
saints and the darling of God. The woman herself also
enjoyed the life of an anchoress until God gathered her
to Him. Now she will sit at his right hand for all eternity,
and contemplate His presence in bliss. So do not you
despair of your virginity. With God's grace the passes
may be closed for a long time, and by spring your servant
may have forgotten where to find you.'

'I would be happy if it were so, but my father's servants are very cunning. Yet I would not have you thinking
I am down-hearted, for although I have no great liking
for the man my father has chosen, he does not disgust
me, and I would like to know what marriage is like.

'But, now, please tell me. How shall I prove to the
people here that I am not going to betray them? I would
never be so base, believe me. What oath shall I take?'

'There is no oath a pagan could take that would sway
these people. They are frightened now, but when no
raiding follows on your arrival they will start to accept

you. Only be patient and in the meantime, if you need a friend come and talk to me, and I will show you the wonders of our faith.'

It fell out as he said. As the days passed I helped with the work that came to hand, carrying baskets, hauling nets and driving the animals to the byres at evening. For the most part, however, I walked the narrow path round the bay to the Abbot's house and back to the main lodge. By the time of the first light snows I had been accepted as one of the sights of the town, if not as one of its fellows.

At the Abbot's house I began to learn about the Saviour and His Father, the Creator, and how those who call themselves His lovers dedicate themselves to His service. I read the Scriptures and the lives of the Saints, and I listened to the scolog as he taught the boys, but I wondered at some of the things I heard. It seemed to me that not everyone agreed about the nature of the Creator and His angels. And after the death of the Master, the Anointed One, His disciples did much in His name that would not have met with His approval. I kept these thoughts to myself, for I was there to learn, not to dispute, although it would have been good to talk about this.

I wish I had the instruction of this woman. She would not have been confused like this. It is clear that this city is riddled with heresy.

I even attended the Sabbath offering with the faithful in the monastery, and I found that some of the people had travelled a great distance to attend the celebration. I listened to the Abbot as he stood preaching beside the cross. I learned the songs and the psalms, and some of the joy the Christians felt at the elevation of the Host began to glow in my own heart. Truly it was a miracle to see the faces, pale and shrunken after a week of hard, endless labour, lighting up as the poor meal turned into the substance of their Lord. Once I even felt a pain in my eyes and found that I was weeping. I began to understand that, whatever the disagreements that might arise among His followers, the words of the Master were food for the souls of these hard-pressed people, and that this was the source of their endless patience.

It is a pity she was exposed to this. The answers are in the church. But she shows excellent humility. Or was she there to sow the seeds of disharmony?

She is certainly an able student.

At last I decided to seek baptism, but before I could begin my instruction everything fell apart. One night, when all those in the main lodge had fallen asleep, a man came up to the gate calling for help. He was recognised and the gate unbarred. When the fire was

28

A healing woman? Why did none of the brothers attend him?

They seem to be expecting the men from Eirinn but they left us in peace many years ago. And she has learned of the Saracens even though she cannot put a name to them.

stirred up and the lights brought, we found that he was wounded and covered with blood. Bean Ailien sent for the healing woman and we listened to his story.

The previous night, boats had slipped out of the darkness and before they had a chance to flee, Vikings had fallen on his people with fire and sword. They had killed the men, emptied the stores and carried off the younger women and children. He had been left for dead in the ruins and come to himself the next morning, nearly dead indeed from the cold and his wounds. He had found no others alive and had come to this, the next village, to warn us and to find shelter. At this news some glances were cast at myself, but nothing more.

'You see how it is,' said Bean Ailien, 'there is nothing here that the black strangers might take for plunder other than the people and the food of their mouths, yet these men will not keep from stealing, for all that it is late in the season. Will there be no end to it?

'The only prize left to us is our children. These they will take away to the south and sell them to the men with skins burned black from the sun. They like our children because they have white skin and pale hair, and they will give the pirates much gold for them as slaves. Then they will do terrible things to them, so that it would be better for them if they were dead. Tomorrow let us go to the Abbot and see if we can find a way to keep this evil from us.'

But in the morning the Abbot said, 'I tell you you have nothing to fear. You are good people not given to drunkenness nor adultery, nor to the secret worship of demons. Neither do you rob your neighbours, and you are patient, diligent and humble. Raids are sent as scourges for the backs of heretics and sinners. We have seen that God is just, for he has given us, his chosen people, peace and plenty when others have poor crops, sick animals and death at the hands of Saxons and Vikings.

'Therefore I say to you, that if a raid should come you must greet it with joy, for you will not die the eternal death of the sinner. No, for you there lies ahead the greatest treasure of all, greater than all the gold and riches of this world; greater than the esteem of your fellow man; greater than fertile land and sleek cattle: before you lies the crown of the martyr.'

When he said this some of the people cried aloud and
fell to their knees where they stood, their faces lit from
joy greater than any I had seen at the offering. One of
the women sang;

'Come to me, my Lord, and my Master,
Come and show yourself to me.
Come from the field with arms raised to bless me.
Come from the sea with sword in hand.
We are ready to receive you at our last great love
    feast,
The cup is filled and the bread is baked.

From my mother's womb leaping I have longed
    for you.
With every inch added to my height my longing
    grew,
To know that you are close to me now makes my
    heart blaze.
I could not see you, though you stood beside me,
But soon I shall see you, bathed in everlasting
    light.

I have stood at the foot of the cross weeping for
    your pain,
My champion, while the sweat ran down your
    slender body.
But now our sufferings will end and we will be
    together,
Entwined, as the hill stands locked in the arms of
    the sea
Washed by everlasting joy.'

*I have not heard this in
any monastery in Alban or
Cymri or in the Sudries. Has
Marighal invented this? It
seems improbable but we must
be on our guard.*

'Yes, truly I say, rejoice,' the Abbot went on, 'for soon
you will see the faces of the Blessed welcoming you, and
you will be received through the gates of heaven. Not for
you the waiting, locked in the grave until the day of days;
nor for you the long purging of your sins. If this death
comes, bow your heads before the sword in gratitude,
for that blow takes you to the feet of your Heavenly
Father.'
But I saw that Bean Ailien did not share in this
rejoicing for she stood apart, and when silence fell
she said, 'You speak of a martyr's crown with joy,

30

The woman is correct. A martyr's crown is only for those who lovingly accept it, and prepare themselves, sometimes for years.

This was a long time ago.

And a long time ago our blessed father Adomnan made it the law that women should not have to suffer by going into battle. It is scandalous that an Abbot should go into battle, although many of them do. In Frankland I saw bishops bearing arms, and many more maintain their own armies. What are we to do? The Adversary is very near.

father, but I am not of one mind with you there. We are, as you say, ignorant people, and although you call us guiltless, it may well be that we are unworthy. We may have sinned in our hearts by error and omission. You, who have spent your fleshly life in study and in prayer, have made yourselves acceptable to God. You may be well prepared to die, but I doubt if this is true of us, poor sinners.

'When we came here today I had hoped to hear some words from you on the matter of our defences. We need guidance there, not on martyrdom which will come or no as God pleases. In my grandmother's time things were different. She told me that when she was a child the men from Innis Gall were harrying the coast from the isle of Maun to the Bay of Gulls and hundreds of people died. Then the Holy Father of the city lived among us and showed us how to prepare ditches and palisades, and how to wield a sword in our defence. He had seen many battles himself, and there was none better than him to face an enemy in the field.'

'Those were dark days you speak of, woman,' said the Abbot, 'I remember those stories myself. Our ancestors spent too much of their time in matters of the flesh, and almost forsook their duties to the Prince of Peace. They forsook His word 'do good to them that harm you and pray for those that persecute you' and took up the sword and battle-axe like the priests of olden times. Those of you who claim to serve the God I serve stay here with us. Let us retire to the oratory to pray that our souls will be ready for the fate that awaits them.'

I was amazed and deeply troubled to see how many of the people were preparing to meet death with joy. Before that time I had always found that the common people would go to any length to save their lives, and would even sacrifice their friends and their children before they would abandon their bodies for ever. I thought that life was the most precious thing to them, but now I saw women and men kissing each other and exulting in the death which threatened them all.

Nevertheless, not all the people were of the same mind, for when Bean Ailien said, 'Those of you who wish to stay and spend the night in vigil must do so, of course, but I shall go back to my house. There are still sick and old there who need my attention. Those who wish to may come with me, for we must see to the state of our defences. It seems to me that pirates who go raiding this late in the season will be truly desperate and weak. It may well be that a firm and steady resistance will drive them off,' many followed her, including myself.

I hope Selyf explained the woman's error.

I knew that the highest rewards of their faith would be beyond my grasp unbaptised as I was. Back at the other village we counted the people and found that more than half the women and one third of the men had stayed with the monks. I wondered then why it was that women, who were not allowed to share the retreat of the monks, were yet the most ardent in the faith among the secular people.

A good woman, such as a virgin of our faith has a simple and loving heart which knows its Saviour from the moment of baptism or sooner.

On returning to their houses the men started to dig in the floors and pull about in the thatch, and they produced a number of swords and daggers.

Bean Ailien came to me, handed me a broken scabbard and said, 'See if you can stitch this, though I doubt if your thin white fingers can sew hard leather. It is old but it is very strong. I wish the same might be said of the sword it held, for since the last Abbot died we have no one here who can work metal.'

'I can sew it,' I replied, 'and I can do better than that, for I can also mend the broken sword you took from it. Indeed, if you have much metal work to be done I will see what I can do, for I have some skill at the forge.'

Bean Ailien's face showed me she doubted this. She said, 'My husband was the son of the Abbot and he tried to learn the secrets of metal working before his father died, but they are not a long-lived family, and he spent most of his own life trying to build on the knowledge his father had left him. Yet here you stand, a child, a girl child, raised in a noble house to all appearances, and you say you can work a forge. You will agree it seems unlikely.'

I can only share her point of view. I saw metal workshops in Gorze. The work was fine, not arms and such like but even so it was only men that could do it. As to forging arms — she must be lying or using black arts.

'I understand your doubt, yet I tell you I am speaking the truth. My foster father, whose house I left only weeks ago, was no ordinary man. He had many skills and much learning, and showed me all he could in the few years I was with him. Under his guidance I made a set of tools to use at the forge myself.' And so saying I showed her the tools in my satchel — the hammer, the plate for drawing wire, the tongs and the pincers.

Does she mean the ones St Columbcille devised or later ones? He would have said a prayer against herself.

The ignorant will always do this. We show them the blessed truth and they hang talismans on every tree and dead animals litter the township.

I think this husband of hers was perhaps the natural heir of the Abbot, but the practice of election by the brothers took over. That would explain why she is at odds with the Abbot and clings to her pagan habits.

I think this confirms what I just said.

At that the woman blessed herself and raised her hands between us saying,

'What black arts have you brought with you? I warn you, I know prayers against smiths and magicians, and I can use them.'

'Patience, woman. There are no black arts here,' I told her, 'I am speaking of skills which can be taught to any child like growing food and weaving. Here is no darkness, only knowledge.'

'That is easy for you to say,' she replied, her hands still making the warding sign, 'we who do the work here know that there is always a chance that darkness will take its portion of our produce. There are things we must do that we may not tell the monks about.'

'That is as you wish. All I know is that when I work in the crafts my foster father taught me I do nothing that I could not speak of to any man or woman. If you do not believe me set any one you like to watch me while I work, and listen to the songs I sing, for I have nothing to hide.'

'I wish to believe you,' she said, lowering her hands, 'and I will send my son to work with you. He may learn something useful to us if what you say is true, and if not I can tell the father we did not let you go unattended.'

She sent him to me straightaway, and he showed me the house her husband and his ancestors had used for metal working. The hearth was well made and had not crumbled in spite of years of neglect. In the floor was a bowl furnace but there was not enough charcoal in the two towns to fire it. The hut smelled damp and sour with the soot from a hearth which had not been used. Rain dripped from a hole in the roof, and the anvil had moss on it.

'Since my father went to his reward we have not used this hut,' said the youth, 'but all the tools he and his father's fathers used are here, since most people feared to touch them. I was not afraid, but I knew nothing of the craft and I was angry to see it all wasted, so I kept away.'

I set him to work cleaning the tools with sand, and I made sure that the bellows were not rotted away. We asked for the services of a boy to fetch water, but the little girl who had waited on me before asked me to let her do it and I was pleased. I also asked for someone to mend the roof, for I needed dark to study the glow of the hot metal and its colour. It is most important. I found the tools were many and most were well made, and I knew that the Abbot's family had been fine smiths. I said as much to my apprentice, and he was glad that he belonged to a skilful line. I could see he was eager to learn as much as he could.

I welded the first sword, and it was strong. When the people saw that it was good they gave me all manner of weapons from battle axes to women's knives to temper or to put a fresh edge on. I worked until my arms ached, and the night was well advanced, and then I slept for a while in a bed in the corner while the youth kept the forge hot. After I woke and took up the work again it came to me that for the first time in my life other people truly needed the work of my hands and the knowledge of my heart, and the thought was like honey in my loneliness. All that day I worked with the young man beside me, and he asked me all the time what I did and why I did it. He learned quickly and I would have been very happy to have gone on with that life.

If this is true it is a sign of grace. Such satisfaction in the service of others is a great virtue.

Outside in the thin, grey rain the people mended the palisade and salted away meat and fish. They worked mostly in silence, but sometimes when there was a halt in our work I heard singing above the roar of the forge.

'Deliver me, o Lord, from the evil men; preserve me from the violent men who imagine mischiefs in their heart. Continually are they gathered together for war. They have sharpened their tongues like a serpent; adder's poison is under their lips.' Then, suddenly there was no more charcoal; the last blade was quenched and polished, and silence fell around us. My apprentice fell asleep where he sat, his hand still on the handle of the bellows. At some time during the day the girl had left food for us and I ate, but I was not yet ready for sleep. Lost in my idleness I walked out of the township and down to the beach, where most of the people were standing.

Psalm CXL

Bean Ailien was sitting on the red rocks, staring out to sea as if the force of her stare might show her the enemy. From the oratory across the bay came the sound of chanting, and the rattling of the bell. Smoke rose from the kitchen. The sun was setting into the sea and the sky around it was a bright red. I looked down at the

Red rocks, — it must be further north than I thought. You will not see them until you get into Kirick.

34

sea as it rippled over the shingle, and I saw that it was
red as blood.

'Bean Ailien,' I cried to the woman, 'look at the waves.
They are red as blood in the sunset tonight. Tomorrow,
I have seen it, they will be red again, but it will be with
the blood of the people of this city.'

'I have seen that also,' she said, quietly, 'but there is
nothing we can do. We must stay here and fight, and if
God wills it, we will die.'

With a sigh she produced my rings from her pocket
and handed them to me saying, 'At dawn tomorrow you
will leave us. If you are travelling alone, you may find
shelter further north.'

I shook my head at her, and tried not to take them,
saying, 'These are very valuable, and you said that the
pirates love gold above everything. Will you not give
them the gold so that they will leave you in peace?'

*The Ætheling of Wessex was
successful in buying peace, but
he had a large citizenry to tax.*

'That is nobly said,' she answered, 'but I cannot
take them. Not because I would refuse a generous
offer — only a fool refuses help in a position like
ours — but because the pirates will come back next
season looking for more fine gold, and when they find
none it will be as if we had never paid them.'

'Then why do you not go yourselves to another village
and escape?'

'Here we cannot leave,' she said, and sighed again,
'for the monks and our fellows in the other place will
not go and they need us to defend them. Also, others
in times past have taken to the hills, but when the
foreigners had gone and they returned they found the
nets ripped to pieces, the meat and grain stolen, and
the houses burned. No other village could feed us in
these hard times so with winter so close we would starve
before long. Besides that, we may survive, for in this
town we have had time to mend our defences, and we
will not be taken unawares like those others. Some of
us may see the day out.'

Second sight?

'That is not as I saw it,' I told her, but she looked me
in the face and said,

'This is our home and we will defend it, and if we
die here it is no more than we will do in God's good
time. We may comfort ourselves with the thought that
if we fight well each pirate we destroy will be one less
left to plague our brothers elsewhere. Scoithin tells me

that my faith is weak and that I should be joining my sisters and brothers in joyful song. I have been cursed with a doubting mind, it is true, but I think that each of us has a different part to play in this mummers' show. I had hoped that, given time, I would learn to see with the Abbot's eyes instead of my own, clouded ones, but there is no time left, now. I must throw myself on the mercy of the Almighty.

At least she is meek and thinks of her fellows rather than her own skin. She is not without some grace. I will pray for her.

'But here is no place for you to die. I entreat you to go as soon as it is light. Your help to us has been a great blessing, and whatever may come, while one of us yet breathes your name will be remembered. Go with God.'

Once again we see the contrast between the sisters Martha and Mary.

And she blessed me. The next morning I left at first light with salt meat and hard bread in my scrip. I headed inland across the plain to the hills. At first I dropped out of sight of the sea, but around noon I looked back and saw two towers of smoke lifting into the sky. Then I knew that my friends were dying, and the thought that my apt apprentice would never learn all he wanted to know filled my heart with grief. At those thoughts there came a terrible pain in my eyes, and I wept.

Some days later I was found by one of my father's servants and I was taken home, safe. That was the end of my learning.

The woman Marighal ends her history.

Marighal dropped her head to her hands and gave a terrible groan.

'Comfort yourself,' said Cadui, 'and be sure that some of your friends have found the bliss of martyrdom. Certainly those in the monastery, and most of those in the other half of the city, for they were innocent of back-sliding. Of the woman — the leader of the heresy — I will not speak, but God will judge them and we will all be known on the day of days.'

'I have always been sure of it,' replied Marighal, her head still in her hands, 'for they died at the hands of the heathen and bowed their heads patiently before God's inscrutable will. It was this patience I wished to emulate when I came to you here. Already I begin to see again what your faith meant to me then.'

'Then why do you grieve for them?' asked Cadui, 'when you are sure that they are in eternal bliss? That shows a spirit ungrateful to God. There was nothing for you to do and, unhallowed, your death would have destroyed you.'

She shook her head and turned her face to us saying, 'There was much more I could have done.'

And we saw then that tears were running down her face. But God have mercy on me, they were not of water, but of blood! We stared at her face in mortal terror while she said, 'Those people were my first friends. They took care of me when they might have driven me off. They gave me my first glimpse of what men mean by love, and I left them to be destroyed. God may forgive me, and I pray he does, but I will never forgive myself.'

St Brigid and St Martin!

'Your noble heart does you credit,' I said hastily, and left her hut.

Cadui came hard on my heels crying, 'Alas, what manner of woman is this your meddling has brought to us? A monster? A demon? Lilith is in our midst and you were eager to give her shelter.'

There is a legend that St Beya wept bloody tears each time she read of Christ's martyrdom, but there are no witnesses.

'Bloody tears are also a sign of much holiness,' I answered him, 'for did not St Anthony weep blood in his temptation.'

'I do not believe so, and if he did, remember he was a baptised Christian and a man, not a godless woman.'

'We must pray to God for guidance in this. One thing I am sure of, we must not tell our brothers of this manifestation. Cienach and Edern would not doubt that it is the sign of a demon, but there needs many hours of meditation before we can find the truth of the matter.'

'I do not care to keep matters hidden from the others, but I too am uncertain, as yet. Be sure, though, that one day I will bring it to light. I am only silent because Nuth and the other innocents would be filled with fear.'

Selyf continues his story.

The mornings were frosty and as late as the ninth hour our breath was white as it rose to heaven. The days passed while I searched my heart, but I came to no conclusion. As long as the woman remained meek and received instruction with gratitude it was not possible to treat her as other than human. My brothers loaned their books to the woman, and she seemed to read Latin, English and British equally easily, which was a greater wonder than her tears would have been to some of them.

Nuth was with me the day when I asked the woman about her husband and he will witness in his innocence that our conduct was always proper.

'You have told us that your father was fostering a boy who was to be your husband,' I began, 'did the marriage take place, and was it consummated? Your virgin state or otherwise will affect your state of grace, so as your instructor I must know.'

'I am still a virgin,' she answered, blushing, 'even though I did exchange oaths with the man my father intended for me. The marriage was not consummated in my father's hall, where we were put to bed, nor later, when we had won clear of my father's lands for my husband was then lost to me. I was again compelled to return to my father's hall, a virgin still, nor has anything happened to change my state since.'

'How did you lose your husband, you poor woman,' cried Nuth, 'and so soon after marriage? Was he killed in battle, or did wild animals take him in the forest?'

'Indeed, neither of these,' she answered, 'My husband was a fine warrior and a very courageous man. Neither animal nor man could stand against him when he was in the prime of his life, how could they, when he was taught by my father in all the arts of the hunt and of the battle?'

'Forgive me,' I said, 'we do not seek to slight your husband nor your father, but surely it was a terrible thing for a man to break his oath to you, even though you say you had no great liking for him?'

'By the time we came to marry I liked him well enough, though when I was young I thought him a coward and a simpleton. My father made sure that I knew his finer qualities before we were hand-fasted, and his oath-breaking was not his choice. No, I would have been proud to be his wife.'

When my father first brought him to our hall he had been in terror since he left his own house, and he sat in my sister's lap weeping and trembling. Like myself, he was in his eighth year at the time, but I had never shed a tear and I was dismayed at this miserable creature who had been brought for my husband. My father had filled my thoughts with what a man ought to be. That he should face hardship and death with good cheer, and

This is true. I went to Kyngaradh to see Nuth and he speaks warmly of Marighal and calls her 'Our lady.' In his innocence he does not see the blasphemy, and I will not show him. Of such is the Kingdom of Heaven.

The woman continues her story.

38

*This is what the pagans
I know believe. They give no
thought to life after death and
think that the only immortality
is if you make a name for
yourself in battle. The lowly
ones have no future which is
why they are the first to be
converted.*

hide the fears in his heart from the world, and make sure
that a good name lives after him — these above all were
the qualities I valued.

I protested to my father and pleaded with him to find
me another man, saying, 'A daughter of your house
should not go to one so ignoble. Is it not bad enough
that his father is no more than a thegn of the king's
household with no blood and no land of his own? In
himself he is nothing, a girlchild, a wailing infant. When
you said I would be married I did not think you would
pack me off with a ninny. I would rather be an old virgin
like my sisters than bed with such a one.'

'Do not alarm yourself, Marighal,' said my father,
more mildly than he might, 'I have told the boy's father
that he will be taught to be a man, and more than a
man, and my word is my bond. With all my cunning
and knowledge of war and my skill in hunting he will
become one of the greatest of his generation, and a
fitting husband for a daughter of my house.'

'It seems to me you have much work to do,' I replied,
but my father's patience was not long.

'That is for me to judge,' he replied, 'I have made
more out of less promising material than he. Go and do
not plague me any more about him. You will see what
sort of a man you have when I have finished teaching
him.'

Until he was ten the boy stayed with me and my
sisters, and spent only a few hours each day with my
father. I spent most of that time in the weaving-room,
where no man creature was admitted, so that I would
not be annoyed by seeing him. Then, as time passed,
he spent all his days in my father's company, and slept
at the foot of his bed like a servant. I went to my foster-
father's house, so that I saw nothing of him till we came
of age. The first time I did so it was a source of great
misery to me.

I must confess that after I was returned to my father's
keeping I was foolish enough to want to see what had
become of the silly boy I was to marry. One day in spring
when the leaf-buds were a red mist about the trees, and
the bracken struck out of the ground like a clenched fist,
I went out onto the moor above my father's hall. Below
me, at the lochan that feeds our river, I saw two men
netting fish. I saw that it was my father and his ward and

I hid myself in the old bracken stalks. A devil must have whispered to me that day, for I watched them as they stripped and swam in the water, and then I learned that my betrothed was my father's catamite. Even though I hid my face at once from their filthy practices, I could not hide what I had seen from myself as I lay alone at night. Before that day I had been completely innocent of the lusts of the flesh, but now such a flood of tormenting visions followed that evil morning's work that I almost wished to give up my raging body for all time.

There is native wisdom here, for what is lust but an agony of the flesh and a torment to the soul?

I am sure my father knew I had been on the hillside that day for his servants spied on our every step, and the next day he sent word to me that I must prepare my bridal gift for it would soon be needed. All that summer I worked on it, and that winter I saw my bridegroom once more, when my father brought him to me.

It was my father's custom to summon his daughters to a feast with him on the longest night of the year. We would sit, all of us, at one long table, and he at another facing us. The heat from the two great fires that he must always have burning at either end of the hall made us drowsy and we would sit in stupid silence, eating only a little and pinching ourselves under the table. Father would sit watching us and if he thought one of us might have gone to sleep he would shout a toast to the woman and laugh to see her scramble to her feet. He would also ask us about what we had done that year. He knew everything from his servants, but it made him laugh when he caught us attempting to conceal the truth. I was questioned the most often at that time, for I was the most restless of the sisters. I would sit, the banners over my head waving in the hot draught from the fires, and try to stay awake to recall the details of my adventures.

Who is the mother of these sisters? She is never mentioned but she must exist.

The winter Kynan — my husband — was returned to me, we gathered as usual, but this time my father had him seated on his right hand like an honoured guest. I was not surprised by this, but had made careful preparations. As the feast proceeded I drove the stupor from my head, pushed my chair back from the table and stood up to say, 'I see that at our feast tonight we have a noble visitor. Let me make haste to do him all the courtesy due to one of his kind.'

40

*Why not? What was he
fostered for?*

*She can manage to use
the flowery speech they use at
court. She must have had
some training.*

*On the other hand the
father does not seem to value
the use of rhetoric.*

I raised my cup to him in greeting. My father smiled
and his mouth was wet and red in his beard. Kynan
looked ill at ease for he had not learned gentle manners.

'Many years have passed since you were last with us,
Kynan White Hair, and the days in the women's hall
have been long without you. I hope that for yourself the
time has passed pleasantly and swiftly, for a young man's
days of glory are short. For ourselves, since you left our
care the time has hung about us like chains, dragging us
to the ground with grief.'

My father laughed and watched Kynan to see what he
would do. Kynan looked at him but there was no help in
that quarter.

Finally he stood up and said, blushing, 'Thank you,
Marighal. I am happy to see the women of this house
again. The time has passed quickly for me. I have
learned a lot. Your father has been teaching me the
practice of arms, and hunting.' And he sat down again.

'We had thought so,' I replied, 'for this is the practice
of our family. Our father is a truly wise man and none
fitter than he to teach all the arts of manhood. Many a
proud young man has left this hall to find his place in the
stories of heroes and their deeds. I am sure than when
your skill is tried you will prove to be a most apt student.'

Kynan had taken a large draught of mead, and now he
spoke more easily, saying, 'There is no man more able
than your father to train a young man for war, but in me
he had a difficult task. Now that we are nearly finished
I am sure, though, that I will not disgrace my name, for
I know more of the arts and skills of battle than any
man alive. But not only can I fight with axe and spear
and sword, and defeat any opponent your father sends
against me, I understand the crafts of the smith and the
huntsman.'

'I am truly glad to hear this,' I answered, 'for I have
a gift for you and a token which shall show the bonds
between yourself and our family. I have made it myself
with all the skill I have learned over the years of my
fostering, and only one who knows the craft of the smith
will see what effort has gone into my poor offering. If my
father will give me leave I will send a servant for it.'

My father nodded, and the servant I had prepared for
this fetched the gift and placed it on the floor between
the tables.

'You do me great honour, Marighal,' said Kynan, 'for I have heard your great skill praised many times by your father's people. I am glad I will have the chance to pair my skill with yours.'

'Better to praise the gift after you have seen it, for I am sure your skill at war is greater than mine at the anvil.'

'It is true no man can stand against me. The only one whose strength I cannot withstand is your father's, for there is none mightier than him.' At this he looked at my father from under his brows, and my father looked at me and smiled. I signed to the servant to spread out the gifts.

First the whole was bound up in a fine blue mantle that I had furnished out myself with embroidery in red and green and gold. Inside there lay a shield, with a boss set with rubies and cairngorm, and inlaid with pictures of beasts I copied from my father's books. Then came a bright coat of mail made of links so fine they were like the scales of a fish, and even my sisters roused themselves to look at it. There was a sword and helmet of the strongest steel I could achieve, and damascened with leaves in copper so that it would bend and not shatter. There was a short bow of yew which I had smoothed myself, and lastly an axe with a long head of steel and a handle of well-seasoned ash. Kynan ran round the table and with one hand lifted the byrnie like a stream of fire and with the other joyfully brandished the sword.

'Oh, generous woman,' he cried, 'I shall surely be first among warriors now.'

'And here,' I said, 'is the sword belt and scabbard I have just finished. It is decorated with jewels which my foster-father gave me as a wedding gift.'

Kynan was beside himself with delight. 'When did a young warrior ever set out on his first campaign with such fine gear? They will remember my name for ever.'

At last my father spoke, 'Fine gear does not make a fine warrior. You would be better clad in the rustiest mail and fight bravely than be recalled as a bejewelled craven. You talk like an unmarried girl.'

At this Kynan's face went fiery red with shame.

'You are indeed wise, father,' I said, 'the finest armour will not make a great warrior if the creature

Insofar as she talks about fine work I can believe her. I have seen women draw wire, and so she might be able to make a byrnie if she were very skilful. But the forging of a sword needs the use of a big hammer with a massive head. This must be swung as if it were a bell-clapper, often and regularly. The men who do this have arms like the legs of cattle. There must be magic about.

She makes no mention of leather-work. Is it a question of caste? I know some think leather work is unclean. How much better if all this skill could be used to refurbish our ruined churches.

This is a cruel humiliation. The girl and her father are both unjust and uncharitable.

42

inside it has a poor heart. But since you had the training
of him yourself, you should know if his heart is firm. We
can be sure his skill is great, for your servants cannot
defeat him. But, then, what are your servants? Poor
mindless creatures which have nothing but speed and
skill. They do not have the heart of a warrior which may
prevail against terrible odds by courage alone.'

My father stared at me as if the light from his eyes
would burn holes through me. I had to lean on the
table as I continued, 'Poor, mindless slaves. What has
he learned from them but the rapid waving of a sword
in the air? He might have stayed and learned weaving
with us women for our fingers are nimble and our arms
are strong from that work. We knew from the first day
he came that he would be good for the weaving, for he
told us that when they fetched you to meet him first he
had been plaiting dolls out of straw. Then he told us of
his terrible journey here with you, when he was so filled
with fear that he soiled himself. Since that day, father,
what more has he learned that might make him more
of a man?

'You took him from our company, and taught him to
fight out of vanity and fear. He knows well how to run
and ride and leap and set out a line of fighting men
for battle. But what is this? Only more doll play and
mummery. How will he fare when he sees the face of a
real foe-man before him, with teeth bared in battle-rage
and howling in his throat. What will mere skill serve him
then? Will his legs turn to water under him, and will he
fall sobbing onto his shield like an infant?

'How much better for him if he had been with us
women and girls while he was growing to manhood?
It is only by protecting the weak and the helpless that
a warrior learns the good of his strength. Then, no
matter how his heart misgives him in battle, at the
thought of those who need him his blood will thicken
again; and when the blood runs round his feet, his arms
will never become heavy. I have learned that men who
fight for wealth and vanity make miserable the lives of
the weak through all the length of this country, for when
the Saxons give over the Vikings take their turn. Gold
and glory waste the land and make the people desperate.
Yet you would have him one of these — a red-handed,
black-hearted ravisher of children! Is this a fitting man?'

Ah, she learned her lesson at the holy city. There is no other duty of which a warrior may boast and claim to be

As I spoke Kynan sat on the floor beside my gift and his face was pale and sweat glinted round his mouth. My father rubbed his eyes and smiled at me.

'Well, Marighal,' he said, 'you have been most eloquent in your ideas on the training of a warrior. Perhaps I should have consulted you before I began to instruct him. You could have shown me what pitfalls to avoid. I recall you were about seven summers old when we began, or was it eight? But then, we would have sorely missed the benefit of your advice for you went off to learn the skills that made your fine gift to him. Talking of which, I must tell you not to be so slighting of your finery for it has been my experience — the experience of many, many years of battle — that what gives a man the greatest hardihood and courage is nothing but vanity. Once he knows that his name will stand or fall by his conduct of himself he will do all that a warrior must. Once battle rage takes him he forgets everything, soonest of all, believe me, home and hearth, and nothing is left to him but the thought of his comrades. If he does not give the enemy point and edge and the sorrow of wounds they will report it and his infamy will be everlasting. This drives him, like a hind before hounds, nothing more.

'But now that I have the benefit of your advice I have taken it to heart. There is a king some days travel to the north who is mustering an army. Pirates from Eirinnn have begun wintering deep in his kingdom and he is of a mind to send them back whence they came. When the roads open you and your man here will leave this stronghold and go to his aid. If your man returns with his sword blunted I will have been proved right for these pirates are on the far side of Dun Brytain and are no threat to my hall, but if he shirks, perhaps your word will be made good. And so that we can be sure he has not blunted his sword on the nearest tree, you will accompany him as his bound servant, Marighal. You will see what a great warrior I have made for you. Now all of you, go, for my eyes grow weary with the sight of your stupid faces.'

So it was that a few weeks later, when the fields were dun and the trees black and dripping with melting snow, my father sent for me and said, 'Now is the time for your travels. You will follow your man and though you

virtuous. If he cannot do so he would be better to have been a monk.

This old man is a deadly cynic. This bitterness is God-cursed.

Which King?

44

will hear everything he says to you, you will not speak to him.' And so it was.

We travelled north over hills for many days till we came to the wide, wide river. On the far side stood a tall peak, riven in the centre as if a great axe had struck it. It stood alone at the mouth of a river which ran down a wide, flat valley. In the cleft there was a mighty stronghold.

Alclyth! It must be there. This ancient fort has been our seat and our protection for generations. It has even kept the Vikings out of northern Cymri, thanks be to God.

We had to wait many hours till the tide was slack enough for a crossing, since the melt-water had made the river dangerously fast. The ferry was a log raft and my master's horses were terrified and half dead with the cold when we came at last to the foot of the peak. There was a palisade round the foot of the peak, and we arrived so late that the sun had set and the gate was closed. Nevertheless my master walked up to it and pounded on it with the pommel of his sword.

A porter appeared in the tower at the side and said, 'Who is this coming to the gate at this time of night? The wine is in the cup and the knife is in the bread and the king seated with his men beside him. This gate will not open before dawn.'

Kynan the Unknown. Kilidh died in retreat some years ago. His heir still reigns in Sulwath but he is called Fillan the Black

'I am Kynan, son of Kilidh, and as loyal a follower as the king would find though he searched his kingdom for a year.'

'I do not doubt it,' said the porter, 'but the king will not open the gate until sunrise tomorrow. That is the law and has always been so and he could not change it himself even if he wished. Go now to the guest house the monks have set up there beside the river. It is a fine house and you will be as well fed and bedded as you would be in the king's house itself. Better perhaps, for since this campaign started this hall has been as full as an egg.'

That will be the monks of St Padraig. They would not remember them because there was a numerous host that year.

'But I must see the king, for I have heard that he is gathering men to go and fight the Danes, and I have come to offer him my sword.'

Then the king must be Maelcolum Mac Domhnall, under-king of Cymri from great Kennach.

'Fine that,' said the porter, turning away, 'go the the guest house and you will find young warriors like yourself all waiting to offer service to the king. At dawn he will see you all, but before that he will not be disturbed.' And he disappeared into the house.

In silent rage my master went to the guest house, and the next morning I saw him offer the fine sword I had made him to the king. With him there was a crowd of youths, none as well born as he, but my master would not speak up and claim his place. When one of the earls put him in the third rank of battle he ground his teeth and glared angrily from under his brows, but he held his peace. It was as well he did not grumble under the slight, for he had no kin there to help his claim, but he kept silent out of pride alone. The king's great army strode off into the rain, and we travelled west along the marshy bank of the river. My master was quickly dubbed kinless on that march, and was made the butt of jokes for his fine horses and his hound and he in such a poor place, but he stared at the jokers and they soon fell silent.

'I have much to do to make my name here,' he said to me that night, 'and if we do not engage the enemy soon I may prove my courage on the body of one of those 'boys', though they have no honour, and it would be beneath me to strike them.' But I could not speak to him to comfort or advise.

The next day the army struggled on round a headland till it faced north. I made sure my master was always well fed and all the men there envied him. The next day we went round the top of a sea loch and headed up a long, twisted pass where the snow still lay. We continued on a high road with another long loch below us and camped that night on the the heights for the Vikings might have caught us unprepared on the beach. The next day and for two days more we travelled high passes where storms threatened us and the way was so steep that men fell to their death from it. At last the march was over and we saw the sea shining below. There beside it lay the seamen's town and the fleet at anchor, and the fields they had started to plough. We hurried to make camp for the night.

That evening I saw the Vikings' herald going to the king's own tent and heard him make speeches to frighten him and to demand tribute as had always happened before. This time, though, the king laughed and said, 'You are not going to win treasure here as you have in the past. My uncle has sent me men so that I could show you his strength. We are many and we are brave and we have not come so far with thirsty blades just to return home at the words of a pirate.'

So the exchange of honour went on and the thegns crowded round to hear the long list of warriors who would be joining battle the next day. All of them there, except for my master, were waiting to hear their names spoken. I went to guard the baggage. At nightfall my master came back and he unpacked his battle-gear while the thegns around us looked on enviously.

'Where did one such as you get such fine gear?' they demanded, 'We have never seen mail that shimmered like that. You must have stolen it from a great warrior, for no landless man could make such a showing.'

'I did not steal it,' said my master without looking up, 'it was given to me freely by the greatest smith in the world.' I was well pleased with this answer, for all that it was wrong, but the thegns were not.

She is modest, at least.

'We say you stole it, or you won it in a fight against a man you had no right to challenge. You should give it to the king as his due.'

These warriors are as touchy as girls.

'I am as good a man in the king's army as any, and better than those I see here. This armour was a free gift to me and is due to no man. Now go and do not provoke me further, for the king has put his word against all quarrelling in his camp.'

They left him alone, but someone must have taken his tale to the king's companions for one of them came to us and said, 'You have armour here which no landless man could have by right. You must come at once and render it to the king, or else confess that you are no more than a pirate yourself.'

'I will gladly speak to the king,' said my master, 'for I have wanted to speak to him since the first day I joined this army. I have been kept from him only by the meddling of fools. I am Kynan, son of Kilidh, son of Fillan the seaman, and the king's own father honoured my family for courage and loyalty by a generous gift of land.'

He strode off with the officers to speak to the king. I stayed to watch the baggage, for I could see the spite in the thegns against my master and I knew enough of this manner of quarrelling to see that it could lead to theft and even murder.

On his return my master was smiling, and well pleased to say to the thegns, 'You must hold your peace now, for the king himself has recognised me and my kinfolk. He

has given me my sword again in front of his companions
to show that I am no landless thegn. Tomorrow I will
prove that I am fit to be in the first rank, so take your
last look at the gear you envy so much.'

The night was chill and showers of grey hard rain
blew across the camp. Nevertheless we woke refreshed
to find the sun warming our backs.

'It is a good day to die,' said my master, but he was
very young.

The king had said we must fight early in the morning
so that the sun would be in our enemy's face, thus we
hastily broke our fast and made for the firm ground
beside the river. The Danes saw us moving and made
haste to meet us and the metal of their arms shone
brightly in the white sun of the morning. A cry went
up and overhead the ravens began to gather. The
armies advanced towards each other and soon there
was nothing to hear but the loud clashing of sword
and shield.

Then I sighted my master, and I felt a chill in my
bowels for he stood amazed and looked as if he might
turn and run from the battle-field. All about him men
were screaming in rage and pain, their terrible wounds
gaping, and I feared that this had taken his courage. He
said to me later that he was unused to a press of bodies
so close to him and he was afraid to swing his sword in
case he hurt one of them. Whatever the truth of it, as
he stood irresolute one of the shabby thegns who stood
behind him began to taunt him.

'It is true what they say,' he shouted, 'fine gear does
not make a fine warrior. Look at the landless one, now,
with his dear sword fast in its sheath. He is afraid to
spoil the beautiful blade with the blood and bones of
heroes. He is afraid to take a dent in his fine helmet.'

My master could not have heard them for he still
stood and I saw him shake his head like a bewildered
animal.

'See where he stands,' cried the vermin, 'shaking
down his golden locks. You would not know that this
is a battlefield. You would think it was a wedding feast
and he himself the bride.'

My master heard that, at last, and it woke a rage in
him that might not have kindled all day. With a terrible
cry he smashed his spear into the body of the nearest

This must be the 'battle-fetter' I have heard the warriors of Orkney talk about. It is said the priests of Othin can call it up in a man and make him as weak as a woman. They will do it to a whole army. I think it is a sign that body, will and intellect are at odds but why this can be done I do not know.

Is this a 'bearsark' rage. It is another of the demon Othin's tricks. But the devotees

48

*of his mystery spend hours in
preparation, singing, dancing
and going into ecstasies so that
the demon can possess them.*

Viking so that the shaft splintered in the man's body.
Again my master looked amazed as the corpse fell at
his feet, but this time he soon recovered for he drew his
sword and charged to meet the next man. Now he was
engrossed in the battle, and I could not see him well for
the mass of men around him. My father's training soon
gave a good account of itself, however, for he stood firm
and hewed about him till the bodies lay deep piled at
his feet. Time and time again his sword tore the body
of a man and the bright blood leapt after it, nor did he
grow weary as the hours passed, and when lesser men
fled back to the river he would not give ground.

I heard him shout, 'Stand! and die as a warrior
should, with a sword in your hand. What glory is
there wallowing in mud, a spear in your back, your
blood staining the water. Stand fast.'

Then one of the cowards making for the river said
that the king's Hearth Companions lay dead and the
king with them, and the princes and earls had fled.'Let
us flee into the hills, now,' he cried, 'and send a herald
to the foreigners to arrange safe passage home.'

But my master knocked him to the ground and said to
all the rest, 'If there is a warrior left who would sooner
die than bear the name of coward let him stand now and
avenge his lord. If there is no man who cares for his
honour, I, Kynan son of Kilidh, will die here alone.'

At that many men turned saying that the landless one
should not shame them, and they advanced again. This
time, after hard war play, the pirates broke rank and
fled for their boats. Soon Kynan had to stop fighting
for there was no one left to fight, and I saw the oars
being run out and sails being raised as the pirates made
for open water.

Unhindered now, the king's host burned the houses
and cut down the children with their swords. The
women were hunted down and those of foreign blood
were raped and killed most foully. These were the
sights I had been spared back at the holy city, and with
horror now I found that I had common cause with the
murderers.

The only good I knew that day was that Kynan did
not join this butchery. He stood on the beach with his
eyes blank, splashed with blood to the knees. There was
blood running down his forearms and dripping from his

hands, and blood soaking his tunic. There were dents on his helmet and shield, and holes in his byrnie. His sword alone would take many hours of work to refurbish, and it would be weeks before his gear could be restored. Men went to him at last and opened his fingers for they had clenched round his sword and would not budge. He was as helpless as an infant. They brought him to the camp and left the ravens to feast on his offerings.

This is very like Othin's bearsarkers. I heard that they will sleep for days after a battle.

It could no longer be doubted that my betrothed husband was a true hero. He had led the battle back from the brink of disaster, and saved the day for the king, who was not dead, but only wounded. But I was sick at heart, for I had seen my father's words proved true, and there was nothing I could think, but that men fight for vanity and for riches, and that the weak are only toys for their pleasure.

This is why it is a vile thing when priests and bishops go into battle.

When we returned to my father's hall Kynan hastened to my father's chambers with me to tell the glory of his exploits, and called me to witness the truth of his daring. I was glad to do so for I had come to like the man, but my own unhappiness must have revealed itself to my father.

The next day he summoned me privately and said, 'Have you seen the truth of my words, Marighal — vanity is the reason why men fight, and nothing more?'

'Yes, father, your wisdom is paramount, and your knowledge of the human heart unsurpassed.'

He laughed, loudly, 'Well, Mari, do not be downhearted. There are few who know more than you about materials for making objects. Perhaps in time you will also know about the making of people. But now, rejoice, for your admission has made me feel generous, and I have decided to free you from your betrothal. You are no longer obliged to marry this bloody-handed coxcomb.'

'Thank you, Father,' I replied, 'you are more than generous, but I will marry the man, if you please.'

'Marighal, cleverest of all my daughters, why do you want to be married when you do not need to? I am not like other fathers who see their girl-children as nothing but a scourge on the house, and use them only to make marriage alliances. I want to see you all around me while I am alive.'

Who is this trainer of warriors? He is as fickle as spring weather.

50

This is a most uncommon father. He wishes to keep daughters beside him. Only Great Carolus was more affectionate. Or is it truly fatherly feeling? These godless men know no bounds to their lust.

Bravely said, but, I fear, unlikely with a pagan for a husband. It would be far better for a woman of her learning to take the veil but she would not have that road made open for her.

She remains chaste on her wedding night. But admits to lust.

'Yes, Father, it is true you are generous to us beyond the ways of most men, and I will grieve on the day I leave this house, yet I will marry the man.'

'What advantage will it give you to be married?' he asked. 'None of your married sisters has been made happier by so much as the width of a hair by their mating. For a woman to be coupled to a man means only that she will be his slave. He will make her bear one child after another till her body is swollen and flabby, and no longer pleases him. Then he will be off chasing younger women and boys, and leaving her bed cold at night. What will you do then, clever Mari? These lords have no books in their halls. There will be no weaving of anything more than endless plaid for him and his retainers. Do you wish to become the servant of your servants? You will never again have the chance to work in fine metals. The freedom of the hills will be taken from you, and your lovely weaving will rot on the loom. All your talk will be on the health of your babes and children, or the state of the harvest. A woman in her husband's hall has nothing to do but sit by the fire and hold her tongue.'

'Father, I have given you best in wisdom, but I do not believe a woman of spirit cannot make her life comfortable for herself. My husband respects my knowledge and my skill, and has some learning of his own. His mind will be furnished better than most men of his generation by being fostered here, and I may be able to add to that. Furthermore, though you may release me from my obligation to marry, my betrothed has not done so, nor have I asked him to. I will be married to him, or be dishonoured.'

My father had nothing to say more, and soon we exchanged our marriage oaths before witnesses. Yet that night, despite my own inclination, I would not let my husband enjoy my body, but showed him the places where my father had hidden servants to spy on us. We lay awake on the bed in our wedding clothes and when the night was at its darkest I tricked the servants and we fled on horses I had prepared. When my father discovered our escape we were too far ahead for him to catch us.

We had thought to go to Kynan's father's hall, but did not go there directly being sure that my father would seek us there first. After some days of travelling on the moors we found the ground dropped away below our feet. Ahead of us we saw a long, spreading plain of brilliant green fields with a river winding through it. At the farther edge of the plain, beside the shining sea we saw a fine city, built all of golden stone.

This place should be easy to find but I am still not sure.

'Let us go to that city,' I said, 'for I see by the fine milk herds and the ploughed fields around it that it must be a very prosperous place. Surely the king there will shelter us for the night and help us to find your father's hall.'

We started downhill and when we got to the edge of the plain my husband said, 'I will go ahead and speak to the king, first, man to man, for with no servants we have no evidence of our rank. I do not wish to see my wife slighted at the first town we enter, so I must make sure your standing is known. I will bring him back to greet you himself.' And off he went down the white road.

His experience on campaign has scored him deeply.

The evening came and he had not returned, nor did he the next day. As evening drew on I began to be concerned for my husband, and since I realised that sleeping under a hedge was doing more to take away from my dignity than lack of retinue, I set off for the city. For all my father's dire warnings I could not believe that Kynan had abandoned me willingly, for he had not even tasted my body, let alone tired of it. Then a man hailed me from a hut at the edge of a field.

Perhaps he met brigands on the road. I would not trust this man.

'Where are you going,' he asked, 'so finely dressed and all alone at twilight? Are you an entertainer for the wedding feast? Better for you if you were, for the gate is closed already and the feast well started. They will not open the gates for any other.'

'Yes, I am going to the wedding feast,' I replied, not wishing to show my ignorance, 'but my horse had trouble on the road and I am late. Tell me about the bride, for I know only about the groom and his family. Is there anything I should mention in my speech to her?'

The old man came close to me, and his wet eyes were gleaming over the beak of his nose.'Indeed,' he began, 'she is one of the fairest women that has ever been seen in this kingdom. She is the king's daughter, and she has skin as white as the bloom on the apple tree, and cheeks red as the foxglove. Her hair is the colour of leaves in autumn, or the best gold out of these hills, and she wears it in four thick tresses, two behind and two before. She

Why does she never show fear? She is not like a woman at all.

52

This is all empty rhetorical formula. I have yet to meet a princess of the Cymri who does not have these qualities — according to her subjects and other sycophants.

A truly virtuous woman can walk naked anywhere and not be ashamed. It is known the angels will clothe her in blinding light.

is as tall and slender as a sapling and as she walks she sways stately as a swan on the water. Her hands are long and white and on them she wears many fine gold rings given to her by her father.'

'Good man, I shall soon see her beauty for myself. Tell me about her family.'

'She is called the daughter of the king, but to tell the truth she is not his child at all. He is old and his wife died childless many years ago. It is said that not long ago he found her walking shameless and naked on the seashore, and no one knows where she came from. Some say she is a sea-demon, and she is so beautiful that the old man was enchanted by her, swore she must be of a noble line, and adopted her straightaway as his daughter. It is sure she is as sweet tempered as she is beautiful, and as innocent as a new-born, and all who meet her love her at once.'

'This is a great mystery,' I said, 'and one such as you speak of must be seen at once. I will make haste now to see your foundling princess.'

'No, I pray you,' said the man, 'night is nearly upon us. Stay here with me. and go to the city in the morning for I am sure the gates will be locked before you can get there.'

But I had no notion to spend the night with the old man in his stinking hut, and there was more than kindness in his invitation, for he had looked at the gold on my arms and neck like a farmer pricing sheep. I travelled on to the city where, contrary to his promise, I found no gates barred. Indeed, I saw no soul in the whole city as I rode through it to the stronghold, least of all a watchman to challenge my entry. I began to wonder if the whole population had been taken by wild horses from the sea, but as I got near the fortress I saw lights at the windows and smoke from the cooking fires. The door of the fort was as untended as the town gate had been, apart from one guard lying snoring behind it. I slipped inside and crossed the yard to the great hall.

This is a badly run city! No sentries at all?

It had been my intention to tell the crowd I was a juggler come to amuse the guests, for I had learned some tricks from my foster-father. I had planned to search for my husband among the crowds jammed along the benches, but then I got to the doorway and looked at the king's table. There sat the white-haired, slender old king of that place, his head bowed with years and his hand shaking as he reached for his cup; there sat his red-haired, white-breasted daughter, smiling like the first day of spring, and between them sat the groomsman and guest of honour, smiling back at his bride beside him. It was my own sworn husband.

I found myself a seat by the wall and covered my face with my kerchief. I prayed to my poor deserted father to forgive me for not believing him. He had warned me about the treachery of mortal man, and the misery marriage would bring me. Indeed my fate was worse than my other married sisters, for I had not even enjoyed one night of my husband's embraces before he had betrayed me with another bride. 'Woe, woe is me,' I groaned, 'this is a shame I cannot bear, for I am cast off before he has even taken my virginity.'

Rejoice, sister, that your state is untarnished. It would have been far worse to have been left without your innocence, and with a child on you, as too many have found.

Then I remembered that I was my father's daughter, and began to lay plans with vengeful rage burning hot in my heart. I was determined that my husband would remember who had made his armour for him, and who it was that had taught him how to use it. I stood up and looked at the man and his new bride. She was indeed lovely, like a dewy pink-tipped flower that would fade before nightfall. Her hair was the same colour as my own, and her neck was not longer; when she reached for her cup I saw that her fingers were no longer nor whiter than my own, and that they were exactly the same in number. In truth the more I looked at her, the more I saw that she resembled myself in every respect, even to the pattern of sun-kisses across her nose and the length of her ear-lobes.

It came to me at last that there was sorcery afoot, and that my husband had been most cruelly deceived for he believed that the woman was, in truth, myself. I wanted him to realise the truth, but so that he should not be publicly shamed I set about gaining his attention slowly. I veiled my face and offered myself as a poor travelling entertainer who might beguile the hour with a few paltry tricks. I had started to bring white doves from the sleeves of my tunic when there happened a thing which some there must have known about. The door of the hall flew open wide and in ran a crowd of men armed with spears and knives and sickles. There was about a score of them, and they rushed up to the

Who is the deceiver and who the deceived?

This is very generous of her.

But how can you trust someone with so much dexterity?

54

54

I was expecting something like this.

king's table, threatening the old man, when my husband slapped his sword on to the table in front of them. They fell back.

'Come no nearer,' he cried, 'or I will make raven's meat of you. Who are you who threaten the annointed king like this? I think you are all landless men and I may not challenge you.'

The men looked at each other, nodded and at once pulled the table over to get a clear run at him. The king and his daughter clung to each other and backed against the wall, sobbing pitifully. My husband looked to make sure that his bride was safe and one of the attackers jabbed at him with his spear. The princess screamed and my husband started to fight like one possessed by demons. At one stroke of his sword a man's head leapt from his shoulders, and at another a man was opened across the belly so that he stood looking at his own guts. Without pausing Kynan drew his knife and stabbed a third man up through the heart, and at the same time smashed another in the face with the pommel of his sword. A fifth died with his ribs parted from belly to neck and a sixth had his throat cut so that his head fell back. And when the seventh died, skewered on his friend's spear through the collar-bone to the loins, the fight was over. They were only poor-spirited peasants who had expected no resistance and could not face the carnage. Screaming, they fled back towards the door and were clubbed to the ground by the people at the feast.

My husband called for silence and demanded why they had made such a wicked and ill-fated attack. They said that they had decided that the old king was too feeble and unlucky to go on ruling them. Lately there had been pirate raids all around, also the cattle were falling sick. A younger man would lead them against the raiders to success, but not as long as the old man kept the loyalty of the people. When he adopted a daughter rather than a son and leader as his heir, they decided they must kill him and change the luck of the country.

Then the king stepped forward and said to his people, 'My children, I knew what was in your hearts, and none have been more troubled than I that I have given you no heir to take this kingship from me. Yesterday, when this fine young man knocked on our gate I found hope born

Peasants!

in my heart. It seemed to me that when he had married my daughter, I would soon persuade him to take my place at your head, and I could retire. I have longed to go to stay at my brother's monastery and end my days in peace. But now that you have shown him what a foul, rebellious people he will have to rule I do not think that Kynan will be pleased to take the kingdom. Tomorrow, having taken his bride, he will hasten back to his father's hall as he now proposes, and he will stay in a kingdom where people know how to be grateful.'

The people cried out that they had not fomented the rebellion themselves, but that it had been started by poor farmers and lordless mercenaries who made trouble all over the land. Weeping they begged Kynan to take over the kingdom and lead them in battle, for they had not seen such a fine man in that country before.

So Kynan stood before them and said, 'This is a good kingdom, and I will not find it hard to lead you in battle, for that is what I am educated for. But understand this, my wife can remember nothing of her childhood, and this is a great grief to her. The people here are all the family she knows now. Her life has been troubled beyond your miserable power to understand, and yet leaving her family caused her much sorrow. If ever I see whispering in corners or furtive glances cast at us, my wife or myself, who are the luck of this country, we will depart without a moment's pause. There is no kinship between us to make me stay with you, but I have sworn to take care of this woman.'

At this the bride blushed and hid her face in her hands, and he smiled down at her, well pleased. The the people swore that they would never rebel, and if they heard of plots against Kynan they would treat the plotters as vermin and kill them out of hand. After that there was much revelry, and my husband and his bride were put to bed.

I took myself to a place apart where I could watch the sea and I meditated on my situation as my father had taught me, thus: this country needed a king to lead them and if I made good my claim against Kynan they would be left without a champion. If I tried to make my claim I would have a hard time pressing it, and though I would win, I would pay for my victory with a husband publicly shamed and resentful. The new bride was a poor kind

If he did so I might be able to find him, but where? He was never at Hy Columbcille where the kings of Alban go. He was only a local magnate so he must have gone to a small one. It is safe to assume he gave his brother the money for his foundation and there are so many sites on this coast which are now ruins. He was not at Cyngaradh, Cathures or Caerleul.

The bath-house at Caerleul is a filthy hole!

56

of creature, and though beautiful she had nothing to recommend her but her helplessness. I had seen that this did not displease my husband, who seemed truly to believe her to be myself, and was satisfied to see 'me' unable to recall my grim and cunning family. I, on the other hand, could take care of myself, and needed neither husband nor champion to support me. Indeed, I was now free of my father and his meddling servants and the idea made my heart leap within me for joy.

Finally, and best, I had been proved right about what will make a man fight valiantly. In battle a man will fight both from fear and vanity, that his name should not be lost to memory, or go down through the generations with ignominy. But as years pass and the hot pride of youth fades, a man may come to feel that it would be better to plough the fields and die in bed, and who, then, will keep the lands safe from raiders? It is then that a man needs to feel in his heart the need to protect the weak and the helpless, as Kynan had done that evening. A man must have the thought of children and wife to drive him into battle and take the risks he would have plunged after eagerly as a youth.

I rejoiced to think that I had bested my father at last, even though he would never know it. I took myself to a hut outside the city and there I taught the young men who came to me how to build a forge and how to work metal. It seemed that was the best I could do for my oathbound husband, but as time went by my father came to know of this, and I was compelled to return to his hall.

I let a good while pass before I went to speak to the woman again. I had to study and pray to be sure in my heart that speaking to her was indeed an obligation of charity and that I was not merely giving way to the temptations of curiosity. My brother monks attended her daily for her instruction, but I kept myself apart. Then, one morning an hour of sunshine in a cold, damp autumn tempted me out of my cell to walk across the lynn and join Ælfrid and Edern as they heard her study for the day. As I approached her hut I could hear her voice lifted in joy, saying,

'He has his dwelling around heaven and earth and sea and all that is in them. He inspired all, He quickens all,

Deduced like a true philosopher! It is good that she rejoices in her virgin state. I pray her deductions are true, and her joy also.

She is not like your pagan queen Dido, Maedoc. She shows true patience and humility. To surrender husband, sovereignty, and wealth with gladness is a sign of much virtue.

The woman ends her history here.

And Selyf takes up the story.

He dominates all, He supports all. He lights the light of the sun. He furnished the light of the night. He has made springs in the dry land. He has set the stars to minister to the great lights.'

She saw me approach through the raised door-curtain and stood up to greet me. Ælfrid closed his book and left since there was no more room, and I sat on one of the stools she had made for her instructors. 'It delights my heart to hear you read this way, Marighal, you are an apt student for the word of God.'

'Truly it is a great pleasure to me to study the Word. The books I study are things of great beauty, and in the Word itself, there is much beauty and much truth. Yet there are things here I do not understand. Why, for instance, does Cienach not speak to me, and why does he immerse himself in the sea for many hours at a time? I find no mention of these practices in the Gospels, nor in the Psalter.'

'You have not yet read the lives of the Saints. If you had you would know that men of great holiness will engage in such austerities. Cienach is the holiest of us all here and what he does we all try to emulate to some degree, although you will not see us practicing it. We scourge ourselves and fast and perform other penitential acts which is the way of our order.'

Cienach has modelled himself on the oldest of the fathers, and the Saints Brendan and Coemgen.

'But why should this be so? I understand the scourging for pain is often a source of much strength, but to starve and to lie awake on the rocks all night or to stand with arms outstretched between the hours seem to me strange.'

'These penances are not to benefit the flesh,' I said, 'but to remind us that our flesh, is only of this world and so is unimportant. You must understand that we who profess the Lord believe that there is no greater good than the endless contemplation of God. In the kingdom which is to come the blessed saints and martyrs enjoy the perpetual presence of God. We, caught here in the flesh must strive to be like them which is why we call our regular life 'white martyrdom'. They have shown us the way by their lowliness, suffering, shame, misery and death, and from time to time we can taste a little of their joy here on earth by emulation. We punish our flesh to prove we hold it to be as nothing, and we wait for the time when we will know the bliss of God's presence.'

True enough but not the whole truth. Prayer and labour are the best roads to heaven. Charity, humility and patience are the crowns of the monastic life. I cannot see the grace in endless, aimless suffering. This is the Rule which was given to us by the holy Abbot Ferdacrich, but there has been much backsliding in the far away monasteries. Too many of them have encouraged indulgent fasting and mortifications. I know those who do so claim to

58

have had visions like those of St John and the other mighty saints, but there is much temptation in visions, and too often devils have entered a monk while he is defenceless in trance. Better to stay fully aware and on guard.

God will reveal Himself in His own time, not before. In the meantime, faith with deeds, desire with perseverance, placidity with diligence, chastity with humility, fasting with moderation, poverty with generosity, silence with conversation — these are what Colman taught us all those years ago, and this has never been improved on.

This accords with what I learned in Lübeck and Gorze. I think she may know a little about smelting but as to forging with her own hands — no.

'This is what they told me at the first monastery I found, but will I, too, be able to taste of this joy?'

'Once you have received baptism at the hands of our Bishop, you will become one of us.' said Edern, 'The sins of your past will all be washed away, and you will be born again, sinless.'

'I only hope it may be true,' she said, sadly, 'but my life has been such that I begin to fear that I will not find forgiveness from the Highest.'

'If you will tell us more about your life we will tell you if you have sinned mightily.' I answered, 'Nothing you have told us this far has been a mortal sin. Indeed, you are gentle beyond the common run of mortals. You must remember that God loves a sinner that repents more than any. Show us your sins freely, and God will pardon you.'

She blushed and said, 'It is generous of you to describe me so. It is true that I have no inclinations of the flesh which your brothers describe as wickedness. I wish no man nor woman ill. I love God with all my heart. I do not prophesy falsely, and I have never, to my knowledge, harmed anyone. These are all the sins which have been spoken of to me, and I am free of all of them, yet I am sure in my heart that I am a very great sinner.'

Edern said, 'You have told us you worked with a smith. It is well known that such people use spells and incantations to control the demons in the fire and the metal to work their way. When I was young I remember the monk who worked our forge would always recite the names of the Holy Trinity while the fire grew hot, and when he was swinging his hammer he would chant all manner of saint's names in time with his blows. But his metal was not good, and the others said that it was because he had not mastered the demons by name.'

'This is news to me,' said the woman, 'for I never had to call on demons when I worked at the forge, nor did the man who taught me. The work was hard, and he was sometimes like one in a dream while he worked but he never spoke any names. He told me that our task was to get the forge or the furnace to the right heat, and once the metal was heating to watch it carefully so that it did not become too hot or too cold for our purposes. Then the metal was shaped by moulding or hammering or welding. If you need metal that will bend and yet be

strong you must let it cool in the air slowly. If you want
a keen edge but do not need a strong blade then you cool
it swiftly in water. Now the key to all of these processes
is time, whether it is the rhythm of the hammer blows or
the duration of a quenching, and to make sure that the
time is the right length. I was taught to sing. But I was
not singing spells, I was merely chanting the names of
my sisters in order. I never spoke to demons. The only
time Grig, my master and foster-father, ever spoke of
hidden things was when I went with him to the mine.
Then I did see things which might come from the
wickedness that walks in shadows.'

'You must tell us about that,' said Edern, 'for it may
be that you have sinned by communing with such
things.'

My education began one day when I was in my eighth
summer. I was in the weaving hall of my father's house.
Like all my sisters I was taught to weave and spin almost
as soon as I could stand and apart from the stuff we
made for clothing some of us learned to make pictures
by weaving them into cloth. We had taught ourselves to
do this by studying garments my father brought from
far countries. We had also learned to embroider from
some Saxon women and to add all manner of detail to
a picture to make it look like life. These pictures take
us years to complete, and we never like to be watched
while we are making them, for we each have our own
tricks for giving life to a piece of work. At that time I
was making a picture of hunters returning with kill on a
winter's evening. I had sewn on little red beads to look
like blood dripping from the deer's nostrils and the jaws
of the dogs. The trees were to be black against the snow
and the sky green, as it can be in winter. I showed the
sun dipping into the sea, and I wanted to make the sight
when light makes water seem like polished gold. I had
thought to make it with gold wire but there was none in
the basket. At once I was filled with a longing for the
wire and I could not work on for thinking about it. I
went to see my father for he was always the one who
fetched it for us, but he was away from home and his
servants did not know when he would return.

That night I could hardly sleep for thinking about the
wire and when I went back to the weaving hall I stared

The woman takes up the thread of her story again.

Concupiscence?

60

at my work with a sickly gaze. Now the weaving hall was a long, narrow hall with the looms all down one side of it lying out from the wall so that each of us sat on our bench with our back to the one behind. On either side of the hall there were pairs of arched windows to let in a great deal of light, and these had all been glazed with round panes of green glass, so that even on the hottest day the room was cool and pleasant. Although it was our custom to pay no attention to each other in the weaving room, I noticed that the rack of oil lamps had been lit over a loom at the far end and I could hear the sound of someone beating down a weft. From the position of the loom I knew that it must be my older sister, Olwen, working there, but as I had been taught, I did not turn the mirror over my loom to see if I was right.

I began work at last, and went on well enough until a draught of air from the windows made my lamps flicker. Angry, I went to shut the casement. As I reached the window I saw a shadow approaching, and I leaned out. There I saw the gold and jewelled form of the Queen who lived in the fortress with us. The enamelled eyes of her mask seemed to stare right at me before she turned away and crossed the yard back to the hall. Her stiff golden skirts touched the ground, so that she did not seem to walk at all, but slid across the stones like a swan on the water. The crystals on her gold filigree crown shivered in the sunlight and the golden wrought flowers in her outstretched hand trembled as she passed over the ground. Behind me I heard a gasp, and I turned to see that Olwen had fallen against her loom. Being yet a child I was not troubled by the presence of the Queen, but the older ones among us could not withstand her closeness and suffered much distress. I went to see if Olwen needed my help. She had fainted and fallen against the loom and the warp was cutting into the skin of her face. It seemed to me that if I left her there her face would be scarred and the warp would become stretched, wasting months of work. Yet I knew I should not be looking at her, even now. I stamped my foot in perplexity as I wondered what to do for the best, and at last I decided to help her. I lifted her up and laid her along the bench.

I went back to my loom, but here was no help for me. I could only think about the gold thread I lacked;

That is a fine room to be set aside for weaving alone. It must be a very rich man that can let his women have such a well furnished place for their crafts. Are we to believe all this?

O, Selyf, it was a bad day when you were disciplined against 'curiositas'. Who is the 'Queen'?

about my sister's rage when she revived and realised
what had happened; about the Queen and the other
wicked servants who lived in the castle with my father;
and worst of all, I thought about the boy my father had
brought to be my husband, who whenever he met me
would grin and pull faces like a clown. At last I thought
that the smith who made the wire could not live far away,
for my father would visit him in an afternoon. It came to
me that I could go for myself and fetch what I needed,
and that it would be a very fine thing to get right away
from the stronghold. With no more reflection I snuffed
my lamps, found a slave who could show me the way,
and collected some food for the journey. Essyllt, my
oldest sister at the time, thought to stop me, but with
the slave to guard me, young as I was, I could come to no
harm, and her complaint was only a buzzing in my ear.

Who are these servants and who is the Queen who poisons the older one and not the girl?

I ran across the plain of the stronghold and soon I
was striding through the forest. Even though my father's
servant accompanied me I was filled with joy to be away
from his halls and from the stifling air which always
surrounds them. It seemed that as long as I was at
home a fog crept into my head and made it impossible
to see clearly in any light. I used to feel it was some
enchantment of my father's, but now I am sure it is a
sickness in our souls.

The forest was brilliant in the colours of early
summer, and the green of the trees was almost a
pain to the eyes. The song of the birds was as loud
as the sound of a mighty wind in the tree tops, and
their wings thrummed as they flew about their nests.
Once a flock gathered and mobbed my servant and I
thought for a moment I might run and hide, but I did
not yet know the road so I drove the birds off. We
made good time and soon the track dropped down
sharply towards a river. Then I knew I was near my
destination, and the servant bobbed and bowed and
left me alone. Soon I saw wheel-ruts in the road and
followed this track downstream. I found a mound of
baked earth which had been cut open to reveal burnt
wood tightly packed inside. The wood was hard and
black and like silk between my fingers. As I studied this
strange sight I felt that someone had come close and
I looked up to see a small man, no taller than myself,
staring at me.

Why should birds mob a slave woman?

Charcoal.

She was not yet ten years old and she must have been well secluded not to know that most farmers dress like this on market days.

It is clear there are some mysteries about her father's house we really should know about. I wish she had given more information.

This sounds as if it is on the river at Mailros, but that's a long three days away.

There was a king called Grig in Lothene beside the kingdom of one of the UiNial. It was said that his name was really Ciric and that he was called after the sainted father Cyricus. It appears that in his

He was dressed like a Saxon, with a plain belted tunic over a linen shift and drawers, and his legs were bound with soft red thongs of leather. He had fine brown shoes on his feet, and a long damascened knife at his belt. His face was wide and patched red. His cheeks and swelling forehead were pitted with specks of brown and blue where sparks had struck them. His pale blue eyes were scored all around with wrinkles from squinting into the forge, and under them the little bud of a mouth and the little wart of a nose looked as if they had been stolen from the face of an infant. The hair of his head was white and fine like flax. In a voice like a reed flute he asked me who I was, and I told him.

He said, 'I hope you may be able to prove this is so, for I know how close your father keeps his daughters and — pardon me for doubting your word — you must see it is hard to believe.'

I saw the truth of his words, so I told him some things about our house that only those close to us can know. At last he seemed satisfied, for he said, 'Then you are the one your father told me to expect. You are thrice welcome, for he said that you are cleverer than all your sisters and the most eager to know the world outside your father's stronghold.'

Then he took me to his house, and showed me how he lived. The house was built in the bend of the river and made out of the earth so that grass and herbs grew right over the top of it. From any distance you would not have known it was there. The dwelling was dug deeply into the clay and rock of the river bank and in all the years I stayed there I never discovered how many rooms there were in all. The opposite bank of the river was a high cliff of many-layered red rock and trees were set along the top of it like a line of marching men. Up to that time the little man — Grig — had shared the house with his brothers, but they had gone away to serve the king of the Franks many years before and had not returned. He was all alone, and at the end of the day, when he had showed me all his workshops and answered my many questions, he asked me if I would like to stay on with him as his fosterling and student. I agreed to do so at once, for I had been happier that day than in all the days I could remember. When the servant came to fetch me we said that I would be staying and the message was taken to my father.

For the next ten years I worked harder than Grig and all his brothers together, and I learned how to set jewels, draw wire, to glaze and enamel; I learned how to work gold, silver, iron and copper, lead and tin; I also learned to ride a horse, plough a yard, make fish traps, milk a cow, and many other things about the land. And I learned to use weapons from a woman in the forest. With Grig I also saw my first sight of other men's dwellings. We would take things we had grown and things we had made to the towns to sell them at market there. At that time the pirates were not haunting the seas, and the Saxons had ceased to harry the land, so travelling was easy. Grig said that I was beautiful in the eyes of men, and he would load me with the jewellery we made so that people would see it to advantage. It was very pleasant to me to sit beside his booth and show the gold rings on my arms and fingers, and necklaces set with smooth green malachite and hot jasper. Grig, selling knives beside me would laugh at the way people stared at such a finely dressed child. The jewels I wore to the common market place were not the best, for those were kept for the great lords whom Grig would visit alone. But I knew even then that fine jewels and clothing are of no value if the soul is sick. Grig knew this also for he said to me,

'Gold and silver are our servants, not our masters. Never let either of them tell you how to live.'

So you see he was not a foolish or wicked man. Further, we often saw monks and priests at the markets. We had little to do with them, for they rarely had any use for our wares, but Grig always pointed them out to me as good men, loyal to their oaths, benefactors of the sick and the poor. He said that if ever I were in trouble these would be the men to aid me, and he was right. Surely an adversary of God would not speak so?

Now I will tell you about the only time I ever heard him speak of his mysteries. Sometimes in the making of jewellery we would use tiny globes of metal, and the making of them was something which has always puzzled me. Gold or silver would be heated till they ran like water, and at the same fire we would heat a perfectly round bowl of clay. Grig would make these

ninth year there was an eclipse of the sun on the first Ides of June which is the saint's own day. The people in consequence held that he was also a saint which is foolishness.

Where would they go for such markets? There are not many held now in this kingdom though I believe there were a lot in the days gone by.

While this is a crude and ill-informed version of the truth it could not be said to be malicious. From a pagan standpoint it is reasonable and just.

This is very interesting. I must talk to Mochua at Cathures about it. He is the best smith in this part of the world.

bowls himself and would spend many hours grinding the surface till it was perfectly smooth. Into this bowl we would drop a little of the liquid metal and then the strange thing would happen. The metal would rush around the sides of the vessel like animals fleeing from a terrible, invisible hunter. Some pieces would even fly out of the bowl. I wondered if the metal was trying to escape from the heat of the bowl, but since it was itself hot I could not see how it would be aware of the heat.

I asked Grig what was happening and he said, 'If you had ever suffered from a fever you would not need to ask that question. You would know that in a fever skin is very tender so that anything placed on it causes anguish. Even when the skin is burning, a hot cup laid against it is agony. I conclude that it is the same for the metal. In its fevered state of heat the hot clay is unbearable to it and it tries to escape. When the metal is cool it falls on to the hot clay and slides slowly across it, and I know then it is feeling pleasure from the heat for it soon becomes soft and pliable like a contented infant.'

The only other time he spoke of such things, we were at the place where he found his raw iron and I had been with him for about seven summers.

One day when the stubble was yellow and the bracken lay like fire under the trees he came to me and said, 'It is time for you to see the place where iron begins. The womb of the earth where all the great metals come from has been a mystery of my family for many generations, and I am sorry to let an outsider into our secrets. But I see now that my brothers will not soon return, and I must take you with me in their place.

'If I went alone I would not be able to take all the mules I will need, and I will need your assistance at the minehead, also. You are coming into your full strength now, and you will be of much help to me.'

The strength of a girl of fourteen?

With so many mules the journey to the mine took many days. The first three days were easy, for we followed the river as it wandered downwards, but the morning came when we started to climb up a slope so steep that the branches on the upward side of the tree brushed against it. At the top we were so high that not even bracken grew there, only the thin white grass of the uplands. We followed a track that ran along the tops of the hills, and then sank again into gloomy forest which hung thick and silent round the road. I wondered that we had left the firm dry uplands for a dank forest, but I found that the road continued solid on a stony bank that lifted it well above the tangled forest floor. After a day's march we left the forest and returned to the trackless hilltops.

'Where the great stone road runs now the land has changed,' Grig told me, 'and if we were to follow it we would run into treacherous bogs. The earth moves slowly to work her will but in time she takes all things back to herself. The men who built the road were small and dark of skin and hair, and they came from far over the sea, thinking to leave their works where others would see and admire, but look what it all comes to.'

I am sure he means the Roman legions. The little man clearly did not know that they brought the word of God with them. That is an edifice more lasting than stone. The only road of the Roman type that I know of now is the one that runs north from the valley of the Nyd to the head of Clud water. It is said that this road was built by the Romans but I saw nothing like it when I was in Rome.

I looked where he pointed and saw that the road did indeed sink into the ground as if the earth had wrapped arms round it and dragged it down. Where it had been there was now only marsh grass and reeds. At the end of the fifth day we came to the mine and slept under the stars as we had intended. In the morning I woke to find my clothes sprinkled with snow.

'We will have to sleep in the bloomery,' said Grig, 'and that will be too hot.' He led me to a stone-built shed which held a furnace so big I could stand up in it. Grig left me to take the charcoal from the mules and hastened off to his mine. I started to fire the furnace with charcoal and the crumbling pink and yellow and black stone which stood in heaps at the minehead. About the middle of the afternoon Grig suddenly appeared from the mouth of the tunnel. My heart froze with fear: he was covered head to foot with blood.

'In the name of mercy, Grig, what has happened to you? Have you been crushed by falling rocks, or were there wolves in the cave?'

'I am not harmed,' he replied, laughing, 'this is only my mother's blood. The earth within the cave bleeds water and iron which form a fine red blood, and if her loving sons are not here to drive it out there is soon a great pool of it in the mine. I must stanch her wounds before I begin work, and the first day I am here I must be like a new-born babe, sodden and red. This will soon pass and my mother will let me into her bowels again.'

This is disgusting, but what can you expect?

I have learned that a 'bloomery' is where the rock containing iron is heated so that it runs like water and can be poured into ingots. These are called 'blooms' but they are far from beautiful.

There is no invocation of spirits and no sacrificing to demons such as I have heard is common to miners in Franconia. If there is sorcery it may well be lawful.

Then from behind him, in the earth, I heard a rushing sound which made the hair on my neck stand up. Grig seemed truly to be more youthful, for he rushed joyfully from bloomery to mine and back many times. He showed me my duties, and there was much to do. As well as firing and minding the bloom I had to pack peat into thick trenches to make a poor charcoal. I had constantly to watch the passages around the fires on both of these to make sure the wind would blow through them, and at sunset I would fall to the ground in the stifling bloomery and sleep till sunrise. Grig hardly spoke to me, and I saw him only occasionally as he struggled out of the mine with his baskets of pink rock. But on the nights when we ran off the pure iron in a hot white stream with bright sparks flying round, it was so beautiful that all the labour was worthwhile.

After many days of this we had used all the charcoal we had brought with us, and what I had made, and at the minehead there was only fresh ore and the fresh peat I had cut.

Grig looked at this and shook his head, 'If my brothers had been here there would have been much more curing for next season,' and he pointed to the iron blooms stacked beside the furnace and said, 'and there would have been more than three times that number, nor would we have had to work like dogs to do it. In days past when we were all together it would have been a feast or a holiday. This week should have been the crown of our year. But this is not your fault — you have worked well. Come with me now, you have earned the right to see into our secret world.'

Then he took a black oil-lamp and led me into the mine through the narrow slit of an entrance. The passage inside was so low that I almost had to bend double, and it was then that I realised that I had grown a lot of late, for I was much larger than the little man who danced along the passage ahead of me, splashing through water and kicking at rubble. The passage grew even lower and with each step my heart sank deeper and deeper in me for I was sure that the walls were closing in to crush me. Grig ran ahead, blithely, and once he disappeared round a bend to leave me alone in the breathing darkness. I tried to hear his step but all that came to me was the steady beating I had heard before, as if the living rock around me was flesh. Grig returned and led me by the hand to where I could stand upright. He held the lamp up high.

I saw a strange sight. The cavern around me was coloured like the rock ore, but the colour was stronger and more vivid with the water running over it. The red rocks looked like raw flesh bleeding, and lines of black ran across and through it like veins on a hand. At the back of the cavern where the light grew dim there were many thousands of glinting lights. Grig held his hand out to me and I saw he held a glittering stone that shone with many facets like a crystal.

'This is one of my mother's eyes, with a myriad of faces. Take it, and know she knows you, the first woman to see her secret self!'

Are these precious stones?

I took it, but with a heavy heart for I was dismayed to think of myself in the middle of a living being. This was no place of mine who had been raised in fire and light and air. I began to shiver in the damp winds of this womb world. But Grig was full of glee.

'Now you see her face to face,' he said, 'as only my brothers and myself have seen her before. She stands around you, a stiff, formless, meaningless pile. Everything we might ever need is here, but in what confusion! Everthing is heaped together and mixed like wine in water, seeming inseparable. But she is not like water. She is hard and rigid and sullen. See how red and angry she is! Each kind of stone hates the other and vilely refuses to serve while it is hard packed against its brother. Helpless and meaningless. It is my great task to find out the nature of each one of them, so that all may find form and meaning. And then my mother loves me. Alone she can do nothing — she cannot bring them to birth unassisted. Sometimes in southern lands she tries to bring herself to fulfillment and then great fires pour out of her belly, and the rocks she would smelt gush down her flanks. But she cannot do it alone. All she can make is destruction and pain, and she must damp her rages down again before she tears herself apart.

What horror! I see the face of the Creator everywhere in His creation, and He smiles at me. This dwarf loves his 'mother' yet he sees her as wicked and malicious.

'Even the Alfather who made her shuns and hates her. He leaves her alone here in darkness and misery and it is only by the hands of her loyal sons that anything good is made. We alone have the courage to face her malice. We return to her times without number and drag

How else could he see her? I did not see Vesuvio myself but I was told of its terrible rage, and of Ætna also. How much happier are we who have our loving Father watching over us. All this smacks of the heresy of Manichee, but since the woman is not party to it she cannot be stained, unless it is by association.

68

her separate parts aloft and work on them. We hammer
and mould and draw. Her father and husband turns his
face from her and we must do it all.'

Suddenly he fell silent, and the echoes from his voice
swept downwards and away like the tide. I was chilled
with terror, but he was exultant, his eyes great with tears,
and his fists clenched. I had never seen him aroused like
this before, even at the culmination of the most difficult
tasks. I realised that I had seen a mystery whose whole
meaning I could only guess at. I never heard him speak
of such again.

A few weeks after we returned I was idle for once and
wandered into part of the house which was dug deep
into the earth. Many of the rooms were empty and many
held small beds and tables so that I thought they must
have been Grig's brothers' rooms. I wandered on and at
last opened a door on a sight that turned my belly to ice
with fear. There, sitting on a high-backed chair, with her
brow resting on her hand I saw the golden queen. I fled
before she might lift her head and see me, and as I ran
down the corridor the skin of my back crawled with the
certainty that she was following.

I ran to the workshop where Grig was bent over his
work and cried, 'When did she arrive? I did not see her
coming.'

'She has always been here,' said Grig without raising
his head.

'I am speaking of the Queen, the poisonous queen
who lives at my father's house.'

'That is not she,' answered Grig smiling, 'but her sister who is like her in every way. I must tell you neither
of them is living.'

'I tell you she is alive. She wanders about in my
father's hall and when she passes we sisters fall sick.'

'I know what she does for I made her and the other
who sits within. Come with me and see for yourself.'

He took a light and led me back down the passages to
the room where she sat, and as I watched he took her
head from her body. He unfastened the clothes at her
back, and showed me the myriad tiny wheels and springs
and wires that were fixed inside her head and body and
made her move around.

'That is very great knowledge,' I said, 'could you
teach me to make one like that?'

'The devil reigns in all heresies but he has raised his throne in that of the Manichees.'

She is an automaton. I heard that such creations were given to great Carolus by men from the east, or sorcerers. I was never in his capital to see.

'Surely I could,' he replied, 'it will take many years, but you are an apt apprentice — I could ask for none better — I am sure you will learn.'

But it was not to be. That night the sickness of women came on me for the first time, and my father's servant was sent to fetch me home. I have always regretted that there was not time to learn to make such a creature.

She is not over modest to mention his praise of her.

Marighal sat in silence remembering her past. Edern was still also, and I thought he was asleep, but he looked up, alert, when I began to speak, saying:

Selyf takes up the story.

'My dear child, you must see that his is very dangerous thinking. Clearly these little men have been looking into mysteries which no man with a care for his immortal soul would approach. Your father must have been a very wise man to bring you from that den of Manichee. His actions have saved you and brought you to our faith at last.'

'You are mistaken,' she said, 'my father had nothing but hatred and contempt for your faith. If it were so much as mentioned in his presence, he would laugh or shout with rage. On the other hand, Grig spoke only good of the Christians, and I am sure he would have joined the true faith if he had come to it young.'

Eiriugena teaches us as follows: created things have only a partial being which resembles the true being of God. This partial being is mixed with non-being, so that the created universe is subject to change and ultimately to destruction. This is the evil in nature but not the evil of nature, for that requires action of the will. Evil and non-being are the same since this is the farthest state away from God.

'Whatever your father's wishes you must see that the little man was leading you astray. How can you think that your Heavenly Father, Who is made of love and Who is all good could make the earth itself an evil thing? The earth is part of God's creation, for men to work and turn to good or evil as grace disposes them. Those of us who would do good will build a city which is dedicated to God's service, but there are those who only seek mastery over the tangible world and ignore the growing soul. Neglected, the soul turns rank and poisonous. But the earth has no will of its own and therefore cannot sin, for it cannot choose between good and evil. The earth has no soul, nor can it of itself be evil, being part of God's creation. Therefore the man you call Grig was leading you into damnation. Indeed he and his brothers are the most misguided pagans and heretics.'

'I do not yet see what you would have me believe,' said the woman, 'but given time, I am sure you will be able to make it clear. Yet I feel a very great love for my little father and I cannot remove all his teachings

70

from my heart. It is all the inheritance he can give me.'

'That is because you still cling to the understanding of the body,' Edern told her. 'You will need to discipline yourself if you are to learn the mystery of joy which fills us when the body is forgotten and the soul rises up to God.'

'Show me, then,' she answered, 'for though you tell me you practise great austerities in this place, I can see little that is a severe test of hardihood. In my father's house we sleep on hard beds as you do here, without covering as you do here, and our food is only enough to keep us alive except on feast days. Your brother Cienach is said to be the most severe on himself, but he will not speak to me and casts his eyes down whenever I come near. You must teach me to discipline myself if I am to come near to that joy you speak of.'

'There are practices here which you have not seen,' said Edern, 'for it is not fitting that one unbaptised should enjoy the higher mysteries of discipline. Cienach, the greatest of eremites knows all about them and he is generously showing me his great powers. It is sad for you that you are of the female sex, for even if you were baptised he would not approach you. He has so far left his body behind him that he will not look on a woman's face lest he should find his heart filled with foul lust.'

'Pardon my curiosity,' she said, 'but it seems to me that a very great saint would be one who could look at a woman and yet find no lewdness within him. Why does Cienach find it such a struggle to be with a woman?'

At this Edern sprang to his feet and cried, 'Foolish creature, it is well known that women can cast spells to charm even the most rigorous saint, and the greater his spirituality, the harder the wicked creatures try to seduce him. Know now that Cienach has even had his parts of manhood cut off, yet he tells me that in every place he goes there are women waiting for him, making lewd and filthy gestures to lure him away from sanctity!'

With these words he left us, for it was nearly time for the office, and perforce I left her too with no more said. The next morning I was roused well before the second hour by Edern's shaking me by the shoulder, his eyes nearly starting from his head. He was near to

Indeed this is not a family given to luxury, but then, pagans often boast of their hardihood.

If this is true Cienach should not be serving as a presbyter. His offering the Eucharist is a scandal.

dragging me from my cell with the strength of his one
hand.

'With your permission, brother, may I ask why you
have wakened me, and with such violence? It is both
unwise and unseemly. I have yet to say my prayer on
waking.'

'Forgive me, brother, but with your permission I will
show you that it is necessary. You must see at once what
is happening.'

'Since it is barely past sunrise there is little chance I
will see anything at all,' I answered, all charity gone.

'O sweet St Padraig and St Columbcille, you will not
need help to see at all. Only come with me,' he said, and
pulled back my door curtain.

I went to the door and looked across the beach to the
east. The woman was coming round the point of the
bay with a rock under each arm. Behind her the sun
was rising dimmed by wine-red clouds. As she strode
towards us — my bowels turn to water as I think of it
— her hair swam round her head like seaweed under
water, and from it flew sparks of light so bright that
everything around us was illuminated. I blessed myself
at once and began to pray for deliverance. All around me *Heaven protect us all!*
in the dimness I could see the others moving and their
crys of dismay were like the cry of sea-birds lost on a
strange beach. As she approached I saw that she was
carrying two boulders with the ease of a nurse carrying
infants, and each was so big that I doubt if the strongest
man would be able to lift one alone. Yet she tossed them
on to the ground as if they were bundles of gorse.

Edern stood beside me, wringing his hands and saying, 'Surely I am to blame for this. I told her days ago
that we needed help to fetch stones to mend the oratory.
It is all my fault.'

'It is a fool that says so.' I answered, 'Was it you gave
her the strength of five men and fire in her hair?'

'No, no. I did no such devilry. But after the first office
I went to her, God forgive me, alone, and I gave her the
scourge I use to mortify my flesh. She studied it and
kissed it and thanked me on her knees, for she said
that here was her chance to serve her Maker with all
her power. She said she would find her full self with
it. I thought she spoke of matters of the spirit, not the
body.'

72

He gave her the Sacrifice of St Beya. The woman was not even baptised! That was both foolish and improper, but then, Cienach and his scholars were always incontinent.

'Do not blame yourself for the evil we see here,' I cried, 'you should blame me, wretch that I am, for I have always encouraged this creature to stay among us in spite of her strange ways. Behold her now, Babylon the great, mother of harlots and the abominations of the earth.'

The others were standing beside us now, watching in terror as the woman raised rocks the size of coffins. She came towards us, and we clutched at the crosses and relics we wore about our selves. She smiled at us with delight.

'You see what I have done,' she cried, 'I have found that I can help you and so serve God with all the great strength it has pleased Him to give me. Now all the people in this country can join you in your offerings, for I shall build you a mighty stone chapel such as no one has seen here before.'

Many of the others broke away and fled to the tower.

Things are perilous indeed. Cienach speaks to a woman!

'Stay where you are,' said Cienach, in his rarely heard voice, 'do not come close to us. We thought you nothing but a poor heathen woman come to us for succour and baptism, but now we see that you are a demon, kindred to dragons and other filthiness. Keep away from us!'

At this she stood amazed.

At Tehaphnehes the day also shall be darkened when I shall break there the yokes of Egypt and the pomp of her strength shall cease in her. As for her a cloud shall cover her and her daughters shall be led into captivity. Ezekiel 30:18.

'How can this be?' she said, 'Did you not say to me that God created the world and all things in it? And is it not true that all creatures are able to partake of the perfection of the Creator? My father and my foster-father told me always to conceal my strength from the sight of mankind, but you have told me that they were ignorant and knew nothing of the great love God has for his creation.

'When I left my first friends to die at the hands of the pirates, I was tormented by the knowledge that I, fighting at their side, might have saved them with my strength. I obeyed my fathers and kept my secret but my friends paid with their lives. Now, after what I have learned here I see that God gave me this strength and nature to use for the building of His kingdom on earth. Yet I see you shun me, and run from me in fear. What does this mean?'

On the other hand there was Samson who was God's champion and was given special strength to do his appointed tasks. The issue perhaps is not what she is, but what she does.

'She is not all wickedness.' I said, 'she is seeking God's holy truth.'

Cienach raised his hand to silence me, saying, 'Behold the work of the Anti-christ himself. He turns our own arguments against us, and leads us with gentle words into everlasting dark.'

And he held up his cross against her. Nothing happened — neither did she shrivel up nor did the cross splinter as we know it must when the adversary is present. We were dismayed.

I shouted to the woman, 'Give us now a moment to retire and consider what we must do. There is a mystery here and we must pray a while so that God will reveal his will to us.'

I turned and led the rest to the watch-tower to speak with the others.

Cienach and Edern plucked at my sleeve and said, 'Let us straightaway perform the rite of exorcism, for we must take every step to protect ourselves.'

I have never seen it work.

The woman was left alone on the beach as the white dawn broke, and I felt pity for her. She did not understand her state, any more than I did, and her will to virtue was immense.

In the watch-tower the talk was hot with anger, and our vows of self-restraint might never have been made. We could not agree about what action to take over the woman. Some agreed with Cienach and Edern that exorcism should be recited, but Ælfrid pointed out that the woman had attended the offering many times as a witness and had never shown any distress at the sight of the Eucharist. This being the case it was not probable that the exorcism would drive her away. I suggested that the woman might not be a demon and Cienach rose up in wrath.

'Do you not know that all womankind, save only the virgin saints and sisters are inhabited by demons? You are foolish men and impure if you think otherwise. I can tell you what I know to be a fact, indisputable, for I have seen it in a vision. In the womb there sits a grinning devil, nor is woman free of it unless she takes monastic vows. Then, at the sound of her final vows the devil flies out of her and cannot return unless she falls from grace. I know, for I have seen it happen many times at the installation of a sister. I knew well that this woman was a blight on our monastery from the day of her arrival, but since I would not break my silence I

What can you do with such people as these?

74

did not state my objections. I thought you would all have your eyes opened. Now the revelation has come, and still you stand like cattle at a gate and will not go through. Have you not seen the destruction of the Host which has gone on since she came? The incorruptible body of Christ is lying mildewed in its chalice!'

'And the relic, — it has lost its virtue.' cried Edern, always eager to emulate his master. 'Last month a woman came to me with a sick child and I placed the most holy relic of St Nynia on his neck. Yet the following Sabbath the woman did not attend the offering and the other people said that the child had died.'

'Children have died before,' said Cadui, 'for all that there have been laid on them relic, Host and consecrated hands. You should rather have taken him to Ælfrid for a good posset, that was why his mother brought him.'

At this yet more furious argument began, and to my shame I found myself shouting as loudly as the next.

Cienach finally snatched up his scrip and staff and snarling like a dog said, 'Blasphemy and filth! I will not stay in this place and endanger my purified soul for the drawing of another breath. Far better to die out on the snowy hillside than to stay with this monster beside me. I am going to Candida Casa, and if any will come with me, make haste now before the taint of this creature rubs off on you. I knew from the first nothing would come but evil, for it is through woman that evil came into the world, and so it will always be. I would rather face the beasts of the mountains a thousand times than stay in a place where there are women. And this vile monster is the worst of them all.'

With this he left the tower. Edern made for the door after him, but we said, 'By your leave, brother, you cannot follow him into the mountains. He is accustomed to the cold and the hardship after his many austerities, and he will take no harm from them. You, who through ill-health have come close to death often, might easily perish there.'

'I know it well,' said Edern, 'and I have always suffered when I could not follow my master's example. My frail body will not obey my cloudy will, and it is likely that I will not survive this journey. Nevertheless, Cienach is my beloved master, and he has shown me

I have see this happen before. If no bishop has visited for some time the supply of consecrated bread will mildew. This is why we say that it is not truly the body of Christ until it is in the chalice and in the hand of the celebrant.

As Macarius taught us — wrath is the wickedness of demons.

Is it not a blasphemy to think that a relic in the hands of a mere man can alter God's inscrutable will? The Creator Mundi is not to be bribed like a drunken door-keeper.

He did not survive the journey. Cienach himself told me.

the true path of virtue, though I cannot follow it myself. Now I will go with him, even if it be to death, for he has need of me.' Picking up his scrip he left us silenced.

Cadui was the first to speak.

'Brothers, we have elected to stay here, in spite of the terror that stalks outside. But we have not agreed what action we must take. Let us go now and break into the cell of our beloved Abbot. His words will be a sure guide to us. He is still our father and in the past his decision has always been our best course of action.'

'Five years ago I would have agreed with you,' said Ælfrid 'but our Abbot is a changed man. As our apothecary I have taken it as my duty to speak to our father about his condition from time to time, and he has answered in charity. Over the last months I fear he has been moving away from us, and is now so advanced in spirituality that he understands very little of our earthly problems. That he still loves us I am sure, but his grasp of matters on the sub-lunar world is slight, and he would have little to say that would be to the point.'

'If this is the case,' said Nuth, 'I do not see what else we can do but follow our father's example, and wait to see what God has disposed for us.'

I felt the time had come to propose a course I had been meditating on for some time.

'With your permission, brothers, I suggest we should talk to the woman again. She has never offered any of us any harm, and her nature never seemed other than good. It may be that she is right, and her strength has indeed come from God. She may even have been sent by him to help us in these difficult times.'

We then fell to discussing the source of her great and miraculous strength, and spoke of the saints of old who had been given great strength to accomplish God's holy tasks. We decided at last to see the woman and tell her she might stay, provided that she did not use the scourge again without proper observances.

'Reflect, brothers,' said Cadui, 'if her past has been wicked that is no less than can be said of many heathens that have been brought to our faith. Our sweet St Augustine himself was a mighty sinner before he was a mighty saint. Once baptised, she will die to her past and be born again to the future in God. If He will it her frightful powers will go from her then.'

He is gone to his reward.

Not only people of great sanctity have such power. Sometimes simple men have been given great strength when the lives of their dear ones have been threatened. Also tears of blood have been manifested by people of great holiness. It is a great pity that the brothers have had so few opportunities for study.

There was some disagreement about that and it was well into the morning before we reached a decision. We returned to the woman's cell, prepared to tell her she could stay, but when we got there we found it empty. Neither herself nor her property was there, not even her baptismal veil. Only the books lay on the bed and under them was a scrap of vellum with this message on it:

'There are too many things about my life that you cannot accept. I see now that I can never be one with you. I saw the fear in the faces of Cienach and Edern as they fled into the hills, and I do not feel that I could bear to see it again. I will take myself to a retired place to watch, and if I see that you need me I will help. Thank you for your patience with me, your poorest student. I pray that we will meet again in the kingdom that is to come, but I fear there will be no place for me there. Farewell.'

I stepped outside and looked around to see where she might have gone. Unless the flock of birds flying north, skimming the surface of the sea, marked her passage, I have no knowledge where she went.

While it is true that the first duty of the desert saints who are our example was to do battle with devils there are many other urgent tasks in this world.

St Benedict told his monks that prayer is their first duty, as did St Gregory. Especially in the congregations. Maelruin, the beloved, tells us that our first duty is to love God and our fellow man and to obey our Rule. Nevertheless before the Kingdom can come we must conquer all evil and convert all the pagans. There is still a long way to go.

I am deeply troubled about her, not for the reasons my enemies would have you believe, but because I am sure that this creature must be brought into the service of God. It is our duty to train her and restrain her, for it would be a terrible evil if she or her kind were to join with the heathen. She would then become the worst possible scourge of all Christians, simple and consecrated. If, however, my protestations are all wrong and she is a demon, she and her kind must be sought out and driven from the earth. If such remain among us, it will only delay the coming of the Kingdom, and it is my duty as a companion of God to dispose of them.

I beg you therefore, most holy and virtuous Bishop, release me from my monastery for a year so that I may carry out the task God has laid before me. It is not my intention to desert my vows or my post on the borders of this, God's country, but the issue must be settled. If not even the ground we walk on will be pointed out by our enemies as irredeemably defiled.

Valete.

This is the second letter, written by Selyf to our Abbot, Gwydion, from the town by the long river. The Bishop Cellach sent Selyf on a mission after they met and spoke at the city of Cathures. Witnesses of the meeting told me that Cellach instructed Selyf to destroy the evil one and that Selyf accepted without complaint. If the bishop granted the mission he must have thought that the men of Rintsnoc were not beyond grace, and that the complaints of Sinnoch regarding heresy were groundless. Unless we are to believe that the venerable bishop was worked on by demons from afar. Throughout his stay there no-one heard Selyf say anything scandalous. His actions were beyond reproach and everyone praised his modest and gentle bearing.

I have determined the location of the city mentioned in this text by the description of the landscape. When I was returning to our monastery from the country of lord Sigurd I saw a place where the moorland rises steeply from the coastal plain. I shall return there to see what has become of the kingdom and I shall enquire of anyone I meet for more news of Selyf and his journey.

To the most pious and venerable Abbot Gwydion, Selyf, your humble son sends greetings.

My dearest father and protector, at our last meeting I wept to see how the trials of the last few years have drawn the white hairs from your head and sunk the lines into your cheeks. Worse by far though, than the decay of the body, is the lapse of spirit. You were once the great leader of our house and order and none was more valiant to take the field in the hunt for souls. Yet now, when we talk eagerly of converting the heathen, you sit beside the fire and smile. What shall we do, who are poor creatures, beside one as noble as yourself? The light is going out of our world, and there is no one to guide us, yet there is so much to be done.

I met Bishop Cellach at Cathures and he instructed me in my mission to find the family of Marighal. He told me that he would release me from the monastery provided that I kept you informed of my progress, so that should I be required to perform my duties as erenach, you could send for me at once. I was dismayed, therefore to hear that you had embarked on your last pilgrimage to Hy Columbcille with a few of our brothers, leaving our cells without a guiding light. Since I have not been recalled, I conclude that the monastery

77

is in capable hands and that my presence there is not essential for now.

Over the last few weeks I have tried to obey Bishop Cellach and search for the great evil that lives in the forest. I travelled east along the seaway to Caerleul but heard nothing, and every enquiry I made was met with silence and fear. I walked inland and westward again and asking at every farmstead if they had heard of a hall such as the woman spoke of, but they shut the door in my face. Even steadings which bore signs of our faith were not diposed to speak to me on this matter. The master of that stronghold must indeed have been a terrible man to keep the workers in such fear. Even though he is dead none who might know of him will name him nor point out the road to his dwelling. The gossocks who live in the forest are wretched, ignorant folk, who still worship twisted roots from the soil, and are dark and twisted themselves in body and soul. They would not show me even the meanest hospitality, and each night I had to make my bed in the roots of a tree.

See note above. I have found this location in a similar fashion.

At last, after quartering the forest from north to south and from east to west, I saw that I had covered every mile of that dismal place and turned north again. I was soon out of the forest and crossed a high, wide moor which is visited by every wind out of heaven. At the highest point, with the twisted hills behind me and a broad loch below, I was struck by a furious hail-storm which drove me west again. Then I saw a wonderful sight. The moorland fell away sharply below my feet, and there lay a long plain with a winding river cutting through it. On the farther edge of the plain, beside the winking sea, lay a city of golden stone. I was sure in my heart that this must be the city of which the woman had spoken when she told of her husband's betrayal.

Just below me the white road wound down the hillside and across the plain to the city, and I made for it joyfully. At the road head there was a small shrine to St Maura, I stood a while in prayer, giving thanks that I had been delivered from darkness. Many times in the forest it had seemed to me that I would never see a stone dwelling again and that I had been most treacherously misled by the woman about her home and family. But there below me lay at least some of her history, and it was as fine as she had said. I hastened down to the sunlit plain.

Very pleasant it was to walk on a firm road where no brambles and saplings strove to thwart my progress and take the clothing from my body. Nor did the ground seek to swallow me from feet to crown, as it had on the moor. I passed beside a small river where the birches leaned down to hear the music of the water running on the stones and everywhere rang with delight. No two reaches of the river were the same, for at one instant I could see stones shining through the water, at the next a pool where the water was brown and deep. Then came a clash of white foam over rocks and at last the fair wide plain where all was cheerfulness and the river ran bubbling over shingle.

It was near the feast of the Transfiguration and the summer was crowning the year. The fields round the city nodded with oats and barley and bees were loud in the meadow. I felt the sun on my back, I must confess, with delight. 'This is indeed a blessed kingdom,' I said, 'thanks be to God.'

At the wooden walls and gate of the city I was welcomed by two guards in finely burnished helmet and byrnie. One of them conducted me through the town to the king's hall and I looked about me amazed. Nearest the gate was a great stone granary, and on the opposite side of the road from it stood a mill with tall men turning the stones. There was also a dyer's shop where men and women worked with bright stained arms, and beyond it, a weaver's shed with many looms. All these had stone walls and I was not surprised to see a mason's yard where there was much activity. Beyond again, out on the promontory, rose the king's hall which was a great stone tower. Before it there was a deep ditch with a bridge across it, where the guard left me.

In the stronghold they told me that the household took its meal late in the day in summer, and that I would be welcome to join them then. I rested in the shade of the tower for the afternoon, and as the evening cooled I entered and took a lowly place at table. I watched the household and guests as they assembled for the evening. The hall filled quickly with lively people who talked loudly and laughed a great deal, and at first I thought that I was in the company of youths and young girls, for they wore brightly coloured clothes with much jewellery and embroidery,

Delight is as much man's duty as suffering. Why did God give us the faculty of delight if we were not intended to use it in celebration of His creation? Surely delight is not wicked, unless it is that we rejoice in the degradation of others.

There must have been a long period without war for such a lot of building to take place.

80

It is indeed a prosperous and peaceful place that has so many idle women in it.

If I am right in my speculation then this would be Bishop Chrodegang out of Cantwaraburg and Wiurœmuda.

Different habits in a life will make for very different appearance. I know which of the two I would consider more likely to be virtuous.

yet when I studied them, I saw that they were no longer young.

The king's table was covered with a white linen cloth and a man sitting near me told me that it was changed every Sunday for a clean one. Even the windows high in the walls were hung with rich weavings in bright wools and there were many tapers on the walls. The king and his lady took their seats beside each other at last, and on the king's other hand there sat a bishop with a gold-embroidered cap and vestis and a linen robe. I had never seen him before, and to this day I have never learned his name.

The king's clothes were the most splendid, as was fitting, and his arms shone with many rings. His hair was fair with many white strands in it and his moustache was long and thick, but his face and hands were brown and I could see that he spent much of his time out of doors. The queen sat silent beside him and I looked at her closely to see if she bore a likeness to Marighal. Like her, the queen was tall, and her hair was bound in four tresses, a fashion which had been taken up by other women in the hall. The hair was the same bracken red, the eyes were also long and green, and she too lacked a finger on her left hand, but there the resemblance stopped. The queen's neck was sunk in wreathes of fat where the first was lean, and the queen's hands were white and plump and soft where the first one's were calloused with the work that had filled her life. Furthermore the queen's brow was creased with lines denoting a fretful nature, while Marighal's serenity had been perfect, except only when she spoke of her need for God's love. In youth, perhaps, they might have been taken for one another, but the years and the difference of their lives had left them very unalike.

As the evening wore on and the talk grew loud from wine there was much laughter and brawling in the hall and the men tried to wrestle with each other without spoiling their finery. A bard came in and sat himself in front of the king and played his instrument, but none paid any heed to the old hero story he sang. Finally one of the noble company took his harp from him and began to sing a song which it was not seemly for one under vows of chastity to hear, so I left the hall.

I stood looking at the twilight gathering over the sea, and the bard came out to relieve himself. He shook his head at me and said, 'Did you see how that fine manikin took my harp from me? The time was when none would have dared to touch the instrument of a bard for fear of the great and terrible curses that would have fallen on him. Now, since we are a Christian kingdom, a singer of the great stories must take any dole he can get and swallow the insults that go with it.'

You should stop your ears with balls of wax like St Brendan, although the sounds that offended him were different.

'Why not find yourself a pagan kingdom, my friend?' I asked, 'for there are still many who would be glad to hear the old stories well told. Truly I never heard them told better than you did tonight.'

'There are none this side of the sea,' said the bard, 'and I am too old to take myself off to Eirinnn. Besides, I have taken an oath of service with the old king, and vowed to serve him and his heritors for as long as I live. I was young and ignorant in those days and the people were always eager to hear my stories. If I satirised a man he would lose his followers in a very few weeks. People all grew silent when I struck my harp, but now they chatter on when I play as if it were a thing of no importance. But I must stay and serve this king and queen for all that they were only designated his heirs on the day he left for Hy Columbcille.'

An idle boast, and one that I have heard from skalds before. It goes back a long way into the darkness of the pagan years. They seem to think they were sorcerers of a kind. It is absurd, of course, but the pagans are afraid of nothing more than losing face in front of their neighbours.

'Tell me, on that day did many men come to take the old king from his throne to kill him and did the king that is here slay seven of them with his own hand?'

'That is the very man — Kynan son of Kilidh — and brave and valiant he was on that day. I saw it all myself and I was proud to be sworn in service to such a terrible warrior.' He sighed. 'I was taught that a bard's word is as good as any noble's and I will not be base and forsworn, but I long to be free, and my heart yearns to sing once more in a hall filled with silence and awe.'

'Take heart,' I told him, 'for surely one day the bard will again be heard and attended. There are still the lays of the Christian monarchs to be sung, and they are brave and mighty. But tell me how it was in the days when this king was first in this country, and people still wept and trembled at your songs.'

They do so already. In Lorraine I heard one sing of Pippin, Otto and the great Carlus. He also sang of the beauty of women.

'In those days many times did the men from Eirinnn ground their great black ships on our beaches, and leap into the swirling foam. Then our men would snatch up

82

These words are familiar! And so tedious.

This is done in imitation of king Ælfrid. It is possible to do this if you have a prosperous and industrious nation.

This kingdom has steep hills on the southern flank and north of the river there is only scrub and marshland. West the moors; east the sea. It is isolated from friend as much as from enemy.

helmet and shield, axe and sword and rush down to the seashore to meet them in battle. Soon the sea would be wine-red with blood, and the ravens gathering. Above us we would hear the beating wings of the Morrigan, and the slain would be taken to eternal feasting. But in the first few years of his reign, the king found that the good soil of this country and the strong backs of the people could make much gold. So much gold did they make that he found he could pay tribute to the Vikings and induce them to leave us alone.

'Then we became a Christian kingdom and with the witless bishop at his side, the king spoke to them saying, 'We would no longer see our children dead and our young men lost on the beaches every summer. Ours is a fertile land and if we are spared to tend it we will be able to give you gold each year, nor need we shed the blood of either side. If you continue to harry us neither will profit, for with no people to till the land nor peace for the cattle to grow sleek, there will be neither grain nor gold, nor meat for you to offer to your gods.'

'The seamen were well pleased to find that here was a way to get gold without effort. It fell out the way the king had said, though some of the young men who still had a name to make protested that this was a craven way to live. They went their own ways after a while and it has been like that since. When other kingdoms are pillaged this one stays quiet as a tomb, and only the peasant is filled with glee. The king has only a small retinue since the brave young men went away, and the ones that are here are dressed up like mummers. Now the bishop has persuaded the king that he should set up a congregation of monks, so the masons must be taken off the defences and set to build a stone oratory. The town will be filled with black clad monks and we must huddle behind a wooden wall. I know that this way takes us to disaster, for a time is coming when seamen will seek to take more than what the king gives freely. Each year when they come to fetch the levy I see them look more closely at our crops and our warriors, and they know how peace-softened we are. The time will yet come for me to sing a dirge over the slain heaped high on the beach.'

These dark words troubled my spirit, but I had other business.

'I have heard that in those days there was a young woman lived here, who could forge silver and gold, and perform other feats of skill. Did you ever meet her?'

'There was a woman, it is said, who lived in a cave along the beach, but her teaching was all sorcery. Men would go to her to learn to control the dark forces, but they were tight-lipped when they returned, so we knew nothing of where she lived or what she said. I went to seek her one day for I thought I might make a song about her, but I did not even find the cave.'

I thanked him at that and returned to the hall to meditate. The company were preparing to retire for the night, but the king, his lady and the bishop were still at their table.

As I entered the bishop leaned over and spoke to the king who looked at me and said, cup in hand, 'Ho, monk, what is a pilgrim doing at my court? We have seen no strange faces here for many seasons. What do you think of our city here and of our kingdom? Is it not a very fine kingdom?'

'Indeed, sir,' I answered, and approached the table, 'I have travelled much in this country and Alban and I have never seen a kingdom as rich and fat as this one. I am forbidden to take meat or whole wine, but the meat I have seen passed at this table is the best I have ever seen and the wine is deep red. Blessed is the king who rules here and twice blessed are the people for their days will be long and their children will thrive.'

'Well said, monk. Now, tell us your name and the places of your pilgrimage, for we long for news of the world beyond our valley.'

The bishop said nothing but he watched me closely as I spoke.

'Before God, my name is Selyf, and I was the teacher of boys at Rintsnoc before the lamentable day when raids drove our tenants away. After that our Abbot became an immured anchorite, and for the last ten years our congregation has dwindled till we are nothing but a sad remnant and the lichen covers the stones of our city. We have few relics and our books are mildewed, but we cling with fervent loyalty to the Rule we have been raised to, sure that when God's kingdom comes we will be prepared for it. Lately our Abbot retired to Hy Collumbcille for his last days, and I must return soon to take his place,

It is not accurate to call the mission a pilgrimage, since he is not sent to make conversions, nor is he under penitential vows, and at the end of the journey there is no holy place to be visited.

but I have been sent on a mission by Bishop Cellach Mac Ferdalaig himself, and for now my brothers are leaderless. I pray constantly for their safety.'

I saw that the king was very moved at this sad history, and he said, 'There is little hope for any of us with so much trouble in the land. Here I keep a little haven of peace for my people, but I cannot be sure even of this. At any hour the seamen may sweep into our harbour who are not sworn to our treaty, but what can I do? I cannot keep a larger armed following, for that would cost much coin.'

At his words the queen began to weep and lament, and he paused to calm her. He bade me go on with my story to divert the lady.

I continued, 'My mission is to seek out a woman who lives in the great forest beyond these hills. I met her once before, when she stayed with us at the monastery, and she begged us to give her baptism, but Cellach fears this was a foul mockery of our faith for it became clear to us that she was no simple mortal.'

The queen gasped at these words and pressed her white hand to her cheek.

'I pray you do not speak of such things!' said the king, angry, 'My lady has a gentle heart, and cannot bear to hear tell of the demons and dark things that live in the forest.'

'Truly, sir, I am sorry to offend you,' said I, and a demon I picked up in the forest took charge of my tongue for I then said, 'I had hoped above all to please the lady, for I have tidings of her family.'

On a mission like this perhaps you should have imitated Cienach and laved your mouth daily! For myself, I think it is a better notion to think before you speak.

At this the king sprang furiously to his feet and cried, 'My curse on the liar who says these words. Know now that my wife came here by miraculous means when she was but a girl, and knows nothing of her family, nor do any in this city. How can it be that an ignorant, wandering monk, with no token of his mission, can claim to know her kin? In all the years we have ruled here there has been no word of her kindred, and it is her dearest wish to be united with them. How can you know something no one else knows?'

'Sir, I spoke hastily,' I replied, 'for I do not know for sure who the lady's family might be, only that she closely resembles one of a family I know well, and I thought to do both a service by bringing them together.'

'This cannot be,' cried the king, 'they live in a far country. You are lying. What is the meaning of this? Guards! Take this man and lock him away. He will be confined until I am satisfied that he is not a spy. You are not to speak to him!'

Clearly you have frightened the king, Selyf.

And at that the house-thegns came to my side and took me below to the cavernous cellars of the tower. They bound my hands and feet with iron chains and left me behind a barred door. Then I lifted up my voice and wept for the folly which had brought me to that place.

'If only I had kept my tongue between my teeth. Why did I speak up like that? There is no certainty that the queen is any kin to that woman — why did I not wait until I knew more? Was I possessed? I am an oaf. My mother told me I was born with a mouth like an unlaced satchel, spilling what it should keep close. She said my undone mouth would be my undoing.'

But I calmed myself and resolved to bear this adversity with patience, even as the blessed martyrs and saints have shown us, for is not misery to be welcomed as preparation for the life to come? For two days I was kept confined, and I was obliged to recite the offices for there was no light to read by. Through a little window high in the wall I could hear the sound of the sea tides, and watch the coming and the fading of the light, but nothing more. The king and his guards kept a close watch on me through a slit in the door, but said not a word.

This is permissible in the circumstances, but I hope you did penance for it.

Towards the end of the third day my fast was ended and the guards handed me in some bread and foul water, and when the sun was sinking I was taken to the king. He was preparing to retire but he had me brought to a closet so that our words might not be heard.

'Since your arrival here I have been put to a lot of trouble. After you were confined, my wife plagued me with sighs and said, 'I have always wondered whence I came, and who my kin might be. Do you fetch the monk to me so that I may here more of what he has to say. It may be that he truly knows more of my father's house and family.'

'Now I fear that if I keep you away from her she will disobey me and speak with you yourself, therefore I will tell you this: by an act of the most holy grace my wife's heart was emptied of all memory of her

How is he able to say what is grace? It seems to me he has

been listening too well to this facile bishop of his.

childhood before she came to this hall, and since she became queen she learned nothing more of her family. Yet she is full of natural feelings and wishes to know of her father and mother. I might tell her myself, since I know the family well, but I have not, nor would you if you had my knowledge. They are not simple people, and if you say you have news of them you must be a liar and therefore an enemy. Now tell me the truth. Where have you come from?'

'Before God, sir,' I said, 'I will tell you what happened to me last year, nor will I conceal anything from you. A woman came to our monastery late in the year, and she told us she was the daughter of a terrible lord.

They told me she stayed from All Saint's to the start of the Advent fast.

'She said that she had been released from bondage by the death of her father, and had come to us at once. She it was who told me of this wonderful city. She wished to become a baptised Christian, but before the bishop who could perform the rite arrived she revealed to us that she had a terrible nature, and when she saw our horror she left us. When I told the bishop of the woman, he straightaway sent me to seek out her and her family and destroy them. If by God's grace I can come to them I will, but so far all I have managed to find is this city. I had hoped you might set me on the road to her dwelling.'

'If you seek evil, monk, then I know the place you must look. But who is the man who is newly dead? I tell you now, it cannot be the father of my lady, for he died about the time I came into this country.'

'The woman I spoke of said her father had died recently. They may not be sisters but she was in many, many ways like your good queen. Furthermore she spoke of her numerous sisters, and mentioned the queen of this city as some form of kin.'

This is a small prevarication, but in this case it is permissible.

'I do not recall that any of my lady's sisters ever came to this city, yet they often had knowledge of things in a manner I could not understand. Truly there were sisters without number in that dark hall. When was it that the terrible man died, as that woman described it?'

'It was near the night last year when the earth shook and the lochan below the farm of the peat moor was swallowed by the earth.'

'I heard people speak of that night,' said the king, nodding. 'There was a mighty storm down here also.

Waves broke even against the walls of this tower. Tell me the name of this woman, and by what name she spoke of me.'

'She named you Kynan White-hair,' I answered, but I could not find the tongue to name the woman aloud, so I said, 'the woman called herself Mairidh.'

'I cannot recall a sister of that name, but there were many. It is sure Kynan White-hair was the name given to me in that hall, although here I am known as Kynan Bright-Helm, son of Kilidh. It seems to me you may speak some truth, but I am certain my lady's father died more than twenty years ago.'

He brooded for a while, then said at last, 'Listen to me, monk. Tomorrow my wife will send for you and ask you about her father and kindred. Tell her only that her father is dead, and that she may have a few sisters living, but make no mention of the quaking earth, nor the lochan which sank, for you will only trouble her heart to no purpose. She must never learn more of her family than that.'

For that night I was returned to the sour straw of the cellar, but the guards gave me a mattress and a blanket and a mouldy pillow, all rich in fleas. I am used to hardship, but I chose the hard stone floor of the cellar rather than keep bedfellows. I slept well, nevertheless, for my heart was much lightened. The next morning the king and queen sent for me early, and I was taken to them in the meadow outside the tower. There the queen asked me courteously about her father's house, and I recounted to her what the king had instructed me. When I had finished the queen wept pure water, and lamented the father she would never see. Then she asked me to remember her in my prayers, which I was glad to do, and she left with her woman.

The king said, 'She has no children, poor creature, and she is nearly past the age when she might bear, but I will not set her aside, for it would mean more than my life to me to do so. I have a nephew named as heir who is nearly a man, so my hall will be secured.

'Now tell me, monk, what did this woman whom you call my lady's sister tell you of her home?'

'Very little, sir — she spoke more of her education and fostering. She told us of a Queen made all of gold

This is the same man as mentioned before, but I doubt if his city is now as it was.

He is eager to keep her in a state of ignorance.

She must be of a different kind from the demons. Thanks be to God.

88

*Not merely mechanisms,
surely. Such machines as these
could only be worked by
sorcery. Were there invocations
or incantations? That is the
issue.*

*It is difficult to see
what can be the motive power
of these things, other than
captured spirits, but I am not
learned. Furthermore I have
never heard of machines that
could watch like this in all my
travels.*

who was a machine, and who poisoned all the sisters when she passed by.'

'Yes, I recall that one. She would wander about the halls at the new moon, passing in silence from one chamber to another, but I never felt the poison in her look, myself. Before I left the stronghold I was sure that she was a machine, for she was made of metal of the same colour as other machines my master had as servants. Some of them were tall, taller than a man, and they could carry a great weight; others were very small and could slip under doors, so that they were used to spy on other people in the halls. There were many machines in that place. The only one with human form was the Queen. Most were globes with one red eye. One day I came upon my master in his closet and he had a small globe on the table before him, split into two pieces, and inside I could see that there was much wire and wheels and jewels. When the master saw me he clapped the two parts of the magic machine together and hid it from me. Later I found that my wife could master the machines also, and even made one give her father a false message so that we could leave his stronghold.'

'What you tell me is very strange, sir, for such wonderful machines have never been seen in this country.' I still hesitated to tell the king what I knew of his marriage, so I went on, 'I would ask, with your permission, what took you to the castle of this terrible lord, for surely you would not go freely?'

'You speak the truth there. It was the grim lord himself who took me there as his fosterling, for he had some command over my father, and I stayed there for about ten winters. All the heritage I got from him was a little part of his knowledge and one of his daughters. Terrible he was and ageless, and no-one knew the place where he had been born. I recall that his skin was as hot to the touch as if fires burnt inside him, yet he always complained of the cold and fires would burn in his hall winter and summer. He was a very strange man, and I loved him when I was young, though I fear there was a devil in me then, for he was great abomination.'

'How can this be?' I cried, 'his daughter also spoke of him as all evil, yet she herself seemed all grace, and with great yearning to know the love of her Creator. Right up to the day she left us I was sure she would become one of the elect, and I remain uncertain despite my mission. I would have sworn that after tasting the joy of baptism there would not have been a fragment of evil in her.'

Then the king laughed and took me across the meadow to the bank of the sea.

'Monk, I see you do know a little of my lady's family, but it is only a little. If a man knew what I know about them he could have no doubt. Many of the sisters could behave with charity and sweetness, it is true, but if I had not had my loving, gentle wife to bed with me for the last many years, I would never have thought that a daughter of that house could show so much grace and serenity of spirit.'

'Then, sir, if one sister may find grace, may not another?'

'She may, monk, but there is much room for doubt. Since you show yourself willing to discover the truth about my lady's kindred I will make my confession to you.'

'I beg you do no such thing, sir. I am no longer a priest, I am only a simple monk and an indifferent scholar, with no powers of absolution.'

'That is not to the point,' said the king, and he fixed me with his eyes. 'If you had not come, boasting knowledge of the family I would have taken this secret to the grave with me. I cannot make a public confession of it, as the bishop would advise, for it would ruin my wife. I have been in torment for many years with this knowledge in my heart, for the facts of that appalling race are too grim to bear. God has sent you to me so that I might unburden my heart. Now hear me.'

My father was a thegn and chieftain of a small holding in the southern marshes. I was the oldest child, and had neither brother nor sister to grow up with me, since my mother was at variance with my father for a time. There was no one of my rank nearby so I kept company with the sons of my father's steward and huntsman. I longed for my seventh birthday celebration, for it was the custom of our family to send boy children for fostering in their eighth year. My mother was unhappy at my approaching departure, and quarrelled with my father about it. He had told her nothing about the family I was to be fostered with, other than that it was a great

You could not read her heart, Selyf. That is where true obedience begins, and that is why the bishop has sent you on this mission.

You know any baptised person can hear the confession of a believer if there is no one else to do so. Whether or not you think the bishop was suitable is your own conclusion, but I have my doubts.

The king begins his story.

household, and that I could learn more there to fit me for a high position in life than in any other hall in the country. My mother wanted me to stay until she had another child to take my place, but my father would not listen to her, and I stayed away from the stronghold to avoid the sound of her pleading voice.

My eighth year began in mid-winter, and there had been much snow. On the beach the wind had blown the drifts into the shapes of dragons and wolves, and my companions and I were doing battle with them with wooden swords. When we returned to the hall at sunset we found the gate to the stockade had been pulled across before the customary time. We were met by my father's steward, Gwalchmai, who took us, not to the hall, but to the byre on the other side of the township. I looked across at the hall, and I saw that all the windows were dark, above and below, and it was silent, with not a soul coming or going. Gwalchmai gave us all food, then told us to be very quiet and go to sleep. We did as we were bidden, for my father had told me that in danger it was my place to do as any adult bade me.

In the morning Gwalchmai came and took his son away with him. The huntsman's son and I passed the day in any way we could, plaiting straw, telling stories, fighting or some of the fouler tricks boys alone will practice. Again we were fed at sundown, but the soldier who came with our food would not tell us what was afoot. That night we slept only a little in the damp straw, for we were sure that there was a pirate raid coming and we were eager to do our share. The next morning the huntsman came and took his son away and I was left alone, warmed only by my rage at being kept out of the battle I supposed was going on. I passed a wretched night, with the rats jumping over my feet, and found that while it had been amusing with companions to trap them and entertain ourselves with them, alone I thought only of their sharp teeth.

In the morning my father came for me and took me to the bathhouse. He washed me and put on a heavy tunic, thick leggings and a sheepskin cloak, and led me towards the hall. At the door we met my mother who was wearing her finest bleached wool dress under her purple mantle, but her hair had been shorn like one in mourning, the braids cut off nearest her head. Neither

Boys unsupervised are not to be trusted even when they have been baptised. At least this one knew how to obey his elders. There is little enough of that, God knows.

did she wear her rings but only a round cross which she put on my neck. Then she wept and threw her arms about my neck and kissed me and I was moistened with her tears. My father was angry at this display and struck her and she ran from us. Then I began to be afraid, for I had never heard of a woman so dismayed at her son's departure. My legs became weak and I hung onto my father's hand as we went into the hall and approached the figure standing at the fireside. My father said, 'This is my own son.'

I looked up for the first time at my foster-father. Like my own father he had a thick dark beard, but his eyes were the pale blue of a winter sky. All children are the children of giants, since their parents stand twice their own height, and they must tilt their heads back to look them in the face. Now I saw that my father bent his head back to look at my foster-father, like a little boy. My foster father's head brushed our roof-tree.

He was truly a giant, the last, and most dreadful of his clan. My father lifted me onto his shoulders and the giant stooped to look at me.

'Is this your whelp at last? You have been long enough in finding him,' he said.

'This is he and no other. You will not find a better boy in this nation.'

'We shall find him out for ourselves,' said the giant, and his voice was the booming of the sea when it drives foam onto the shore. The sound of his breathing was like the rushing of shingle down the beach after a great wave has retreated, and I grew weaker still with fear. The giant bent over me and swept me into his arms, and without another word he strode out of the town and into the marshes.

When we came to the edge of the forest he did not hesitate but walked straight in among the trees. Towards the middle of the day we came to a clearing where the gloom of the trees gave way and let in a chill blue light. The giant stopped his rapid march as suddenly as he had started, put me on the ground and squatted in front of me. He pulled food from his scrip and, showing me dried beef in one hand and barley bread in the other he asked me if I was hungry. I had to keep my mouth shut to stop my teeth from chattering

I assume this is the father of Marighal. The size of the man, however, is no proof of a malevolent nature. Consider the history of St Brendan — he found a young female giant on the beach and he baptised her. She chose immediately to die and go to heaven proving that she was full of grace. Then there is the story of St Maeslo, who found a young male giant and gave him baptism also. He was as virtuous, and soon died. However, both of these were more than a hundred spans tall, and they appear to have come from the sea so it is possible they were of a different species.

and nodded, trying not to think what might be hiding in the forest behind me.

'If you wish to eat, then answer these three questions,' he said. 'First, what will your father be doing at this hour of the day?'

'Not hard to say,' I replied, wondering at the ease of it. 'My father will be out hunting, for today there is no rain or snow falling.'

'And where will he be in the crowd of the hunters?'

'In the lead, in the place of honour, surely, where the leader of his people should be, unless he has a guest he wishes to gratify.'

'Second question: when the sun sets, what will your father be doing?'

'At sunset he will be taking his place in the hall where his people will be feasting.'

'And where will he be sitting? At the top table or at the end of one beside the door out to the kitchen?'

'At the very top, surely, in the place of honour, unless he has a guest who is greater than himself.'

'Finally,' said the giant, taking a hazel-wand from his belt and handing it to me, 'if your father had a stick like that in his hand what would he be doing?'

'He would be in his hall in the morning of one of the feast days, hearing the petitions of his people, and later he would be helping the priest at the sacrifice.'

'He would not be whipping his dogs or beating lazy servants?'

This is an unholy catechism to find out the nature of the boy.

'No, indeed,' I cried, 'he has a huntsman and a steward to do those duties for him. He has no need to do them himself.'

'So I have you at last,' said the giant, and gave me food. I had thought him to be testing my knowledge of courtesy, but after I had eaten I went behind a tree for a necessary purpose, and I found Gwalchmai's son lying in the snow. He held his head twisted far, far round and the side of his face that was turned towards me was the same blue-white as the snow. The eye that I could see was open but it did not see me. I turned his face towards me and found that he had turned into a monster. The far side of his face was swollen like a pillow and coloured deep, vivid purple like the stain of bleaberries. The socket of his eye was so deep I could have laid my two fingers into it. Beyond him I saw the huntsman's son and I thought that he had been buried in the snow up to his neck. Then the notion came to me that the ground would be too hard from frost to bury one in it, yet all I could see was the face, snow-white and the two eyes closed. I went towards him to see if he would speak to me, then I saw a bundle of clothes lying beyond him, and the snow round his neck which was deep red, and I understood what I was looking at.

The giant came up behind me and said, 'Do you like it, my prince? It would make a pretty toy for a king's son.' And he bent down and picked up the head by the hair, and something bobbed where the neck had been, and then merciful God sent a blackness over my mind. I knew nothing more until we were at the giant's stronghold and one of his daughters was feeding me broth. I lay in a fever for many days, and for weeks I could not see my new father's face without my heart stopping in terror.

This monster is not endowed with grace.

God have mercy on their souls.

It is a great grief to me that the fine spring of my life should have been blighted like that. When I should have been running on the hills and the seashore with other princes for company I had no one of my own age but the giant's daughters. Little comfort I had of them, for they were a silent, lonely sisterhood and had no time for play and laughter. They would sit day on day, spinning and sewing, and scarcely spoke to each other, still less to me. They saw to it that I was fed and clothed, and they bound up my wounds, but they never left the stronghold, and they let me know that they did not like me to do so either. The one who became my sweet wife, Marighal, was kept from me or shunned my company. After a couple of summers I found that my master wished to have me at his side to teach me all the arts and skills of arms and by and by I forgot my snivelling fear of him and gave him my devotion.

I forgot that the bodies of my people lay unavenged in the forest. That was my crime and its curse has lived with me to this very day; I betrayed my first friends and I am forsworn of my oaths to them. My only happiness is that their murderer is dead, though I had little to do with it.

This is reported by Marighal also.

The end of the king's tale.

By now the sun was sinking towards the horizon and the wind had changed. The king led me back to the hall and

Selyf takes up the story again.

94

*Your body perhaps. But
more important is your soul.*

*It was we, poor exiles, that
kept the light of knowledge
burning in this country, and
saved it for the world. If
it had not been for 'our
kind' the whole of the northern
world would be sunk in pagan
darkness.*

we went in to dinner together. I was given a seat closer
to the king and I saw that the bishop was watching me.
During the evening I withdrew to read my office, and
when I did so I offered up a prayer of thanksgiving that
the king's foster-father was dead, and that I would not
be meeting him if I found his daughter. Though you
say she is a demon, father, I am sure I will be safe
with her, but the king's account of her father filled me
with dread.

In that place apart, when I had finished the office,
the bishop sought me out and questioned me about my
knowledge of the king's wife. I said to him merely that
I had known her sister slightly, for the king was anxious
to keep her secret, and I do not owe such as him the
whole truth.

'You spent a long time with the king today talking of
God knows what. What does the king have to say to one
of your kind? You must tell me, for I am appointed the
spiritual guardian of this city, and the king's soul friend,
and I must know all that happens here.'

'Truly, sir,' I answered quietly, 'the king was seeking
news of the country where he grew to manhood. In my
travels and missions I have seen many places and the
king asked me how things fared in the south.'

'Even so,' the bishop said, 'your kind must always be
rushing about the country. No good can come of it.'

I concluded that the bishop was a Frank, and by
his cross and pall I saw that he had been sent from
the see of Jorvik. He was not pleased to see one
of our ancient and venerable remnant at his gates.
But I had no quarrel with him, nor did I seek one,
for I would not be staying and I saw no need once
again to defend our practices to him. He was not so
content.

'Know that I have been in this city for many years,' he
said, 'and before me a brother of the sacred order of St
Benedict was adviser here. It was he who brought the
light to this barbarous kingdom in spite of the terrible
dangers that beset him. He baptised the people from the
mountains to the sea, and from the beaches of stone in
the north to the sands of the south. To me has fallen this
heavy burden, to continue to baptise the new-born and
to spread the word of the true faith till darkness is fled
from this kingdom for ever. But this would not please

you, would it? I hear your kind do not baptise infants, even to this day.'

'Sir, I have not come here to join the debate about our differences with you. Since you have raised the matter, it is true that we hold it a blasphemy to approach the sacrament without the power of reason, but I leave the disputation to my betters. I am not versed in rhetoric.'

The bishop was eager to show me my place for he went on, 'Did you not see the fine church the king is building for me? It will be all made of stone, and there will be no equal to it in all of Cymri.'

'Indeed, sir,' I replied, determined to remain true to my Rule, 'you have been most like the builders of the temple in Jerusalem in your very great endeavours. I am sure you had a wisdom as great as Solomon's to guide you, for it is said that the serene St Benedict was a clever and a forceful man. I wonder, though, what it was that happened all those generations ago when the bell-shaped cells were built. Was it perhaps the work of mighty bees, do you think, that raised the stone walls of those little pointed houses — the ones that litter the coast and the forest? Truly they were the source of much buzzing.'

'Buzzing, indeed, and buzzing is all it is,' cried the bishop.

'Yes, sir, and glad we are to hear it for it is the sound of joy, contentment and industry while God's mercy shines on us like the sun shines on the bees. What else should we do but raise our voices in the best way we know how ?'

'In blasphemy and error, that is how,' he cried, 'your kind still operate as if the holy St Gregory had never sent you the one true Rule and Calendar. Sweet Jesus, some of you even keep concubines.'

'Not concubines, sir, wives — handfasted wives. And is it not better to keep a virtuous wife in public than a whore in darkness and shame? And once our heir is born the woman retires and no more shares her husband's house, as did the Levites. Is this more of a scandal than that a consecrated priest should be seen in a brothel?'

'Those bell-houses are not beehives, they are the droppings of Satan and his host. They left them when they visited this country and populated it with demented monks!'

Your restraint is a credit to your discipline, Selyf. We are known to be a contentious order, and cannot agree even among ourselves. You may be sure he was trying to provoke you.

Apis humilis casta, indefatigiblis.

This was incontinently done, but God will forgive your eloquence. Only remember what Climacus said also, on wrath being the wickedness of

96

demons. The clergy do not love us. They only love fat cities and wealthy people. They never could have borne the hardships we underwent to bring the truth to this country.

I have seen this practice in Rome.

I am sure I am right about this city.

I forgot that you had been out of Brytain. You were in the company of Berach Abbot, were you not?

Pride goes before destruction, and a haughty spirit before a fall. Better it is to be of a humble spirit with the lowly than to divide the spoils with the proud. Proverbs XVI.

With that the bishop fled back to the king's side. Had I stayed in the city I am sure the bishop would have had me murdered. After the meal I was given a place in the hall to sleep and no one interfered with me when I read my office, though none joined me either. In the morning I watched as the household went to the wooden chapel at the site of the new church, and attended the Offering. To my great amazement the king and his wife both took part in the communion meal, even though it was not a feast-day, and as he handed the cup to the king, the bishop looked up at me. After that I went down to the beach and stood for most of the day with my hands raised in prayer for patience. At the end of the day's business the king sent for me again, and we walked round the top of his great tower as we talked. Far out to sea, the pointed island of rock they call the Devil's Milestone floated on a haze above the water.

'How do you like our fine church, monk Selyf?' said the king, 'Will it not be one of the finest sights on the coast, or in the whole kingdom?'

'Indeed, sir, I am inspired to delight and wonder at it. It will be as great as the temple of the Great Carlus, the Emperor of the Franks which I saw as a young scholar. You will be able to say with truth "The Lord has said that he would dwell in thick darkness, but I have built a house of habitation for Thee and a place for Thy dwelling for ever." '

'Is that from the Gospels?' asked the king, 'I am not familiar with it.'

'It is from the chronicles of the sons of David. The words spoken by the great king Solomon when he had completed the temple at Jerusalem. They sprang to my lips when I saw the stones of your chapel.'

'I would like to know more of king Solomon. The bishop does not speak of him, but I have heard that he ruled his people in peace for many years, as I have done. But he lusted after many and strange women, unlike myself. My wife is mostly woman enough for me, though she was passing strange in her youth.'

'That I can well believe,' I said, 'for the woman I met manifested a great and terrible strength to me and my fellows so that we fled from the sight of her.'

'If she were of my wife's family she would have great strength of arm, and much more besides, although I could not tell you all of it. I spent ten winters in that hall yet I could not tell you half of the mysteries there.'

'I would be glad to hear as much as you could tell me, sir, for I need all the knowledge I can gain if I am to survive this mission.'

I knew from the first that I would be marrying one of the daughters when the time came, and I knew which one, for she made herself known to me at once. She did not like me well at first, and would torment me cruelly when her older sisters were not at hand to restrain her. In those days I would often see my mother in dreams at night, as she was the last time I saw her. When she turned and fled from me I would try to call her back, but I would waken at that and find my betrothed watching me. She laughed at me for my tears and took my mother's round cross from me saying it was a toy for babies, but at the last she gave it back to me.

Kynan continues his story.

One day I saw her no more, and I heard that she had been sent for fostering. About that time I went to live in my master's hall, and my education began in earnest, so I did not look for her.

This confirms what Marighal said.

In my whole time at the castle I had not seen any male person other than the giant. I wondered how it was to be that I would learn the skills of the warrior with no person to oppose me. Soon I found that the giant had many devices which he caused to be made by the great artificers in the forest. When I was first shown them I thought them toys, but they were most ingenious and skilful toys. There were the slaves that were globes that flew, singing, and from them I learned to use sword and shield. Indeed these could strike much faster than any man I have ever fought, and worse, no stroke I could make would stop them. The first time I was in a true battle I was stricken motionless for a while for the men around me screamed in pain and rage. I had been accustomed to opponents who fought in near silence. Even when the giant himself stood as my adversary there was no sound, other than the din of metal on metal.

Trapped demons or damned human souls?

So he was not suffering from the 'battle-fetter' that the men of Orkney dreaded.

The giant was a great teacher. I learned to trust him and, at last, to love him, but that was not because he never injured me. He gave me grievous wounds in practice, but he would tend them himself with much tenderness and great knowledge so that I would heal swiftly.

98

Hawking? Is there nothing this giant did not know?

Who was the giant's wife? Why do you not think to ask, Selyf?

He names her at last!

Some grace has been shown him by this.

No matter how swift or cunning I became I could never return his blows. He showed me how to undergo great hardship, fasting for many days with nothing but a few sips of water. I could stand watch for half a day at a time in baking sun or freezing cold, with my byrnie and my helmet on and shield and sword unslung till the metal tore the skin off my neck and hands. I could pass many nights without sleep; I could hunt and hawk and live off herbs that he showed me. I manned my own hawk and tended my own blades, for my master said that one who did not understand all these things and know good from bad would be a poor sort of warrior.

Once I asked him why he was so careful of my education and he told me that he had no son of his own, nor ever would have, and since he had no wife living I believed him. The children of his line were all female and this was a source of much grief to him, so he took the son of a good man to teach him as if he were his own.

Those days were very happy ones as I grew quickly in strength and skill, and I had not time or inclination to reflect upon my state. I had heard from one of the slaves that could speak that Marighal had gone to one of the great makers for training, but I did not think of her. I loved my master dearly and my only happiness was to strive with him and to learn from him to become one of the greatest warriors of my generation. Anything that I showed an inclination to learn was shown to me, and I even learned how to read and write a little.

But of his black arts I learned nothing, nor did I seek to learn them for all my study was to be as mighty and as cunning in war as himself. I did not wish to follow him into shadows. Then the day came when I asked for a sword and mail shirt of my own, for the pieces I had for practice were not suitable for a young chieftain. He said that I would have my own battle gear soon enough for I should soon receive them from my lady, and I must prepare for that. I worked hard for a while but when I was told that the arms my lady was bringing me had been made by herself I was dismayed.

I thought that my honour was being slighted and I said to the servant, 'How can it be that a girl-child should make a sword when a woman cannot even lift a hammer, let alone use one. Surely the weapons she will make will be poor stuff?'

'Not so,' sang the servant, 'she has been taught by the greatest smith of all and there is nothing she cannot do in the making of fine gear, for she is the daughter of Usbathaden, and none are mightier than his kind.'

I was content, and waited till the time of the midwinter feast. Then I saw all the sisters who lived in the stronghold assembled for the first time in years. They all drank to my health and to my manly years now started and without doubt my lady was the finest among them. She alone stood tall and keen-eyed, nor was she cowed by the presence of her father. She was fierce and proud and when she presented me with my gear she made a challenge to me and to her father to prove that I was worthy of her work. I had no answer, but my master said that I was worthy and I would prove it by joining king Maelcolum in campaign against the Vikings in his kingdom. For a moment I doubted myself, for the gear was the finest ever made in the whole of Alban and Cymri — I still have it in the hall if you wish to see it — I do not let many do so. The sword is as keen as the day I received it from her, but my worth to wear it as a warrior is long gone.

Did you see it, Selyf?

Loud laughter from the great hall told us the king's household was gathering for the evening and he must leave me.

'Before you go, sir,' I said, 'I must tell you that this is what I heard from my lady's sister when I met her. She also told me that she went on campaign with you. If this is true, perhaps it will prove to you that I met your lady's kin, for it is not customary.'

'It is true,' he replied, musing, 'she was my servant on our campaign.'

'Indeed, I had not expected to find it true, for it seemed to me ill-advised. Was she not abused by the warriors you travelled with, for women who travel with warriors are licentious and coarse. Was she not derided by them for her gentle ways, or worse?'

'I see my lady's sister did not tell you about her sorcerous ways. You must understand that when my wife went with me it was not as a woman, nor even as a boy, nor in any human shape, since her father did

This is the end of the king's narrative to date. He confirms at least that the woman was with him and that she was a very skilled smith. It is still not easy to believe.

Shape-changing, by Maelcruin and Dafydd. Now we are at the nub of it! There was a healer in Lübeck, a little yellow man from the north-east whose skills were famous in that country. They said that he was a shape-changer when he was younger, and could become a bear, a wolf or a deer at will. When I was there he was a different man, for he had accepted baptism and attended the mass every week.

Having submitted to the one God he could no longer do so, of course, but when I asked about it no one would tell me anything.

not wish her to speak to me. She was my servant, true, but silenced, for she ran beside my horse as a mighty hound.'

For the first time in many years I was unable to find words and my amazement was complete.

The king smiled at my stupefaction and said, 'Tomorrow is the feast of the Transfiguration, Selyf, and I will be at leisure. Come to me after the morning offering if you wish, and you shall hear more of my wife's strange ways.'

And he left me to watch the island draw close to the land as night came upon us.

The next day I attended the offering, then said the office for our order alone again. I took it as an ill omen that my voice shook on the words, 'tremble, thou earth, at the presence of the Lord — at the presence of the God of Jacob which turned the rock into a standing water and the flint into a mountain of waters.' I had begun to fear what I would hear next from the king. I went to him at about the third hour, and the Frankish bishop saw us walking together along the beach. He frowned but did not make to join us, and we walked over the firm sand of the estuary to the side of the sea.

The king said at last, 'You may be sure that my wife looked after me well while we were on campaign together. I never went to sleep hungry, though it was a lean time of year, and game was scarce. At first I found it strange to think that the hound could understand my every word. I had only to say what I needed, and soon, panting, she would drop it at my feet. Men envied me my dog as much as they envied me my gear.'

Then he told me in detail of the battle the woman had recounted. He told how the king had given him a ring in token of the pledge between them, and he smiled joyfully to recall his feats.

But then he became sad again and he said, 'My wife remembers nothing of this, nor are there many living that can recall those days, and I could wish I had been properly attended for that alone. Yet I rejoice to think that she has forgotten so much, most of all the terrible task I had to perform to win free from her father's stronghold.'

'My lord,' I said, 'some things are blessedly forgotten. Why do you not make a proper confession of your deeds and do a penance for them to remove them from your heart?'

'I wish that I could, monk, for when I left the giant's hall I had done things which it were far, far better to forget, and yet to this day I am not sure if it were sin.'

'Nevertheless, if a man truly repents, no sin is too great but the blood of our Saviour will wash it from his heart.'

'Of what value is my penance if I am not sure that I have sinned? Those deeds that trouble me most are in no catechism, no penitentiary, nor has the bishop mentioned them in his homilies, for all that he is a very learned man. I truly wish those deeds had not been done by me, but they were needed, and I do not wish them undone.'

'My lord, I am not a clever man, nor yet a good one, but I think that a sin, though necessary, will not be expunged unless truly repented. I will try to discover what might be a suitable penance, if you wish.'

'Very well, I will tell you what I did, and you can be the judge of my actions.'

A tangled situation, true, but surely the man's regret of itself is proof that the deed was sinful. God will always illumine our hearts if we will only give Him time.

After that feast was over the women of the house were hidden from me once again. I could not discover them this time, though I sought them throughout the stronghold. You must understand that it was vast, beyond the power of mortal man to build, and the halls and passages were so many that I might wander in them for half a day nor see the same place twice. Many of the halls were empty and in the silent passages and windy courts it would have been easy for any to pass in secret. I roamed this emptiness for days, and found only metal slaves and empty space, and strange things which I cannot recall, though I have tried many times. There were mirrors, all of wonderfull smoothness; there were great globes of glass where the surface was coloured like rainbow yet ran like water; there were rooms filled with sparkling light like the dancing lights that appear in the northern sky at night. Some of these sights might have driven other men from their senses, but I had been reared with strangeness and I kept myself in hand. Often I came to doors which were locked, and if I tried to enter I would find at my side a metal slave which struck me with a bolt of stinging light, and I would leave the door alone.

Kynan resumes his story.

I wish he would give us more details.

This taunting is most unpleasant, but not at all unusual when a young nobleman is going to be married.

During that time the giant only came to me at meals, but he knew what I did by day, for he would mock me saying, 'Our young stag's horns are sprouting and he wanders alone in his rut. What shall we do to help him to a hind? Once he had a bitch to hunt me but she is gone. What will he do now, but use his own nose to find a quarry, and though it is as keen as any man's it is not as good as a deer hound. What shall he do, but use his ears and follow the music of the distant drum?'

But in truth his words were a guide to me, for one day as I was crossing the outer yard, I heard a sound coming from one of the buildings there. It was one of the largest of the outer buildings — bigger even than the stables — and much longer than it was wide. Along the sides there were tall windows fitted with round panes of green grass, and one of these was open. It is strange to tell, but I had seen that building since my first days at the stronghold, yet never had I thought of it as a place which might be inhabited. Now, for the first time, I heard a sound coming through that window, and it was a steady beating sound as if someone were striking a drum with muffled sticks. Then that sound stopped and there came a sighing and a singing as if someone struck a harp's strings.

I began to seek the door and soon found I had a metal spy following me close. Had my master not spoken of a distant drum I might have stopped at once, but there came no stinging light from the slave and the hunt was on. I found the door at last, low down on the south wall, and as it had no handle I opened it with the blade of my knife. Inside I was instantly blinded by light from the other side of the room. I fell back into the yard to save my tormented eyes. At once the door closed nor could anything I did that day open it again.

The next day, early, I heard the beating sound again, and at once I went to the door and opened it. This time I was prepared for the blinding light and put my hand before my face. Once inside, the door closed and the light was less strong. The spy had followed me in and hung in the air close by, singing a loud and dismal song. I looked at the wall of light and found that it was a wall of mirrors, entirely smooth. There was no door that I could see, and each one gave me back a full image of myself from the crown of my head to the soles of my

feet. Then as I walked before the mirrors a great wonder
was revealed to me, for I changed as I moved, from a
man to a dwarf with legs short and a chest wide and
deep. A few steps further on and I turned into a sprite
with legs like reeds, twice as long as my body. This was
a terrible blow to me and I stood stricken to ice and
could not move. Then, as I watched, I changed before
my eyes and I melted and flowed like water between
rocks and became once again comely and proper. This
did not continue for my head swelled and shrank and I
became a dwarf again. I confess I was now stupid with
terror like a beast, but I found my feet no longer rooted
to the floor and fled through the open doorway.

The spy flew after me, passed my shoulder and hit
the stable wall so that it smashed into a spray of wheels
and wire and ruby eyes. I looked down at my body, and
behold, all was as it should be. The hideous creatures
I had been a moment before were gone, but I ran in to
the hall where there was a great mirror, and studied my
every line.

When I looked closely at the mirror, I saw that at the
edges the image changed because the nature of the glass
changes, becoming thin and bent. I pondered on this for
a long time, and I was glad that the giant did not come in
to eat with me, for I was sure that I had a very important
problem to solve. Like a huntsman on a trail I followed
the notion till at last I saw that I had not changed in the
outer hall, but the mirror had done so. No man knows
all the secrets of a mirror's nature, but this was one. I
was sure that I could come to no harm, so the next day I
went into the yard before the sun rose over the palisade.
Even so I found a spy at my elbow.

As soon as the sun struck the door I slipped in
through it like a snake off a rock, yet I was not too fast
for the spy-globe. It flew in after me to hover keening
like the one before it. Then I was able to strike it from
behind and break it on the stone floor with one blow. I
turned to face the mirror wall and reeled as my strange
image appeared in front of me. I told myself not to look
at the mirror's image but at the edges of the mirror itself
and by and by my eyes stopped plunging like a fish in
rapids. I pressed on one side as if it were the edge of
a door, and behold, the mirror moved, not away at the
side, but at the top, and the bottom edge swung towards

*A simple soul might think
that this was sorcery, but I
have thought about it and I
realise that these strange sights
are produced by mirrors that
have had their surfaces bent. I
remember that the first one I
saw gave back the image of
a soul in torment because of a
dent in the metal. I concluded
that the light from my eyes
was bent by the bending of the
metal and returned to my eyes
distorted.*

*The slave machine was
destroyed by the sight because
it did not have the faculty
of reason. Perhaps they are
invested with the souls of
animals.*

*This man has much
presence of mind for one so
young. It is a great pity he
does not play a greater part in
the affairs of the country.*

104

me. I was very fast and was able to spring clear before the thing smashed my legs. There was now a space under the tilted mirror that I could crawl through.

Next I found myself in a room walled on two sides with mirrors so that I saw myself, back and front, repeated many times. This time the mirror swung about a fixed mid-point, and there was a gap between two mirrors just wide enough to let me through. I pushed the mirrors aside and stepped into the next chamber.

There before me stood my lady, with her hair in four braids and her fine green mantle swinging round her feet. She was standing at a loom, weaving, and as she beat down the weft there came the muffled sound of drumming that had fetched me there; and as she threw her shuttle there came the sound of strumming that had kept me there.

I looked past her into the long, long weaving hall, and I saw that the great chamber held many looms, some so old that the warp was weighted with stones, and swung in the breeze from the window. Some of the looms were hung with weavings of beauty and strangeness that showed beasts and plants and countries which no man could know. The hall was lit with green light from the windows, but also, above the loom where my lady worked, there hung a rack of brilliant lamps, charged with the black oil my master prized above all for illumination. My lady did not look at me, but beyond her, where the light gave way to shadows by the wall, there sat an old woman with mumbling, hairy lips. On her knee sat a beautiful girl-child, little more than an infant. These two were gazing full at me, and while the old one did not move by so much as a blink of her wet eyes, the young one stretched out her hand to me. In it she held the round ancient cross that my mother had given to me. I did not take it at once.

Without turning my lady spoke to me, saying, 'Take the cross, Kynan White-hair, for it is a sign that I did not lie to you all those years ago when I said I was to be your wife.'

I took the cross from the child and my lady went on, 'Son of man, soon it will be time for us to be married. I have brought you here so that we may talk without my father's knowledge.'

In my opinion this is very much like the way that faith operates. We retain an image in our hearts which is unshakeable, and no matter what our foolish senses tell us we are not deceived provided that we keep our inner eye on the image within.

I note that even though Kynan was fostered by the monster he never refers to him as father, but only 'master'.

The crone and the infant, is there blasphemy here?

'What need have we to speak in secret, woman?' I said, 'Your father has decreed that we should marry. Why should I hide from him whom I love more than my own father?'

'Understand this, Kynan,' said my lady, 'my father does not truly wish us to be married. His desire in bringing you to his stronghold was to find a son for himself, but he knew well that it is customary that a foster-son should have a daughter of the house as a wife, and he must respect custom. He knows that when you take my virginity he will die. So he will do everything he can to stop our marriage. Throughout the years many men have sought us women in marriage, for to wed a giant's daughter will give a man much power, but till this time only two have succeeded in getting away from the stronghold and in consummating the marriage. They succeeded because they fled to a far country in secret. Of the others who stayed too long and too near some live married, but in a virgin state because my father took the man's lustiness away; for the rest, my married sisters have been cruelly treated and abandoned, and even killed. If you and I succeed we will only be the third couple to win free, but that will destroy my father. You may be sure that if you marry me and stay in my father's house you will not take me and live through the night. He will not surrender his flesh lightly.'

Sorcerers are very clever at this. They can make a man impotent for years.

'If the effect of your marriage will be so grievous why do you wish to marry? Surely a woman must hesitate if her father's doom waits upon her wedding day?'

'I cannot deny that this causes me much pain, but it is a pain I must accept, for if you and I do not unite, you will never leave this hall alive, and I will be a prisoner here till God's kingdom come.

On that day of wrath they will be released and judged.

'Once before a young man came to seek the giant's power without taking the wife offered him. He studied for many years to understand my father's arts, yet when he came to leave this hold without his bride, the knowledge in his heart possessed him and he ran mad through the forest till he turned into a monster. Such would happen to you if you tried to leave without one of us to help you.'

'Truly, I have no wish to stay here for the rest of my life without sight of my fellow man, but I do not believe what you are saying. Your father told me that when the time came to leave I would be examined to find out my worthiness, and if found worthy I would be returned to my family with my bride. He showed no sorrow at these words, nor by any pause did he seem to show he felt harm in it to himself.'

'He only told you a part of the truth, nor would he seem troubled by your leaving, for in his heart he does not believe that you will. Many obstacles lie in the way of our leaving, and we must plan carefully how to overcome them.'

I still could not believe her.

He has been duped by the magus.

'This is the first I have heard tell of these terrible things, and I am finding it hard to take your word. You tell me, of a sudden, that we must seek a way to destroy the master we both love, and if we do not the loving master will destroy us. It would be easier to believe that the grass beyond that wall is red and the leaves purple.'

How can all these females be sisters? They are of such different ages. Furthermore there has been no mention of any women other than the sisters and daughters of the house. Is there incest here? It is woefully common among the godless pagans. This 'oath-helping' is another of their ways. One oath taken by the holy scripture is enough for a good Christian.

'There stand my sisters,' said Marighal, pointing into the shadows at the other two. 'They stand as oath helpers to my words. Essyllt, the oldest among us yet living, and not long for her mortal habitation; being so close to her death she is beyond lying and her mother was a true queen of an ancient line. Elayne, the youngest, whose mother came from beyond the sea to bear her, and left a nobler house than any to do so; she is too young to know deception. Both of them will give you warning if I have departed from the truth.'

At these words the crone and the infant bowed to me in silence. They continued to watch me as Marighal went on, 'Consider how you have won your way into the weaving hall. Time after time my father has sent his spies to seek a way into this room without success. At first he even made the attempt himself, but his eyes are too weak and his body too big to find the path through the mirror maze. You, not as powerful as he, nor as swift as the slaves, have attained access to this chamber. How may that be?'

'I do not know for sure how I have prevailed,' I answered, 'but it seems to me that though my eyes are not as keen as a globe's, being human I cannot be so easily deceived. I used my body's knowledge to confirm what my eyes were trying to tell me, and when they lied I could follow my memory to find the truth.

I am ready to test the truth of any sight if it does not please me.'

'Well answered,' said Marighal. 'Now consider this: you know in your heart that what appears may not be true, yet you have been happy to believe what my father said to you because you had nothing to gain by thinking otherwise. But if you shed the illusion as you did before you must see that you have nothing to gain by staying within these walls another day.'

Well answered, indeed. It is a wise man who knows that his eyes may deceive him.

'Perhaps you speak without deceit. I cannot yet see what you will gain by your deception. Tell me what lies ahead and if your words come to pass I will know you are not forsworn.'

'Good Kynan, you are as clever as you are strong,' she said, 'now listen to my sisters, and they will tell you truly what will happen.'

'All this is true, we swear it by our hands and by our eyes,' said the sisters. 'If you would live, you must do as she will tell you. Usbathaden is our father and we love him, but before the tombs of our mothers who did not live to see us grow we warn you he is cruel beyond belief, and though he truly loves you now, his love will turn daily into hate as he sees you growing in wisdom and strength. Look into your heart and recall the day you came to us. What happened to the companions of your childhood?'

At last they mention their mothers.

I wondered as they said this, for they spoke with two voices yet the child could not have been of an age to speak so fluently.

I turned to Marighal, and said, 'What will you have me do?'

'Listen closely,' she said, beckoning me, 'already your discovery of this place has been told to our father, and soon your presence within it will be found out. Tomorrow or the next day, he will speak of me. When he does, tell him that you wish to exchange oaths so that you may travel with your bride to see your family. Say that you are weary with longing to see them. My father will agree to the feast readily, but he will say that you must complete the tasks he will set you as a final test. You must agree to all of them without hesitation, for he will be trying your obedience. Whatever the task you must set about it with your heart high, for I shall soon come to you and help you.'

Is this no more than the loyalty to be expected from a fosterling?

As the son of a land-holder it is his clear duty to marry and beget children. And tradition and his own interest make it important that he should marry into a powerful family. It is a pity that there is no-one to teach him after Radbert that even in marriage lust must be curbed and used only for blessed procreation.

'I will do as you have said,' I told her, 'but with a heavy heart for I do not seek evil for my master.'

'We must all accept what God sends for us,' said Marighal, 'but now you must leave us and return to the armoury, for soon another slave will be sent to find you.'

I slipped out through the mirror maze and at the door I put the remnant of the spy-globe into my scrip. Once outside I took the pieces to the far side of the strong-hold, and scattered them so that the wily giant would not know that two of his servants died in the same place. The next day fell out as Marighal had predicted, for the giant sent for me to hunt with him. When we were returning with deer across our saddles he spoke of his daughter's great prowess with the bow.

'Have you given any thought to your marriage with her?' he asked.'The time is near, for you are both long since old enough.

'Indeed, sir,' I answered, 'she is a fine maker and a woman of great courage. When I was on campaign she saw to my provision, and looked not at all to her own safety. I look forward to marriage so that I may take her to my father's hall. I know that there she will receive full honour, both as the bride of the young chief and as a noblewoman in her own right.'

'I am glad to hear this. Nor will any rejoice more than I when a brave youth takes my daughter as a wife. But before your oaths may be exchanged, there are condi-tions that you must satisfy.'

'I had foreseen this, sir,' I replied, 'for the noble daughter of an ancient house is not to be won like the daughter of a herdsman. But please let me be tested soon, for I am weary to see my father's hall, and it is many years since I embraced my mother. I almost fear that they will not know their son when I return.'

'I understand your haste,' said the giant, 'but I would not have you rushing into marriage like a young ram. Come to me tomorrow at daybreak and I will give you a task that will try your courage and your skill. It will be a humble task, but so easy for you with your strong legs and back that you will finish it in half a day. Indeed you may think it beneath your manhood to do it.'

'Not so, sir. No task could ever be too low for me to
do if it is yourself that sets it. I am your obedient and
grateful son.'

Now he speaks of himself as son.

The next day at daybreak I rose and went to my master who laughed when he saw me. Then he led me out
from the stronghold and into the forest till we came to a
wide clearing. From it we could see across to the giant's
hall, where it stood with its towers gleaming in the newly
risen sun.

The giant said to me, 'That is my own place. I built it
nor can any man come at me while I am in it.'

Then, in the clearing, he showed me a great stone
building which was begining to decay, and he said, 'This
is a place I built many, many years ago when I first came
into this country. I thought I would show the people
here how to raise the finest cattle they had ever seen,
which could survive even the winter here. They would
not listen to me, because they were afraid and preferred
their old ways. So I left them to their traditions and gave
them the byre to do with as they pleased until the roof
fell in.

So, he has spared some thought for those less wise and strong than himself. Why did he cease to do so?

'Now I have taken a notion to use it again, but I will
not use it with all the dirt and waste those ignorant fools
have left here. If you would marry my daughter you will
clean it from end to end so that none of my globes will
find a speck of dirt, though they search all night.'

'I will gladly do so, sir,' I said, though my heart turned
cold at the news. The stallings were as deep as my knees
in places and in others were trodden down until they
were as hard as rock. I had only a wooden spade, a
birch-twig besom and the strength of my back, but
Marighal had told me she would help me so I pushed
my way in through the brambles and began to scrape at
the floor.

Heracles diverted the river to do this. I doubt if Kynan is up to that!

After a while a shadow crossed the doorway and I saw
her.

'What is your task?' she asked me, and I told it all.

'You must now go outside,' she said, 'and leave the
place to me. Climb into the rowan-tree on the western
side of the byre, nor yet move from there until I summon
you with my own hand, for if you do I will not be able to
save you.'

I did as she bade me and sat myself in the fork of the
tree where I could see what she did. She walked out of

This is certainly sorcery.

Was she silent all this time or were there incantations?

Sorcery again.

Those who wish to reach a closer communion with the one God will always seek to change nature. He is the one thing beyond nature, and if we wish to know him we must model ourselves on His incorporal being.

Demonic wrath?

the south door of the byre and knelt on the grass. After a while there came over me a feeling that I was swooning, and I found that I could not move a single limb, though I tried with all my strength. I could still see and hear, however, and what happened made me wonder.

As Marighal waited a mouse crept out of the grass, and came towards her, and with my last breath I will swear that she spoke to it saying, 'I have a task for you. You must gather all your brothers and sisters, cousins and all your tribe, and you will come into the byre through the one door and leave by the other and as you go you will take the dirt from the floor with you. Nor will you leave so much as a speck behind you.'

'Why should we do this thing for you?' asked the creature, 'we owe you no allegiance, nor can you compel us.'

'I can compel you, you foolish creature, but I will not, for it is not to the point. You owe the man in the tree yonder a great debt of obligation, for if you had not stolen from the wrens that day and started the war all those generations ago, he would never have been caught in the giant's trammel.'

'What if there was stealing that day? That is our way. Would you have us steal no longer and our children and ourselves starve in the winter? Are we to change our nature, and so changing die — for it is sure the farmers will not give us our provisions freely.'

'I do not seek to change the nature of any creature. I know that stealing from the farmer is how you live, but I say you had no quarrel with the wren, his hireling, and no cause to provoke her and her kin to anger and revenge.'

There was no reply to this and at last my lady said angrily, 'You know I speak the truth, for it is talked of daily by bird and animal kind. You know what is due, why do you hesitate?'

'Mistress, we are simple creatures and we do not see why our grandsire's folly should bind us now.'

'Thieves and wretches,' cried my lady, 'do not awaken my father's rage in me. You have just been pleading with me to show lenience to you on the grounds of your nature. Where do you get your nature from but from your grandsires? As you inherit their nature so you inherit their duties. Do your duty now and discharge

your debt to this man or fetch more suffering on generations to come and they will curse your name for ever.'

'We are already a cursed people,' said the mouse, 'and
all revile us and drive us away when they see us.'

Silence fell again and nothing was said for a long
time, then the mouse's voice came again, saying, 'Will
you reward us?'

At this my lady laughed a laugh so great I felt the tree
shake under me.

'Yes, I will reward you,' she said, 'if the work is well
done, and finished by sunset.'

'May we call on our sisters the insects?

'You may do so if you can. The means are yours to
decide. I have told you what I want.'

By now the sun was well below its highest point in
the spring sky. As I waited I watched the shadow of a
branch creep across the back of my motionless hand.
After a very long time I heard a great murmuring start
in the forest, and it grew and grew till I raised my eyes to
see what caused it. Out of the south I saw a great black
cloud coming, and beneath me, on the ground there was
a vast rippling sea of brown, and the noise was like the
roaring of a mighty wind. Both the cloud and the sea
gathered to a point and entered the byre through the
south door. Of my lady I saw nothing, but I was filled
with fear lest she had fallen in the path of this flood of
creatures.

What passed next I cannot say for sure, since it all
happened out of my view, but the din I could hear was
like a marching army. I gazed across the glen to the
giant's hall, and I could see the shadows growing and
the light on the castle walls turning from gold to red.
I began then to fear that the sunset was upon us and
the task was not nearly finished. My terror then was
greater than any I have felt in battle since I was bound
and unable to help myself. If I live a thousand years, I
hope never again to know that state where my doom is
made and I can make no move to change it.

At last the sound in the byre seemed to fade and
dwindle and I heard my lady's voice speaking to the
mice again. 'The byre is truly clean, daughter. I am
well pleased with you. And with the dirt you have
spread on it the grass in the glen will grow the richer
next summer.'

*II Corinthians 12:14 For
the children ought not to lay
up for the parents but the
parents for the children.*

*We are all in God's hand.
And must lie like children
there.*

112

Virtue is its own reward.

She has mastery over these creatures, yet she is also in their debt. Yet they were discharging one themselves. This is very like our relationship with God. Why does He bother to bargain with inferior creatures? He leaves us free choice over our actions even though he could compel us because he wishes us to choose the Good freely. He does not reveal His whole purpose to us for we could not understand, but he asks us only to have faith and do our simple duty.

'That will be our reward for now,' said the mouse, 'but one day we sinners will have need of your voice. Then we will remind you of your debt to us.'

'I will remember I am in your debt.' said Marighal, 'and now you must go, for the sun is setting.'

Then she came to me and touched my breast, saying, 'My father is on his way, come down.' And at once I found I was free to move again.

'You have nothing to fear, for the byre is as clean as the day he built it. Go in now and wait for him and the slaves he will bring to do his searching for him, for it is sure he will not be able to see for himself. I must leave you now in order that my part in this should remain a secret. Tomorrow you will be given another task, but whatever happens, do not be afraid. I will come to help you before the middle of the day.'

It was as she had said, for the byre was so clean that even the moss was gone from the walls. The giant arrived with his globes and they flew backwards and forwards over the floor singing to him, but they found nothing.

Then he said to me, 'You have done well today, Kynan, though how you have done it I do not know. Those stallings had been gathering for many generations. Do you meet me here tomorrow at sunrise and I will give you another task.' And he strode off swiftly, leaving me to find my way home through the darkening forest.

The next day I returned as the sun rose behind me and found my master there. At his feet there was a bow and a great bundle of arrows, and he pointed at them saying, 'Now the byre is so fine and clean I have a notion to put a new roof on it. The turf is long since dried up and blown away in the wind. It is said that the feathers of birds are the best thatch, for they are light and keep out all the rain. Your task today is to collect enough feathers to cover the roof of the byre, but see you do not use two feathers of the same colour, for such a fine byre as I have built should have the finest sort of roof.'

He does not say how the feathers are to be fixed in place. The first breeze will take them away.

'Indeed,' said I, weak with fear, 'that is a hard task, for the shooting of birds is not learned quickly, and the foresters who do it for their sport practise constantly. How shall I do, who have never tried it before?'

'Do not fear, Kynan,' answered the giant, smiling, 'I know that one as wise and cunning as yourself will soon devise a way. Are you not the cleverest fosterling I have ever taught? I will return at sunset, and if the task is not completed, not only will my daughter be forfeit, but you will surely die.' So saying he left me.

The giant reveals his foul purpose.

My fear grew stronger at these words, for I saw that the women had been speaking the truth. He no longer had kind feelings toward me, and he would destroy me if he could. I took the bow and arrows with shaking hands and shot at some birds nearby. All the time I was waiting for Marighal, but she did not come and the sun rose higher in the sky till it stood at its highest. Then I saw the little few birds that lay before me and the fear I always felt for the giant grew in my heart, and unmanned me so that I began to weep. Suddenly Marighal stood in front of me, and I spoke like a complaining child.

Even the bravest are unmanned by a hopeless task.

'I have been sore afraid this morning, for I have to kill enough birds to thatch the byre with their feathers, nor may two feathers be of the same colour. And today for the first time your father said to me that if I do not complete the task I will die, and he is no longer kind to me. Where have you been?'

'Be sure that I came as quickly as I could,' she answered, 'but my father suspects my part in your success, and his spies were thick about me this morning. It was many hours before I could leave without being seen, and even now two of my sisters risk themselves by going about in my likeness.'

All the sisters are part of the sorcery.

'Is it true you father will kill me out of hand if I fail this task?'

'Any time you have spent with my father you have been in peril of your life. Surely you must have known that, for he killed your fellows on the road here.'

'That was many years ago, and I thought he loved me.'

She shook her head.

'He may have loved you, but now you are a threat to him. Only remember that your danger is no greater now than it has ever been and keep your courage up. Tell me again, what is the task? You need feathers, but did father say that the birds must first be killed.'

'He did not say so, but he gave me the bow and arrows so I tried to use them.'

114

The giant was trying to confuse him. He takes too much on trust from the monster.

My lady looked at me in silence. Then she said, 'Go and sit in the rowan tree again and leave the task to one who understands what is needed.'

A magpie flew overhead with a great clash of wings and my lady looked up and trembled. I returned to the tree and at once my limbs would not move, nor my head turn, but I sat and watched like one in a dream.

Marighal looked carefully at the little mound of bodies I had made, and shook her head. Then she turned into the forest and returned at once with water in her hands which she threw over the birds. As the drops hit them they began to shiver and tremble, and one by one they stood and shook themselves. My lady raised her arms above her head and when she lowered them again she had assumed the form of an owl. The birds bowed before her and humbly thanked her for their lives, and asked how they might repay her. She told them of the task and begged them to give her their aid.

'Mistress,' they replied, 'we will do what we can, but our understanding is weak. You must guide us and tell us what to, do for we birds do not work well all together.'

Not all birds can build. Swallows build like the Romans — with mortar; terns use just a scrape on the beach.

'Not hard to do,' said Marighal, 'there are some among you who are the most skilled at making and building. They will stay at the byre and build as it were a vast, flat nest. Others, who are strong lifters, will carry baskets, and the gatherers among you will fill them. Go to each bird in the forest and fetch from them but a few feathers and there will be more than enough.'

'May we seek the help of our kindred?'

The owl is the symbol of wisdom and deadly cunning.

She organises the birds in the same way that wisdom assembles ideas in the heart. Ideas are a defence for the soul; the foundation is faith.

'Indeed you may, and swiftly, for time is running out. I will be with you all the day and show you what to do. Your skills and strengths added together will be enough. I will watch and guide you where to do your work.'

At these words the birds lifted into the sky with a mighty throbbing of wings. I saw them no more, but all the rest of the day I could hear them behind me rustling and scratching and twittering. Sometimes I caught sight of my lady circling overhead, watching the work, and the sound of her cries oppressed my spirit. As the short day wore down to evening I began to fear that they truly would not finish in time. At last, as the lord of the sky sank glowing behind the hills, silence fell in the clearing and Marighal appeared before me again in the shape of a woman. She touched my breast and released me from the tree.

'The task is done,' she said, 'nor has any drop of blood been spilt. Remember always that it is not necessary to force creatures, beast or human, to do your will. You need not seize what may be freely given.'

I turned and saw that the byre was covered with a fine, shining roof, and though the evening breeze blew strongly across the glen none of the feathers lifted.

'O, wisest of women,' I cried in delight, 'is there nothing your wisdom cannot conquer? This roof will satisfy the giant mightily, and there is now but one task left. By tomorrow evening we will be freed from this terror.'

Marighal did not share my glee.

'Nothing you or I could do will satisfy my father. Yet he must bow to fate, no less than ourselves. Tomorrow's task will demand more of yourself than me. But keep your courage high and we might yet be free. For now — farewell.'

Soon the giant came up with his golden spy glinting in his hand, and straightaway he cast it up to the roof of the byre. After the thing had viewed the new thatch it came and sang to him, and what he heard left him displeased, for he said, 'So, son of man, you have triumphed again. I can see little hope of ever defeating you. Come here tomorrow at sunrise and I will show you to your last task, though with the cunning you have shown today I am sure it will not trouble you.'

The next morning I met the giant and he took me up the hillside some distance. There he pointed out a very tall fir tree which grew at the far side of the glen.

'That tree is nearly as old as myself, and it has grown year by year till there is none other like it in the world At the top is the nest of a magpie where there are always three sky-blue eggs. Many times has that maggot pie flown in through the window of my hall and carried off precious objects of mine. I long to be revenged, but I cannot climb that tree myself for I am too heavy. Today you will climb it for me and steal the eggs from the very king of theives, and justice will at last be served. I will expect you at sunset.'

'You will not have to wait long for me, sir, for even from here I can see that the branches of that tree grow up its sides like the rungs of a ladder. Tonight

116

the eggs will be in your hands and I will claim my bride.'

The giant smiled his winter smile again, but I left him with joy in my heart. In my folly I thought that this task was the simplest of the three, and all around me the forest seemed to share my pleasure. The buds on the trees glowed, and the light sparkled as I leapt over streams and rushed through the undergrowth like a proud, silly young stag. But when I came near to the tree I was surprised to find my lady there before me.

At her feet lay a black iron axe with a double blade curved like two half-moons. On the grass beside her she had spread a white linen sheet, and on the other side she had built a great fire over which hung a black iron cauldron. A river ran at her back and a rowan-tree hung over its bank. She had filled the cauldron long before my arrival, and a thread of steam was rising from it. At that moment the sun hid his face behind a cloud, and the air became chill and grey.

My heart began to fail me but I spoke up boldly.

'Well, my lady, you have wasted your labour today, for the task your father has given me is a simple one. It needs only strong legs and a steady hand and these I have myself and have no need of your powers.'

'Before you say any more, look at the tree you must climb. It has the widest bole you will ever see.'

I looked to where she pointed and saw the bole of a tree so wide that three men could not join their hands around it. As I walked toward it I saw that I had been deceived, for the tree stood apart so that I had not been able to see how great it truly was. The trunk itself rose to the height of an ordinary tree as sheer and as smooth as glass, nor was there any branch growing out of it on any side. Above the tops of the other trees the great one spread its branches in plenty and flourished them in the wind. And I saw that I would never reach them.

I turned to my lady and said, 'Surely this is a terrible task! Though I have strong arms and legs, and know how to climb, I can see no way to conquer this tree before sunset. There is neither stump nor branch nor crevice in the whole length of that mighty trunk.'

'Be cheerful, Kynan White-hair, and summon up your courage. There is a way to do the task, but it will need all the spirit in your mighty heart.'

I saw an axe like this in St Basilio, in the Scala Mortuorum. What was it for? I cannot remember. The ignorant say that rowan-trees are magical, and hang their talismans in them.

He should have learned not to trust the monster by this time.

'Tell me the way, Marighal, for my life is in your keeping. If there is a way to scale that awful tree I will try it even if I die in the attempt, for it would be better so than to die a craven at your father's hands.'

'Well said, my lord, now you must listen to me and remember all I say, for once you have begun this road I will not be able to guide you further.

'First, you must take the axe lying at my feet and cut my head from my body, then my limbs.'

'What are you saying to me, Marighal?' I cried, 'I could no more kill you, my friend and helpmate, than I could kill myself. Indeed I would rather take my own life than harm your smallest finger.'

'You are all tenderness, my lord,' she answered, smiling, 'but do not fear. You will not be killing me. You, who found your way through the deceiving mirror maze should know well that what seems to be is not always what is. I will save myself from harm by the sorcerous powers known only to the women of my house. There is no danger to me if you will obey my every word.

She admits to sorcery.

'Once you have removed my limbs you must strip the flesh off my bones. Put the flesh and the guts on this linen sheet here, then tie it up and hang it from the branches of the rowan tree that hangs over the river. The bones you must place in the cauldron and there you must boil them until they are so clean of flesh not even a mouse would find a scraping. All the time you are doing this you must repeat a verse that I will teach you. Once the bones are clean take them to the tree and pierce its bark with them to make footholds up it. You will find that they go in easily, and as easily come out again when you descend. Only remember that any bone you do not touch with your foot will stay in the tree, and I will be damaged so. When you have returned to the earth you must lay out all the bones in the way they were when they had flesh on them, then you must throw the water from the cauldon over the bones. Once you have done that go as quickly as you can from that place, for what will happen afterwards is not fitting for you to know.'

My eyes are starting from my head as I read this. I call the saints to witness, there is monstrous evil here!

'Lady,' I cried, 'what you ask of me is not possible. I am a warrior, not a butcher, and I cannot strike down a woman who does not oppose me or offer me threat.'

His fear is understandable.

118

'You will do so — you must do so — or you will die and I will be a prisoner till God's kingdom comes. How many times must I tell you that?'

'I recall it well, but still my heart fails me.'

She sighed and shook her head at me, and said, 'You have hunted many times with me and my father, and I have often seen you gralloch a deer on the hillside. Keep in your heart the picture of me as a deer you have just caught and will take home for eating, and strike me quickly. If my flesh and bones are kept clean and kept together no harm will come to my body. Only be sure that you collect all the bones from the tree bole and I will be safe, I swear it, by the living, merciful God.'

'Lady, there must be another way. I know my hand will not fall steady if it is not raised in the heat of battle or hunting. Let me try once, at least, to climb the tree unaided.'

'I told you last night that this day would take the best of your courage, ' she said, 'I swear to you that there is no other way than this to do the task. If our freedom costs us dear then the more worthy are we to gain it. Come now, it will not take much strength to sever the neck of a woman. I have seen you pierce the body of a warrior with one hand.'

'The warrior came at me with his face twisted in rage, and a sharp sword in his hand. He challenged me to battle with him to prove himself the stronger and the better man, and in hot rage I took the challenge to keep my pride in manhood. What valour is there in striking down a defenceless maiden?'

'There are many men who should be forced to answer that question,' she said, and her face was grim as she spoke.

Picking up the axe she thrust it at me saying, 'Your reluctance speaks well of your manhood. Only remember, Kynan, I am as good a warrior as any in this kingdom, and my father's fierce blood runs hot in my veins. Be sure that if you do not strike me down with this axe now, it will drink deep of your blood before nightfall — if not by my hand in revenge for my betrayal then by my father's for your cowardice.

'Do you not think I would rather be dead than kept here half alive in my father's power? My hatred will follow you for all eternity if you abandon me, and you

This is truly a terrible threat, and a terrible creature makes it.

will see then that I am one with my ancestors and your dearest enemy. Strike me now before that comes to pass, or are you truly a coward?'

I went to her then and took the axe, but it was heavy in my hands.

'Do not try to provoke my battle-rage, Marighal,' I said, weary. 'I could not strike you even in the reddest anger. Nor can I strike you to save my own life, for my hands turn to lead at the words you speak. But I will strike you, for I believe you when you tell me that this is your only hope of leaving your father's hall.'

At these words she took off her clothing, even her thin shift, and knelt before me naked on the broad white cloth. She knotted her hair up so that her long neck was clear for the blow and she told me the chant that would keep her safe even though her body was broken and scattered. Then I struck her head from her body and caught it before it could fall, and as it sighed its last sigh I laid it gently on the fine linen. I severed the limbs with one blow of the axe apiece, and cut the skin from these with the hunting knife she had made for me herself. Time after time my gorge rose in protest at this terrible work, and I would have to pause, retching and weeping. I cut her breasts and the rest of her skin from her torso, and with my hands smoking and red I lifted the guts and all the soft, strange things it is not fit for a man to know of a woman and placed them on the white cloth. And I peeled her face and her wonderful hair from her skull and put them and the brains and the eyes into the cloth. Nor in all this time did I cease to weep for the horror and the outrage I was committing. Finally I tied all these things tightly with a red cord from her hair and hung it in the branches of the rowan so that her blood dropped in steady, slow drops into the river below. Then I flung the bones into the cauldron where the water was now boiling fast, and I stoked the fire underneath it saying the rhyme she had told me.

'Bone without flesh alone is pure,
Dry and clean it will endure,
Bone is white as flowers of May
Thus woman spotless is alway,
White and perfect, clean and sure. . .'

And I repeated it many, many times, for I could not stop it coming to my lips. Indeed it kept the vision of

Is this anything more than a blasphemous mockery of our Lord's death? Am I to believe that by her death and resurrection this creature hopes to redeem her mate? She could not hope to emulate the purity of the Lamb, for by her nature and her heritage from Eve every woman is contaminated.

Only one woman has ever attained perfection, and only one ever will till God's kingdom come — The Mother of God.

my horrible deeds from my heart. About the middle of the day, as I waited for the water to cool, I looked up with the incantation in my mouth and, as it hung white and dripping red over the river, I saw the cloth move. At that I stilled my tongue, for I did not know what I might conjure.

I climbed the tree as my lady had instructed me, and I used her skull for the first step, as a guardian for the path. Each bone slid easily into the bark as if there were a hollow ready carved for it, yet when I removed them there was no mark on the tree. I took no time to wonder at this for the day was turning towards its close, and the climb above me was long. I found the eggs at the top and all of them were as blue as the fairest summer sky, and yet it seemed to me that, as I looked at them, I was seeing something beyond like the depths of a pool below a blue surface. There were so many mysteries about the giant's life that I did not pause to wonder at a fresh one, but put them in my scrip and made haste to descend from the tree.

The sun was dropping fast and as I neared the bottom I looked up and saw that his rays were fading from the glen. I knew that the giant would be leaving his hall to seek me, and in my fear and haste I missed touching one of the bones with my foot. At the foot of the tree the skull leapt into my hand, and I laid the bones upon the grass. My lady, wherever she was then, must have guided my hands for the bones were laid out the right way almost without my effort. It was well they were for the sun had taken his light from me. I took up the great black cauldron, and flung the water over the bones, and lifting my scrip carefully, I fled from the clearing.

Behind me I heard as it were a flapping of mighty wings, a long keening cry, and a hot wind followed me down the path. I put my hands to my ears, nor did I lift my eyes from the path until I came near the place where the giant waited. Then I saw a sight that made me stand still in wonderment, for I saw my lady beside the path, restored and in her tunic and mantle as if the events of the day had never happened. I could not speak for joy.

'You see now that I spoke the truth to you,' she said, 'You did no harm to me when you struck me with the axe, for here I stand, whole.'

'Truly, my lady, I will never doubt your word again.'

It is possible, I suppose, to see this as a picture of the church of Christ as it is in these troubled times. Constantly she is being ruined and dismembered, but because of her faithful she can restore herself to wholeness once again.

So she is restored to us.

'Look also at this,' she said, and held out her hand.
'As you descended the tree you missed one of my bones
with your foot and behold I no longer have the smallest
finger of my left hand. The bone is in the tree, and will
stay there until the tree dies.'

'Alas, what have I done,' I cried, 'I have failed to make
you whole again.'

She was blemished by this outrage, but this is a small penance for such a hideous blasphemy.

'Be sure now that this is no bad thing, for before we
can exchange our wedding vows my father will bring
myself and all my sisters to stand before you and you
will have to chose me from the crowd. You will know
me then by this left hand, and we will be united. But
hurry now, for my father is waiting for you.'

So saying she ran off into the trees. At the byre the
giant looked angrily at me.

'Well, son of man,' he said, 'have you come to tell me
you have failed, for I see nothing in your hand?'

'No, sir, I have them here in my wallet where they
will come to no harm.' I lifted them out. The giant still
frowned.

'Was it the easy task you thought it to be?'

'No, sir, by my hand, it was not, for that tree was taller
and straighter than any I have ever seen.'

'That is because it was not truly a tree, but a road to
a world you could never reach without help.'

Which world does he refer to?

He looked at me in silence but said nothing more. I
also said nothing but handed him the eggs and waited.
At length the giant spoke and told me to go back to the
stronghold without him.

'Why do you wait on me? Surely you do not need me
to guide you in this forest.'

Thus dismissed I left him, and sought him on the
following morning in his hall. The door was locked, nor
would he answer me, so I laid myself across the threshold, and stayed there until the third morning when he at
last came out.

I sprang to my feet and said, 'I have come now to
claim the wife you promised me. Bring her forth and
show her to me so that we may exchange vows, for truly
I am longing to take my bride to my father's house.'

'There was a time when you thought of this hold as
your home,' said the giant, 'nor would you have sought
to leave it, with your bride or alone. Why do you wish to
leave it now?'

122

Q. Insofar as the giant is malicious and powerful he can be said to be evil. But if the young man and woman stand against him can they be said to be evil?

A. Opposition is no proof of virtue, for it is known that the demons in Dis contend violently with each other all the time. It is part of their punishment for vying with their loving Father.

Q. Yet the woman bears no ill-will against anyone and seeks only to free herself from the evil one who binds her.

A. This shows that grace may be present, but it is not enough to prove that the woman is one of the elect.

Q. Surely grace is not extended to the damned at any time?

A. God in his loving kindness withholds nothing from any creature.

Q. Can we not then assume that the woman may come to love God truly and in so doing rejoin the angels above?

A. Restlessness such as she shows is a blessed sign of a search for the truth, but we must first see if she will obey God's holy will. This is the test.

'Master, it is many years since I saw my father and my mother, and they will not have many days left to them. I would be a poor son if I had no wish to see them again and to show them my fine woman.'

'They are mortal, and their days have always been numbered — why have you only now remembered your duty, when you have been happy to neglect them before?'

'Master, a few days ago I was visited by a dream of my mother and she looked ill and weary and full of days. Already I fear I may be too late to look upon her living face, for why should she appear to me in dreams unless she has left her fleshly habitation? I hope only that I may look upon her face again before it is put to the flames.' I had learned deceit from a master.

'Woman is a feeble creature,' said the giant, 'we do better not to heed what befalls them. I will tell you now that your haste is without point for your mother died some summers since.'

'If my mother is dead, sir, I must make the more haste to see my father and his sons, if there are any more. The house will be melancholy without its lady, and my father may be contemplating another marriage.'

'He may, but he can always be prevented. You would be better to wait now for another spring before you make your journey, for it is easier to travel before the brush has started to grow and while frost makes the moorland firm underfoot. I must consider my daughter's comfort.'

'She is as hardy as a wolf of the forest, sir, and you know it well. Let me go now, I beg you!' And I wept at last to think that I had been far from home when my mother died.

'Very well,' he said, 'so be it. Tonight we will begin the wedding-feast. Now give me leave to go and make my preparations. There is very much to do.'

'You are generous, sir, to make a wedding-feast for us, but there is little need for it and we must make haste. I am a simple man, and unused to courteous ways. A fine wedding with many guests would only show the world what a tongueless wretch I am. Only let us make our oaths and be gone.'

'A couple of days more will not add much to the sum of your years here, and I would be a poor father indeed if

I let a daughter of my house marry my foster-son without marking the day.'

I began to fear that my protests would provoke him so I agreed to the feast at last. When I entered the great hall at midnight I wondered to find all the guest tables full, but it was not with nobles and princes. No, our wedding was attended by the charcoal-burners and the hunters and fowlers of the great forest. There also were the farmers who made a miserable living with a few pigs and cows in the clearings rather than face the perils of open country; there were the drovers who could not pass through the forest without the protection of the giant, and there were the few, last wandering tribes who passed by once in a few years.

In all that throng I could not see one face that showed joy at being brought to a feast. True, there were many who had never seen so much food at one table, nor yet did they seem afraid, but each face, man, woman or child was like the face of a sleeper, neither did they eat nor drink with any eagerness. At the head of the table sat the giant with his golden servants beside him. At his left hand sat his Queen, and though her hands brought food and drink to her jewelled lips, no morsel entered them.

My master summoned me to join him and said, 'Sit here, Kynan White-hair, son of Kilidh, heir of the southern swamp. Come and greet your honoured guests. Is this not a fine gathering for your wedding-feast?'

'I am indeed honoured, sir.' I said, pretending that I did not see his mockery of me. 'I greet your company gathered here to witness my vows to your daughter. I am afraid I am not worthy of their trouble in coming here tonight.'

'It is no trouble to such as these to come here,' he said, 'they know they are fortunate to see the marriage of my noble daughter to a son of your house.'

'Sir, you know you do me an unecessary honour by this for, I am not nobly born, and though every man of my house is a fierce warrior, our line is short.'

'Nevertheless, it is one all men should respect and honour,' said the master. I saw he was angry at my mildness on finding only gossocks at his table. 'You all have courage, strength and cunning in plenty,' he went on, 'and these are the great lineage a man can give his

This is how it will be in the hall of the damned for all eternity. No joy, no pain, only endless fear.

Adso has said that this is how the Antichrist will lead us all astray in the last days. He will place all the world's sorry goods in front of us, but he will dupe us so that we think we are in the presence of great riches.

124

heritors. Let it be known to everyone that I love this man dearly, as if he were my own son.'

So saying he raised his cup high, and at this sign the company cheered till the echoes shook the roof-tree. Yet there was no heart in it. The master raised his hand for silence.

'Nor will you cease to prosper, Kynan, for tonight you marry into an ancient and gifted house — and again he lifted his cup, and again the cheer rose — and more than this, you are to marry one of the finest women our race has ever sired.'

This raised the longest shout of all. With a trembling hand I raised my cup to answer.

'My thanks to all of you for your greetings. I know I am fortunate beyond all I could hope for, but the greatest source of pride to me is the wife I will be taking tonight. I beg you now, father, let me see her. Bring her out so that men may see what a happy man is here before them.'

He calls the monster, 'father' for the sake of the guests.

The giant raised his hand in a fist, and at that moment the door to the hall flew open and in strode the daughters, every one.

Each looked exactly like her sister, as Marighal had said. No man could have told one from the other, neither by dress nor by face, no matter how hard he might study. Each wore her red-gold hair in four tresses, two in front and two behind, and her skin was as white as the breast of a seagull at sunset, and her eyes were the green of deep water. Each one had cheeks red as the foxglove, and lips like the berries of the rowan. Her brow was wide and white and on her head there was a crown of gold filigree wire where crystals hung and quivered like dew on brambles at dawn. The kerchief beneath it and the shift were of finest linen, and her tunic was of red wool edged with gold and silver, and her mantle was of green edged with a deep fringe of gold and blue; green and red precious stones were set in it so that it swung as she walked. Beneath her shift her little feet peeped out and in with every step, and each was shod with the softest white leather, with gold flowers on the front, and on each hand she wore two rings of twisted gold wire with red and amber beads.

What is this ranting praise of womankind? Was he driven by lust, then or is this just the habit of his countrymen?

They came in, one after the other, all the sisters, and nowhere could I see a difference between them. Olwen,

who had been my second mother; Leborchan the wise
woman; Elayne the dimpled baby; Beatrude whom I
had carried on my shoulders years before; and Essyllt
the crone, all looked as much like my lady as she did
herself — those named and many, many more. Before
that night I had not known how many sisters were in that
house, and as they ranged themselves across the hall and
back again in three files my heart went white within me
for fear that I would not know my lady. Suddenly the
giant spoke at my ear with a voice like thunder, and I
leapt in my chair like a wounded stag.

'There she is, Kynan White-hair. Go and choose your
bride from among her sisters and lead her to her father's
table. Bring her to my side so that we may drink to her
health and prosperity.'

I stepped down and walked trembling along the files
of women. Nothing in those smooth, white faces told
me which was my lady. Each one of them stared ahead
with green eyes as cold as glass, and would not look
at me. The giant's voice came to me speaking to the
company and bidding them to fill their cups. Then a
flicker caught my eye and held it. I looked round and
saw the fingers of a hand moving, and, looking closer I
saw that the smallest finger of that hand was missing.

At once I knew my lady. I stepped up to her and
taking her by the right hand I led her to her father's
table. There I claimed her as my rightful bride before
the whole company. The giant was not pleased by this
and with a wave of his hand he restored the sisters
to themselves so that Marighal alone wore the crown.
The sisters took their places at the table opposite ours
in order of age, and those who knew me smiled at me
at last.

A woman taken by a man is always damaged. A lustful glance alone is enough to tarnish the purity she should take to the grave and beyond. And since in this case the woman is also disobeying her father the mutilation is to be expected.

'Now we will have the entertainment,' said the giant,
'I ask your forbearance for the poverty of my efforts.
Had I more time I would have brought musicians from
Persia, jugglers from Iberia, and acrobats from the land
of the burning sun, but my son-in-law is in such haste
to consummate his marriage I have had to cheat you all.
You will have to be content with a local artist.'

He clapped his hands and in came a poor old man
with a small harp in his feeble arms. The people of the
forest frowned at me as the giant had shown them, as
if to say it was I alone that had cheated them. Yet the

sisters and I knew well that if the master had willed it he could have brought any man he wished from any country in the world.

The bard sang in a feeble voice to an ill-tuned harp and was certainly the worst poet I have ever heard. Even the giant grew tired of his poor voice, and his own mockery wearied him, for he said, 'This is poor stuff,' and sent the old man off with a wave of his hand.

'Let us all drink to the man and wife,' he cried, and all rose to obey him, with another dull shout. In all this time my lady had not looked at me, and even at the toast she stared ahead of her with a face like snow for paleness.

I felt that night that the sun stood still in his place below the edge of the world till the last guest had fallen asleep at the table. Indeed he was well up in the sky before the giant spoke up in his brazen voice to bid his guests wake and witness our vows. Marighal made her oath, and some of her sisters stood by as her helpers. Then to my amazement the giant stood for me when I made my vows to his daughter. Everyone there was now weary, except for the giant himself and he summoned servants to bring more food and drink. We rubbed our eyes and yawned, and tried once again to be joyful as guests at a wedding should.

But when the middle of the day was past the forest people said, 'Master, we have come to your feast as you bade us, but now, we beg you, give us leave to return to our homes. We have spent a day and a night in revelry with you and witnessed your daughter's oath and now we must go. We have flocks to gather, stacks to tend and for many of us the road home is long. Please dismiss us, we pray you.'

The giant lifted up his voice in rage and cursed them, saying, 'For all these generations I have protected you and kept your roads open when all were closed elsewhere. I have kept the pirates from your doors, and the Saxons from your meadows, and I have watched without tiring. Yet now, wretched ingratitude, you will not stay to see my daughter consummate her marriage. Are you to be like the scavenging wolves who smell a failing beast and wait with joy to see it stumble? Be off with you, if you must go, but be sure that there will be no more help from me if you leave me now. After this time, when the pirates march into your lands, and the men from the east

Only God can do this; 'The mountains saw thee and they trembled, the flooding of the water passed by; the deep uttered his voice and lifted up his hands on high. The sun and the moon stood still in their habitation; at the light of thine arrows they went, and at the shining of thy glittering spear.' Habbakuk 3:10-11.

He claims he has taken care of them, but at the price of their souls.

I think the giant is afraid. The damned can never feel that they are safe.

put fire to your homes, and none will come to buy your rotting produce, you will remember me and regret that you did not give me more of your time.'

'Master,' said the people, and some wept at his words, 'by our hands you must believe us, we would stay if we could, nor can you compel us to stay longer than we agreed. Our beasts wait for us and without us they will starve. We wish you well, though you have been a hard master to us sometimes. We have been right pleased to come to your feast today, but we dare not stay longer, even though you cease to aid us. Farewell!'

They left, and suddenly the sisters rose from their places also and spoke in loud voices to each other before their father, which I had never seen before. My master was very angry and he struck the table.

'Go away, now! Go from me! Do not make me sit and listen to the rattle of your foolish mouths. Why do you pause? Is this not the time for which you have been waiting, some of you for generations. Why do you tarry now? Get your sister's bed ready at last.'

At that they fled, and left my wife and myself to wait on their return to release us. The giant said nothing to us, neither of rage nor of greeting, but he watched my lady as she sat eating and drinking wine. She was as calm as if she were watching on the moors alone and I wondered at her patience.

For myself I silently cursed the day that I had ever come to that hall, and raged at my craven father who had put me in this creature's power. At last the sisters returned and led us to our bed without a word. They undressed the bride till she stood in her fine shift beside the garlanded bed, and her hair hung unbraided down her back. Then they shut the doors of the bed and left us.

'What is to become of us? Your father will not permit us to leave, surely?'

She shook her head and put her finger to her lips, then dimmed the light and said, 'My father loves me, and I am sure this marriage has his good will,' but as she spoke she thrust her hand behind the tester and brought out a spy-globe. She twisted it in a way only she and her father knew and it fell into four parts in her hand, then she put it under the pillow. We lay in silence on the bed

128

until we heard the humming of another which she also found and destroyed.

After that she turned the light up and said, 'Now I am sure it is safe for us to talk a little. We cannot stay long in this bed for the stones above us are not part of the wall. They are made so that when the first rays of the sun strike them they will descend and crush us as we lie. If this does not kill us then there are globes set all over the halls which will summon my father, but I know their working and can stop them. I have horses ready in the stable, and your battle-gear lies under the mattress. Now rest a while and we will leave at the darkest hour of the night.'

The monster would destroy his own child!

We dressed ourselves again, and she set about the globes with a thin silver knife. At last I saw through the little window that it was time to go, and we stepped down into the passage. Marighal left one piece of the globe in the tester, one in the doorway, one at the head of the stairs one at the foot, one at the doorway to the yard, one in the doorway of the stable, and as we led the horses out with muffled feet, she left the last one in the gateway. As soon as we were deep in the forest she stopped and took a paper packet from her wallet and scattered what it held over the ground at her feet.

The mice are called into service once more.

'This is grain I have washed well in the juice of certain stinging herbs which my foster-father showed me. My vassals the mice will carry them all about and when my father comes to pursue us with his hounds they will chase a strange scent all over the forest.'

We fled upwards then, and as the sun rose again we travelled fast across the moorland, with our shadows long before us. By the end of the day we were in the forest beyond my master's hold, and there we rested. Nevertheless by the middle of the next day we looked behind and saw the forest shaking as the giant sped after us.

Afraid, I said, 'Now, wife, we are finished, for I had thought your father had no power in this country, yet here he comes and the forest parts before him.'

The Antichrist will be given power over men's hearts so that they will defy the virtuous

'My father's power holds everywhere, for those who wish to see him prevail will always give him way. But I know his limits and I am not afraid, neither should you be. Take the horses down the road till the shoulder of the mountain stands between you and this place, and tether them well. If you wish to see my father bested come back here at once; if not, you had better continue along the road to its end. Remember, though, that you will never be sure of your safety till you see him defeated with your own eyes.'

She dropped from the back of her horse and from the pannier she took a box of black iron about as long as my forearm. I did as she had told me and secured the horses on the other side of the pass, then walked back to see what would follow. She had fixed the black box on to the steep face of a great rock on the hillside by the road, but I could not see how. Now she stood watching the nodding of the trees that marked her father's approach.

'He will be here very soon' she said, 'I had hoped not to use this thing for it will do much to change the face of the forest. Now I see my father will not accept my departure without driving me to the limits of my power. God's will be done.'

With these words she pointed at the black box with a rod and fire gushed out of it with a roar like thunder. The great rock split down the whole of its length and water poured out of it to form a mighty waterfall rushing over the path.

'Wife,' I cried in fear, 'what is this power that changes nature from its course? Surely nothing good can come of it?'

'It is only some scrapings from the byre mixed with charcoal and a yellow rock. Grig, my foster-father showed me what to do. Only nature can change nature, that is the whole truth as I know it. And now it is beyond my power to change it back.'

As she spoke her face grew grim with grief and she waited for her father. Soon we saw him coming through the forest and this time he was alone. When he came up to the side of the new river he stopped and called, 'Well, daughter, you seem to have carried the day between us. I cannot cross this mighty cataract, for the water will carry me away. I could return home for the slaves to build a bridge, but by the time I finished you would be long gone, you, and that long, white-haired creature beside you. I hope you are pleased.'

'I have won, indeed, Father, but do not think that I rejoice in my victory. I am grieved beyond words to think that this marriage will bring your death, but we

and try to thwart them. This is a sign of the last days.

I have heard that the sorcerers of Vinland can do something similar. One of Sigurd's men told me.

By St Brigid and St Martin she has seen something here! But not enough. Change is continual but only in our sub-lunar world. Everything in nature is trying to move towards perfection and change-lessness, but this can only happen through God's will. Grace is that which helps nature to change herself.

130

He makes no mention of her tears of blood, but his fear is stated.

She loves her wicked father.

He left his immortal bride! Who is she and where does she live?

both know well that there is no remedy for it.' And she wept sorely at that. The sight struck fear in my heart, for I had never seen her weep before.

'Do not grieve for me, daughter,' said the giant, 'my doom will come upon me when it must, whether by your hand or by another's, nor should you be troubled by its coming. I could wish to see you more rejoicing in the fine young man at your side, Marighal, for it seems to me you will not be with him long.'

'Father,' said my lady, angry, 'do not seek to threaten me at this late hour. We are on the road out of your lands now and in the new world you will not have power over us.'

'I speak only the truth, daughter, nor do I seek to threaten. I have lived long on this earth, and I have learned to see a pattern in all events. The man will betray you, to his grief, not by any act of mine, but because it is in the way of things. Do not think I wish you anything but well. Whether we meet again or not, you are still my daughter.'

'I love you, Father, and be sure I know there is no man alive who is your equal. If I could have made my fate fall out another way I would have done so, and if there had been a way to preserve your life I would have found it, but once my foot was upon this road there was no way back.'

'Daughter, I know it well. The price of our power is always higher than we think. Many generations ago I left my immortal bride to seek dominion over mankind. She warned me when I left that what I sought would bring me no joy, but would only increase my emptiness. I would not believe her and left her weeping to find that she only spoke the truth. I never found the road back to her.'

So saying he turned and left us, and my wife wept many strange tears at his parting. At last I said to her, 'Lift up your spirits, my lady, for we are free and life is now starting for us. We are young and very wise, and we can well take up the duties our training has fitted us for. Mount your horse and let us see what fate is waiting for us. The road is open now and we will soon have many chances to win renown, and what is man shaped for if it is not for noble and memorable deeds?'

At this my lady washed away her tears and we rode north and west to the high red moorland, then we turned toward the sea and came to the edge of the plain that surrounds this city. I left my lady there and came to this place to ask for free passage into the city, but when I arrived at the hall I found she had arrived here before me. By some great miracle, all the knowledge of her youth had been taken out of her heart.

But this is not the truth of what happened if we believe what the woman said. And Kynan is still the giant's dupe.

It seemed to me, to this very day, that this was her father's work. In a moment of kindness he took her up from the place where I left her and cleansed her of the knowledge which would only have been a burden to her as my wife. I made sure that it was my lady as soon as I saw her there, for I looked at her hand and there I saw that the smallest finger was missing. It was my Marighal, indeed, but not, thanks be to God, as I had known her. That night she came to me a simple maid, happy only to have a fine young chieftain to fight for her people and to rule this kingdom with me for the rest of our lives. Nor has the giant's prediction come true, for in all the years of marriage we have never been apart.

That is my strange history, monk. You see I am by no means clean of sin, but I have seen many strange practices and even destroyed the body of the wife promised to me, but God in his mercy straightway restored her to me. I am indeed fortunate. Since my baptism as a Christian I have tried to count all my sins as forgiven. Am I not right to do so?

He could claim that he was coerced into sin, which would be a mitigation, but not a purgation. If he is lying in his heart and took the chrism and the bread under false pretences then he is damned forever.

We had talked for a very long time there on the beach and now we saw the king's steward approaching us to summon us for the evening feast. The noble guests were all assembled, and were wondering at his absence.

Selyf takes up the narration.

The king sent him back and turned to me, saying, 'These guests of mine are by no means noble. There is a fat salt merchant from the east and his ugly wife; a bishop who stuffs his wallet faster than ours stuffs his, and a crowd of hunters who have come for their mead. I ask you to tell me, monk, who is noble there?'

'Sir, I, who am scarcely in the world cannot answer that. But you must make haste, and give me leave also to say my office for I have missed one of my hours and must atone for it before I break my fast.'

This is a bitter man speaking. He should know by now that true nobility lies in true humility.

'Your hardships are to your credit, Selyf, for few men these days will deny themselves anything. I wish you well. Come to me tomorrow after the morning offering — I have something more to tell you.'

He left me then and ran across the plain to his stronghold like a boy. Truly his heart was already lighter for his confession, as we know it must be, but he left me with a heavy one. In a frail voice I said the words: 'Come and see the works of God; He is terrible in his doing toward the children of man, He turned the sea into dry land, they went through the flood on foot; there did we rejoice in Him. He rules by His power for ever; His eyes behold the nations.'

For the blinking of an eye it seemed to me then that the ways of God are so mysterious and inscrutable that for a man of understanding to find hope in them requires more faith than anyone could muster. I drove this devil from my heart and stood for a long time in prayer till the temptation left me. Then I went to a place beside the sea and meditated on my duty to this man.

God's mysteries are beyond you, but do not despair. Your demon has tempted you into thinking that reason alone is your salvation. Where is your faith?

The next morning I stood at the door of the church and waited on the king. He passed me in the midst of a crowd of followers and did not notice me. I spent the day in prayer and the exercise of patience, for it was clear that my time in that fair city was over. Some time after the ninth hour the king sent a boy to find me and I went with him to the king's closet where he greeted me with a nod.

'Well monk, it seems I am to dismiss you from this city. I have had my bishop and a deacon from Jorvik both at my ears like a cloud of midges. What have you done to bring such hatred on your head?'

'Sir, I have done nothing, nor have any kin of mine, other than to belong to the order my mother bore me into. Ours is the oldest Rule in this country, and we brought the word of God here centuries ago. But after the Saxons came, men in black mantles followed them over the sea and sought to tell us that we are sinful and blasphemous because we do not keep the festivals at the same time as they do. And other things. Do not fear to tell me to go, great Lord. I have been told it many times before.'

Our blessed Colman turned his back on the monks of St Benedict and found his way into the wilderness. When God's terrible judgement fell on the rest of the world and the savages overran the proud men, and destroyed the false monasteries, we kept the lamp of learning lit. But now, Selyf, the rest of the world sits round a blazing bonfire while we still huddle around our little light.

'Indeed I am sorry to tell you so, Selyf, for I have seen nothing in you but meekness and good nature. But I have worked hard all these years to build a city where men might find peace and long life, and if your presence here is to bring strife among us, I must dismiss you.'

'What of your good lady, sir. Is she one with you in this?'

'She knows nothing of your conflict, nor need I tell her, but if I did I am sure she would favour the bishop's cause. He is with her many hours a day, and she turns to him constantly.'

'Sir, with your permission I will go, and be happy to do so since I have my mission to complete, but before I go I must exchange honour for honour and give you my confession.'

'Before God, monk, I do not need to hear it. Nor, for all that, did I think that what I told you was a confession of offences. I never sought evil in my master's house.'

'Sir, to the black monks you would keep at your side your lack of volition in the committing of a crime is not mitigation. I have contended with them before on this matter, and I know their hearts. On the other hand it is the belief of my people that a man may commit an act of great wickedness, but if he has not knowledge or will to the sin then he is innocent. But this is one of the causes for which we are reviled and driven from the land.

'No, sir, I must tell you my history which will help you to decide for yourself whether you are free of guilt. And, as you shall answer to God, be sure you do not hide your deeds from yourself.'

'I have no time for monkish argument, Selyf. What can you know that will tell me more of myself? You must tell me so that I may judge you, not myself.'

'Sir, you are forsworn, and an adulterer. The woman you have taken to your bed is not the woman known to you as Marighal, the giant's daughter. I know, for I have met the woman myself.'

At these words the king sprang to his feet and stood in front of me so that his breath was hot and fast on my face.

'You lie, monk, and the bishop told the truth — your kind are a curse on this fair country. I will have you thrown into the wilderness this very night.'

'So be it, sir, you may do with me as you wish, for the fate of my body is not a great matter to me. But I must tell you all I know before I leave you,

Arco fuin, imondaire. Why must we ask permission of all men regardless of their station in life?

By his senses and his intellect man knows himself, but wisdom is born in his heart with his body, and wisdom is how he knows God. Therefore the new-born is born in grace, only to lose it when he follows the prompting of his polluting flesh. If only we could be as the Saviour told us and be like little children all our lives.

for it is not fitting you should go to your grave in ignorance.'

'Be sure you tell the truth, monk, and pray that I find it better than gall on my tongue or you may not be spared even for the wolves. I may strike you dead, unshriven on the floor here, and the bishop will be happy to hear my confession.'

'I told you a lie once before, sir, and I hope I may be forgiven for it. I said that I met a member of your lady's family last autumn, and that I gained from her some knowledge of your strange foster-father. The truth is that the woman's name was Marighal, and she and no other was the woman you butchered then vowed to keep beside you all your days.

'Sweet Lord, you must believe I do not wish to tell you this sad news! She also was without the smallest finger on her left hand and more, much more, she still knew all the secrets of metal working that she had learned from her foster-father, Grig.'

The king seated himself, and was silent as I told him the story of Marighal as she had told it to me. He questioned me from time to time about details of the story and as I went on his anger left him and he began to look pale.

When I told him the history of the night he won the kingdom he groaned aloud and said, 'This cannot be true. The sweet girl I took to bed in this city is as like my lady Marighal as it is possible to be. How could I be deceived in her?'

'Sir, I have no answer for you.' I cried, 'but I can tell you this: the women you left at the road-end bore you no ill-will for your betrayal, and had forgiven you almost before the crime was done.'

'O generous heart,' said the king, and tears ran down his face, 'that is her noble nature. How many times in the long winter nights have I thought of those lost days. There have been times when I longed to run on the moonlit hill once more with the cold wind in my face and my lady hunting at my side. And I have spent my evenings in the company of fools! I have hung my sword across the door and took my discontent as the price to be paid for peace. Yet always in my heart I knew misery, for I had left my first companions unavenged, and eaten the meat of their murderer. And I was happy to do so. No

If the man is so very unhappy it is most likely because he has sins to pay for. In charity you should be giving him a penance. I think a period of exile would be the most appropriate under the circumstances.

deed I have performed since is heavier than this! Why
was I born to this cursed life?'

'Sir,' I said, 'do not seek to choose both your sins and
your penances. God keeps that prerogative to himself,
and He will think it ill if you usurp him.'

'Do not mock me, monk, I have too much to bear.
O, my heart is sore! Leave me now. I must meditate
on what you have told me, and decide what I must do.'

The next morning at the second hour I woke to say
the office and found the boy messenger waiting to take
me to the king again. I saw that he had spent the night
without sleep.

In haste he said to me, 'Selyf, I have made my decision. I must know more of what you said about the
giant's stronghold. If my lady is still a virgin then perhaps it is true that her father did not die when I came
to this city. Yet you have said he is dead now. How did
it happen? Can it be that one of Marighal's sisters has
also gained her freedom or is this an illusion also? I must
find out all this, and I must find the woman you called
Marighal. I will go with you when you leave. Tell me
now what you had discovered when you stopped your
search for the giant's stronghold.'

*The king has volunteered
exile. Here is grace indeed!*

'My search had been completely fruitless,' I told him,
'and I came here to seek more knowledge. I would be
happy to have you with me, for it seems to me that
together we might find the road better than I alone. I
do not even know what I am searching for.

'But what about your kingdom, sir? Are you not afraid
that it will suffer if you leave it. I must continue whatever
you decide, for my Bishop has given me a mission, but
you have pressing duties here.'

'A short absence will not trouble this kingdom. I have
left it strong and well-stocked.'

'Then, sir, if you think it fitting I will be glad to have
you at my side to guide my blundering feet. I may also
illuminate your heart a little.'

'We will go together. And God send an answer to our
questions quickly. Wait in this room for me, and keep
out of the hall till we leave. Those men of Jorvik hate
you, and will not trust me either, if they see me with
you.'

While he made ready to depart I took this opportunity
to tell you of my journey, dear father. I am about to start

my wanderings again, and my only prayer is that I will find out God's holy truth. Pray for me, father, for I fear that I am going into darkness such as men have not known before. I rejoice that I have been given this chance to strive against the wicked with my faith, for truly a sword will not prevail there.

I humbly pray you to tell my loving brothers of my battle, and ask them for their prayers. I pray for them daily in their trials.

Valete.

The conclusion is short. I hope this is not taken amiss.

I am alone here tonight at Riecawr. Even though the leaves are dead and travelling easier no-one takes the road at this time of year. Outside the trees are dripping and there is a pool under the bed-platform for I can see water glinting beneath the boards. I cannot sleep for fear and cold so I sit writing by the light of a filthy smelling dip. I confess it freely, I am afraid. I do not want to meet these women, they change shape so easily. My mother changed into a ruin of blood and flesh under the sword of a warrior — they showed her to me but at first I did not believe them. I thought it was a calf they had butchered. All women change, all the time, and I learned to fear the changes, so do all sensible men. I remember the face of Eithne Cuaransdottir as she cursed and raged and sent her son Sigurd to fight for the honour of God.

I think I have a marsh fever on me, and I see as if it were yesterday how we hanged the men of Innisgall above the nodding machair. We built a great gallows and we hanged them five and six at a time, high in the air so that they would not defile the ground. God forgive us — there were more than three and a half hundred of them, nor could all of them have had a hand in the slaughter of a mere fifteen monks and an old anchorite Abbot. Some of them asked me for a blessing and I raised my hands over them. God will judge them in his good time, but I cannot. To prove I did no ill I was given these letters by one of the pirates. He said he had found them when they raided Hy Columbcille; he was going through the huts looking for treasure and took no part in the killing of monks, but when he saw my short white robe he recognised me as being brother to the one who fled the hut leaving the manuscript. He gave them to me, and God has rewarded us both. He looked to be at peace when they hanged him beside all the others and the smell of burning flesh had ceased to trouble him. Yet it troubles me still.

Below is Selyf's last letter — written from God knows where. I will follow the path as he describes it and see what God will send me in his mercy. Mortal terror is on me — 'Oh Lamb of God that takes away the sin of the world; Have mercy upon me!'

To the most holy and pious Abbot Gwydion, Selyf, his most wretched son, sends greetings,

My sweet father and my most dear friend, in sore distress I heard that you had not gained the refuge of Hy Collumbcille, nor were likely to. At the guest-house of Riecawr I met an old canon from the bishop's household in Brychan. He said that before you could leave the mainland you were stricken with fever from the travelling, and have since been confined to the City of St Modan. You have now but three of our brothers to serve you in your pitiful state. How much do I regret, darling of my heart, that this dreadful mission has drawn me from your side. All that remains for me to do for my most precious father is to pray for your deliverance at every hour.

I have never ceased to think of you and of the days we spent together in the hills round the dear White House. I remember that even in those distant days you would show me the wonderful forbearance that has shone through our life together. It is hard indeed that, when you are about to take your last journey, I am far from you. The dearest wish of my heart has always been that I would see your face when first you catch sight of eternal bliss, but now I see that this blessing will be denied me. We are in God's hands, and how can I complain who have known the great blessing of your companionship throughout my life. I pray only that this, my final greeting to you, will reach you before you close your eyes that last time. I beg that you will think of your kinsman left alone to mourn the light of his world.

I do not question the bishop's decision to send me on this journey. My only doubt is that when I find the evil thing I will not find the strength to put it to flight. Nevertheless, there is so much evil and confusion in this forest that someone had to be sent. In my confusion I have often longed for your spirit to guide me and to keep me firm in my faith, for my adversary has been strong and cunning.

The king and I travelled here on foot and unattended. For the first few days I had a companion like a boy let out of school, so eagerly did he hasten along the road. The first morning we climbed to the moor as the sun rose ahead of us and we travelled for three days. The third night we spent at Riecawr where I learned of your affliction, and my burden was added to a hundred-fold. The old man from Brychan had been left as an oblate at Cudbert's city and, knowing the country he told me of a spring of holy water which the saint had produced beside the loch. I filled a flask of water there before we continued our journey.

I wish the holy Cudbert was here with me now, and his holy water to hand.

The king's recollection of his last journey over that ground was poor, as over twenty years had passed since he saw it. He led me round many peaks and along glens without cease before he was sure of his road.

We were two days journey south and a little west of Riecawr when he turned to me and said, 'We are now in that part of the forest where the giant's power began to be felt. I recall that as we got closer to the stronghold, our power to turn away grew less and less. Are you ready to continue?'

'I am, sir, though my heart is failing within me, for my duty is clear. It may be that the monster being dead, his power is fading from the land.'

'I see that, monk, and I hope it may be true, but I cannot stop the voice of doubt. His power was so very great.'

'Believe me, sir, we may be in danger now, but it is only the flesh that is threatened, and death is its destiny from its first day. How much the worse for us if we leave evil unchecked and damn our immortal souls?'

'My fear is that we may fail in body and in spirit for all our strivings. What then?'

'Sir, we cannot fail in spirit, for we are upon the work of God and his arm will strengthen us. We have only to call on him.'

The king said nothing, and walked on ahead of me. Later I paused for the office and when I raised my hands in prayer a magpie rattled his wings in a tree nearby. Both the king and I blessed ourselves, but said nothing to each other. We passed a lochan where the trees dripped and fogs hung close above the surface. But at last the king had found his road. He led me round the water to the waterfall that filled it where the rocks were hung with moss and slime. He began to climb up beside the waterfall and I followed though my feet slipped and gorse bushes blocked my way. At the top there was a track which at first twisted its way through bushes, but then became straight and led between the trees like a furrow. The trees gave way soon to pale moor grass and still the track was clear, and there, at the top, we came to the edge of a wide plain.

That bird of ill-omen, it is mocking me even now.

On one side of the plain there was a wide, deep river, and on the other a steep cliff dropped away giving a clear view down the glen. Beyond the river the forest grew thick and black and at the cliff edge the trees had been felled so that no man could approach the hall unobserved. Ahead of us the plain was as smooth as a table for the full length of it and at the far edge stood a massive stronghold. In front of the castle mighty hands had made a great ditch and a bank. With great cunning the maker had made it so that the river, which ran round the back of the hold to fall over the cliff, also lent part of itself to the ditch and flooded it. It would be a terrible stronghold to attack, and none had tried for generations.

'This is indeed the work of a great man,' I said, 'for he has turned the course of nature herself and bent her to his purpose.'

'This is only a very small part of the master's power. Be ready to marvel at the strength of his arm and the cunning of his heart, for you will not see such sights again.'

As we crossed the plain we came near sheep and cattle grazing. The cows were tall and sleek; the sheep did not flee us, but stood on the track and had to be driven from it. I saw that the plain was far bigger than I had thought, for though we walked while the sun travelled from one quarter of the sky to another the stronghold hardly seemed closer. When I saw how tall and wide the walls were my spirit was oppressed within me. Looking up at the narrow windows I saw only darkness, nor was there anyone on the walls nor at the gate, and I began to feel that the place was a desert.

I said to the king, 'I can see no one at the walls, and from here I see that the gate is hanging on only one hinge. What can this mean?'

'I begin to think that we have wasted our journey,' he replied, 'for by this time somebody in the stronghold would have seen us and been sent to fetch us. I think the giant's kin have left this place.'

At last we crossed the ditch and looked up at the castle's outer wall. Truly that stronghold was bigger than any that could have been built by man, for the bridge over the ditch and the gate beyond it were built of timbers half the width of a man, and though they were grey and yellow with lichen none of the wood had rotted. The gate alone was three times higher than myself, and the wall perhaps eight or ten times my height, and there was a tower over the gate for the watch.

Through the gate we could see the main hall, and though it was decayed and many stones had fallen from the top, it was yet ten times the height of a man and blotted out the sun. As we passed over the bridge I had to tilt my head right back to see the ravens wheeling round the top. We stood against the gate, and I was summoning

up my soul's strength to pass the last barrier, when I
found that I could not hear the sound of the river. The
sound of the waterfall as it fell over the cliff had been
loud in my ears. Suddenly there was only the sound of
water dripping in the ditch beside me, and the cries of
the ravens overhead. The heat of the day had been a
pleasure to my skin, but now I was chilled to the heart.
Even the insects were silent.

I looked at the king and saw that he was pale and the
sweat was sparkling on his face.

'Well, sir,' I said quietly, 'shall we go in?'

'Why are you mumbling, monk,' he said, 'in the name
of God, let us finish our journey.' And before the echoes
had died he walked through the gate.

Beyond the wall I found a yard filled with great stone
buildings, each of which would have graced a city. Every
building had a roof of split slates, and walls that stood
straight, and pictures carved in the stones round the
doors and windows. There was one building longer
than the others but low, and it had tall glass windows
so that I was sure that it was the weaving-hall. But I
dared not ask the king if this were so, for he strode
about in a rage.

I looked about the other buildings in the yard for
myself and found one that contained a hearth for a
smith, another a granary, then stabling for tens of
horses, a store with hooks and barrels, a kitchen with
oven and mill stones, a well full of clear water, and
many things whose purpose I did not understand. But
nowhere did I find a person nor a sign that any had been
there for many years. Grass and moss grew thick on the
stones of the yard and hindered the doors from opening;
the straw in the empty stables was mouldy, and the tools
in the smithy were rusted. In the kitchen the dried bones
and rotten grain spoke to me of a place that had been
deserted for many years.

*I am sitting in the kitchen
now, and it is dank and stale.
And I am hungry.*

'Well, monk,' said the king, and he frowned fiercely,
'what am I to make of this? You said that the woman
who spoke to you came to your holy city less than a
year ago. But where is the proof of this? I see here
nothing but death and decay. It seems to me that what
I have always held is true, and that the giant died when
I married my lady, and last year you were visited by some
evil, deceiving creature.'

'Indeed, sir, there is deception here, but where it lies I cannot say. There is no doubt that the woman I met was a monstrous creature, and whence she came was a mystery to me. Yet she was a kind and graceful woman, and I was not deceived in that. I must meditate on this.'

'Perhaps you must, Selyf, but I am a simple warrior, and have no use for meditation to see the truth before me. You have brought me here far from those who need me by making false claims and talking of my strange past. Where have you come from, monk?

'Who was waiting to see us leave so that they might slip round the headland and find my city without its protector. Or who stood out to sea and watched till my wife sat alone weeping for the luck of her city, then swept down like a pack of wolves to carry off her sweet person and her treasures? What greedy man set you to this? What did he pay you for your pains? Was it a fine gold cross to wear on feast days, or a gold embroidered vestis?' And in his rage he lifted me from the ground with one hand and shook me like a rat.

'Truly, sir,' I said, choking, 'I swear by the living God that I am none of these.'

He released me at that and I went on, 'It is well said that he who loves silver is not satisfied by silver. If you seek monks who love fine things and derelict their vows of holy poverty go back to your city and your Benedictines. If you fear for your fine stone walls more than for the souls of those within return at once and watch the sea for raiders, but if you would seek out evil stay with me and seek out the enemies of both God and man.'

The king frowned at me, but said only, 'We must wait through the night at all events, for it will be dark in a short while. I will begin my return in the morning. Go now and find us a place to sleep, for I fear I have a long walk tomorrow.'

Alone, I could not find the courage to enter the great door of the keep. I searched the outer buildings for a place to rest, and at last found dry bedding in the corner of the kitchen. I summoned the king and retired myself to say the office for the end of the day, but when I had finished I felt no healing from the words. Instead I wept that here seemed no end to my mission. In my tribulation I paced the yard and above me the four turrets at the corners of the great hall glowed red

Well, Selyf, you find yourself being accused in the same way as the woman. What is wrong with this country that we cannot trust each other? There has been so much bloodshed over the years than no man can take another for what he seems. If only we could become trusting and simple again.

Well said.

in the light of the invisible sun. I saw clearly in that hour how greed for strange matters is a curse, and what wisdom there is in condemning curiosity. That night I felt almost that God had withdrawn his face from me.

When I returned to the king he already lay facing the wall. He said nothing when I lay down near him, but sleeping or watching, he did not stir. I pushed my feet into the straw for there was a frost in the air, and prepared to sleep my little sleep till the morning hour. But a darkness came over me like a cloud before the moon and I dreamt a long and troubled dream. It seemed to me that I stood trembling beside the gate of the stronghold, and a great procession of people passed before me. Yet though I can recall that some of them wept and some of them smiled, their faces were invisible. I shudder now as I recall the fear that filled me as I waited, but I did not dare to move hand or foot in case they should see me. Yet why I was so afraid I cannot recall.

So the night slipped away. In the morning I was wakened by a light shining on my closed eyes, and I thought for a joyful moment that I was back in the forest. When I opened my eyes a great mystery met me. The king also awoke at that moment and we sat amazed to discover that the kitchen was transformed. The oven was hot and the fire was lit, the lamps over us burned with brightness like the sun and the floor had been scoured with sand. Yet there was still no person to be seen.

'Well, sir,' I said, 'some wonder has been prepared for us.'

The king said nothing, but threw his cloak around his shoulders and ran into the yard. I followed fast and we found that the sun was high and the day well advanced. Around us the grass and moss were gone from the stones and the stones fallen from the great hall were restored. The gates hung straight in their portals and were tightly closed. A noise from the stable drew me to look inside and there six white horses and many mules, all well cared for. In the smithy the hearth was still cold, but the tools hung neatly on the walls and glittered in light from the doorway. The granary was full of clean, yellow grain.

The students I met in the cities of Burgundy Lombardy and Saxony would not agree.

Over there they think that man's endless searching for truth is a sign of grace. It is possible that our fathers have take simplicity too far.

These are the denizens of Hell.

Did you miss any more offices?

I have waited here for three days, in vain. I am still surrounded by ruin and decay, and the weather is getting worse. I must soon start for home or the passes will be closed.

144

Deception indeed.

The king called to me, saying, 'It seems we were both deceived yesterday, or perhaps the deception is continuing. Do you know what has happened?'

'No, sir, I do not. It seems to me that we will find out more if we go into the great hall. I see that the walls are standing straight and firm, and there are people standing at the windows. Would you perhaps know who they are?'

'No,' said the king, 'but it has been a long time since I was here. The women I knew will have changed by now. But I think there are some I may recognise. Let us go into the hall and meet them.'

'Will it be safe to enter the hall, sir? The sight of it makes my heart white.'

'What have we come for, monk? Not to stand like a beast frozen with fear.'

Together we walked into the hall, and I was thankful that I had a mighty warrior beside me. I saw that the king blessed himself at the threshold, and I closed my hand tightly on the flask of holy water. I am not like the Abbots of old who entered a battle with no more than a heart filled with holiness and courage. I am only a foolish monk and my wisdom is small.

In the hall we found a great throng of women standing silently watching our arrival. They were so many in number and so different in age that I could not believe that they were of the same generation. There stood a wise matron with grey hair, and beside her an infant stared up at us. Beyond them a tall girl with scarcely a sign of womanhood looked at us boldly. None were dressed in the finery I had heard of from the king, and their clothes, though well made and clean, had not an ounce of silver or gold about them. Modestly they stood, maidens of marriageable age and women past child-bearing; skipping girls and steady matrons.

We know who the father of this group is, but who are their 'mothers'? I fear we do not need to look far.

As we walked toward them they stood aside so that an aisle opened to the end of the hall and there stood the master's chair. It was a massive square bench with a high canopy over it at the head of the table. Seated there was the lady Marighal, and at her side stood the smallest man I have ever seen. Standing he scarcely came to my lady's shoulder, and the hand that rested on the pommel of his sword was like a child's. Yet the eyes in his face held cunning and wisdom beyond that of ordinary men. As we approached the table the king trembled and he groaned aloud, and at last he threw himself to the ground at her feet.

'My lady,' he cried, 'what shall I do to discharge my terrible debt to you? I see now that I have been deceived in the woman I took for my wife, and I am forsworn. You, in your kindness, did not take her from me, nor did you tell the world of my shame, but left me contented in my error. Now I must try and make good the wrong I have done to the most noble of women, and I fear it will take me the rest of my life.'

Marighal stooped and raised him up. She turned him to face the crowd of her sisters, and said, 'Be comforted, Kynan, for you have wronged neither me nor my kind. Hear me now, sisters, see your friend of happier years, known to us as White-hair. You have seen that he has come here freely, to seek me and readily acknowledges his wife. I call you all to witness that he is without stain, for he was deceived by none other than myself, and there is no debt between him and our kind.'

After she had said these words the women smiled, and some of them came to Kynan and greeted him as their old friend. Then they left the hall till there was only the king, myself, the dwarf and Marighal.

'You have not broken fast today,' she said, and led us behind the dais to a little room where the sun shone brightly through clear glazed windows. There we found a table laid with a plain cloth.

'My sister, Evabyth, will bring us food in here,' said Marighal, 'and we will answer the questions I know you are eager to ask. I am sorry for the trouble you have had Kynan, and you Selyf, who have been my messenger. You have had a wretched task. I ask you to believe me when I tell you there is no way it could have been otherwise.'

Then the lady Evabyth returned with food, and with a swift prayer for indulgence I ate barley bread and cheese and a piece of honeycomb. I drank only clear water, yet I could not have felt better fed if it had been a feast.

'Marighal, said the king, 'there are indeed many questions I have to ask you, but some cannot be spoken of freely, so I must wait until we are alone. But there is one I must ask at once: what has become of your father?'

This is Grig the smith and the foster-father of Marighal.

What kindess was there to leave him in adultery? The greater charity is always to show another his sin as St Gregory tells us.

After eating cheese when you are in full health, that is the least you could do. As Berach sang, "Better than any refection is moderation, when one comes to eat."

'That story is not mine to tell,' said Marighal, 'for, to my everlasting grief, I was not here when that terrible thing happened. Evabyth is the best one to tell it, for she was the bravest woman here at that time, and saw everything that took place.'

'Well, Evabyth,' said Kynan, 'you were only an infant when I last saw you, but your sister seems to think well of you. Will you tell me about it, for I am most eager to hear how my master met his doom. Was it sorcery that did it, or was there indeed a mortal man that could stand against him?'

Evabyth blushed and made no answer, but looked, frowning, at me.

'Do not be afraid,' said Kynan, the generous, 'this man has been tested by Marighal and myself, and has been proved to be a wise and careful man. He can be trusted with the secrets of your hall.'

Then the young woman told us of her father's last days.

Evabyth tells the story of the giant's death.

My father died last year to our very great grief. There was a man, at last, who could beat him, though it is true he did not accomplish it alone. It was the man who took Olwen in marriage. (You will not recall her, Kynan, for she was born some time after you left us. The one you knew of that name died soon after you went.) She grew quickly to marriageable age and she turned into a very great beauty. Her long, straight hair was the colour of ripe barley, and her figure was slender as a birch tree and as supple as a swan. The brave man who came to take her said that he had dreamed of her and that her beauty had possessed him from that moment so that he could neither eat nor drink till he had seen her in the flesh. I think the dream was a curse on his house for some evil they had done. He gave his name as Culhuch and said he was without kindred but he was a fine man, no longer a youth but with hair as black as the raven's wing. He had it cut short to fit under a hood of mail that he wore under his helmet.

The men he kept as his companions were all as well armed as he. They were all dark-haired with heavy black brows that met across the nose. There were twenty of them with him and they carried the longest shields I have ever seen, for they covered them all the way to their feet. The horses they rode were black and very tall, for the back of one of them was taller than myself. They had leather mail on the horses also, and below their saddles they had little loops of leather to put their feet in and keep their balance. So well could they cling to their horses that they could fight without getting down from the horse's back. I know this because I watched them one day from a window as they did their morning practice. No man on foot would be able to reach them but would have to take blows from above his head. They were very agile and skilful and dangerous, and they rode into our yard here as if there were two hundred of them.

The equipment sounds very like that which the warriors of Burgundy use. They and many of the hired warriors I saw used straps like these to keep them secure on the back of a turning horse. They are very dangerous indeed when mounted in this fashion.

They rode out of the forest one afternoon in autumn and crossed the plain with sunlight glancing off their helmets. Up to the gate they came and Culhuch hammered on the gate with the pommel of his sword, 'Open your gates to us,' he cried, boldly naming my father. 'I have come to take your daughter's hand in marriage.'

No one here had ever seen a man so full of pride and arrogance. But my father was patient and sent me and Deirdre to open the gate for them. They rode in without a glance round and took their horses to the stable, giving us instructions as if we had been stable-boys. We marvelled at their discourtesy, but told our servants to do what was necessary and followed them as they strode into the hall. In here Roswitha and Barve met them with all courtesy and led them to their beds and even helped them to disarm, for which they got no word of thanks.

It is a brave man that uses a demon's name to summon him — brave, or foolish?

Then it was time to eat and they were led to their places. Most of us were there that night to see what manner of man had come to seek our sister with so little ceremony. We waited on them at table ourselves, and they stared at us boldly and said, 'Where are your menfolk, all you women? Or do you have no men to take care of you?'

Barve answered him for she is young and bold also.'We have no menfolk, nor have we any need of them, for our father takes care of us very well. Our lives are simple and pleasant, and we have no use for men and their troublesome habits.'

Spoken like a bride of Christ!

The men laughed loudly at this and said they would be pleased to trouble her, and other coarse things. She was not dismayed, so one of them said to her, 'What about your mighty father? Is he not at home tonight, for his place is empty. Is he afraid to face us?'

None of us answered such a foolish question. We knew well our father would come at the mention of himself. Nor were we wrong, for just then he strode into the hall with his finest clothes on, and his cloak fastened with a brooch as big as most men's shields. Some of the visitors looked down at the table when he stared at them but Culhuch stared straight back and said nothing.

'Well,' said Father, 'which of you is the man who thinks he will marry my daughter?'

'I am,' said Culhuch, keeping his seat, 'I have had a dream of your daughter and I cannot rest nor eat nor sleep till I see her in the flesh.'

And a daughter of unholy incest?

'Surely you have had a fine dream,' said Father, and I was amazed at his calmness. 'She is a very great beauty, like her mother before her, but I must tell you that she is not at home, nor will she return until she thinks to do so. She is her own woman, and I cannot tell her what to do. Now, tell me, what makes you think that you are fit to join yourself to a member of my ancient line? Are you of a noble house, and gently raised?'

Kynan's family were not noble either. Why is the giant suddenly so discriminating?

'Indeed I am not,' answered Culhuch, 'my father's line is nothing. He was only a thegn of common stock but my mother is of a very ancient line. He seduced her when she was unprotected and too young to understand what was happening.

There are some stories about this in the south of the kingdom. It will be easy to find more.

'When she found she was with child and that her dishonour would be shown to all the world by my birth she ran frantic into the forest. There she stayed, insane, till I was born, and she brought me into the world in a pigsty. She abandoned me there to be raised by an old woman servant. Truly I can say that I am so far from gently raised that I was kindred to pigs for the first years of my life.'

At this his companions shouted with laughter again, but I saw that this news came like a blow to my father. For the first time in my long life I saw him weaken. He grasped the table with both hands as if he was going to fall. The men were laughing too much to see this, and my father recovered quickly and said, 'Then you are twice welcome, Pigsty, who comes here with no other claim than your own merit. Your courage does you credit, if not your wisdom.'

'I am clever and I am very strong,' said Culhuch. 'When I came to my full strength my mother's servant told me of my parents and told me where I should find my father. He laughed to see me and was glad to teach such a fine son all he knew about a warrior's trade. He said he was proud of me for I was the best of all his students, and the cleverest of all his sons. So although I came to the arts of war later than the son of a chieftain should, I learned better than they, and if I am not wise this does not trouble me. I have seen something of the world, and it seems to me that wisdom brings nothing but worry. I will make do with cunning.'

'I see you are a subtle man,' said Father, smiling, and he invited the warriors to eat. They did so, and though they ate well they were not gluttons, nor did they drink a great deal of wine. They did not stop to talk after the meal but soon rose and left to retire for the night. My father said nothing, but you may be sure he watched everything they did.

Warriors who can control their appetites like this are greatly to be feared. Most of them are betrayed by their lusts, and can be defeated in this weakness.

In the morning they all assembled in the yard and carried out their drill with neither eagerness nor dismay. When they had finished they rode off into the forest without a word to us, and stayed away until meal-time. At dinner they sat in silence once again and stared at Father and at the few of us women who came to table.

As soon as they had finished, Culhuch stood and spoke to Father saying, 'We are still waiting to see the lady Olwen. Where is she? Bring her out now, for I believe you have hidden her somewhere in this stronghold. You will not let me see her for fear that she will want to go with me. Fetch her now, so that I may see my destiny.'

'I have told you she is not here.' said Father, mildly, 'I will take any oath you will to that fact, but since you are so eager, I will send to find out where she is and at this time tomorrow I will give you more news of her.'

'Very well,' said the dark man, 'we will wait another day and see what you will do for us, but you may be sure that we are waiting only to see what action you will take. Do not try to deceive us or it will be the worse for you.'

'Most noble warrior,' said Father, and he bowed mockingly, 'I would not deceive one as worthy as you have shown yourself to be.'

Culhuch and his companions retired with no reply.

150

The next day the pattern was repeated, and though Culhuch had said they would be watching us we did not see them again that day. It was all equal to father for he was well able to keep his business hidden if he wished, and his messengers left unseen. In the evening the silence in the hall was grim as the warriors ate. They had taken it as a slight that my father had not sent messengers rushing all over the land to find Olwen, and they were angry. Only myself, Barve and Eadyth joined them that night and we had little appetite.

After eating Culhuch stood and said, 'Well, now, giant, you have had all day to find your lovely daughter. Tell me, when may I look upon my promised bride?'

'Not hard to say, courageous man.' said my father, still patient as stone, 'My daughter has taken herself to visit the Christian women who live south and east of here about two days' march. She has taken a notion to join their rule and will soon complete her vows as an anchoress. If you would see her you must hurry, for at the next Sabbath she will be gone from the sight of man forever.'

'How do you come to know all that?' cried Culhuch. 'We have watched the stronghold all day from hiding places in the forest and we have seen no one leave or arrive. I believe you when you say she is not here, for we searched the stronghold while you slept last night. We did not find her, but now I think you are lying unless you have found news of her by some foul and sorcerous method.'

'How I came by the news is not for you to know, Pigsty. You are vilely discourteous to have answered my hospitality by spying on me. My word is my bond and I take it ill that you doubt it. Olwen is not in my hold, nor is she your lady till she consents to be so with her own mouth. And I have told you, if you wish to gain that consent you must seek her quickly at Caerleul. You will leave this place in the morning at any event, for I do not like the way you answer guest-friendship.'

Culhuch answered with pale face, but whether he was afraid or angry I cannot say. But his voice shook as he said, 'I am not obliged to show you the courtesy I would to a proper man. You are a giant and a demon and your life is all evil. I have come seeking the woman I know to be my rightful mate and I have the right to seek her

Is this the sisters at Caerleul? They would be sure to remember this event if it took place. I shall go and ask them.

Courtesy is always proper our Maelruin showed us, galling as it may be. Even the Adversary himself must be

in any way I see fit. As for my name, you do not do well to mock it. I am proud to be a man of no family. What I have acquired I took by my own will and effort, and my duty is only to the companions who have sworn their loyalty to me. Of all the chiefs I met at my father's house, I alone was free to act as I saw fit, nor can custom nor overlord hamper me. And I will rid the world of evil such as you, demon!'

They all withdrew and my father sat on long after my sisters and I had retired. In the morning Culhuch and his companions left without breaking fast and we heard no more of them for several days.

The next event was Olwen's return, riding on a fine white horse. We greeted her as she came through the gate but she seemed barely to see us as she dismounted and walked, tall and stately to the door of my father's closet. He opened the door when she knocked and asked her in, but she turned without a word and led the way down to the hall before the meal could be served. There she waited till my father had taken his place above us.

'Father,' she said, 'at the convent the other day a crowd of fine warriors arrived. They said they had been seeking me here, and the leader had come to take me in marriage. Is this true?'

'Yes, daughter, it is true, and I am sorry to say that he was a very overbearing and ill-mannered man. He treated myself and your sisters like vassals. I told him that a daughter of my house must consent freely to her marriage before I would approve it, and he left to find you and get your consent. I am sorry I could not conceal your whereabouts from him, for I am sure you would not be pleased to be importuned by such an insolent fellow, but he insisted. How did he serve you? Was he not very uncivil, this pigsty who presumes to be your husband?'

'He was not full of fine speeches it is true, but since I have been with the good sisters I have come to see that all the ways which we call courtesy are nothing but a cloak that people use to hide what they are truly thinking. I found the warrior most pleasant in his simple, honest manner, and from the unaffected way he spoke to me I have decided to take him as my husband.'

'He should be grateful for the custom and courtesy he despises so much,' said Father, 'for it was these alone

shown restrained language.

These new men are sure to be well known. I will ask permission to look for them further south.

If these are the sisters I think then I can well believe it. They are most arrogant and unbending in their treatment of others, and think they have

152

the only truth, yet they wallow in ignorance.

The giant must have had some source of information about this gang to know that they are mercenaries.

An older race than mankind? This is not possible. The scriptures make no mention of any. Only pagans speak of them.

Is it foolishness to seek a life dedicated to piety and learning? Is it a terrible thing to follow the practice and spirit of poverty? It is a woman's first duty to look to the state of her immortal soul, not to fill this corrupted world with sinners. This Culhuch is vain, deceiving braggart. She would do far better to go elsewhere, even to Caerleul and the sisters of St Brigid!

that kept my hand off him when he came strutting into this hall. He was like a cock on a dunghill, and those were dogs he brought baying at his back.'

'It was well for you that you did not,' said Olwen, 'for you could not have prevailed against his cunning warriors.

Father was angry at that, and struck the table with his fist.

'Are you telling me now that you will go with him and be his wife? A man without family or lands? It is not enough that he is a bastard — he was born in a pigsty and raised by a slave who is the only witness to his name. And you will marry this man who sells his sword to the highest bidder. You, who come from one of the oldest families in the world. Our ancestors saw land rising out of the sea in fire and smoke, and the face of the earth when it was covered with ice. We had ploughed fields before men were wise enough to make fire.'

'I know it well, Father. You have told us many times.'

'What, then, of the women at the convent? Do you no longer wish to become one of them? Are you not already a baptised Christian?'

'I have received baptism, and I will make my marriage vow before a bishop. Culhuch is baptised also, though not a devoted member of mother church. But I no longer wish to become an anchoress, for now I see that it is all foolishness. Culhuch has said to me that I have no right to do such a terrible thing as to lock my beauty away where the sun will never shine on it again. I have a duty to make many children as fine and beautiful as myself, and I owe it to the world to stay in it and move through it, for my presence will be a blessing. He said I have a destiny to fulfil as his wife and I may not deny it.'

'And so, with these fine and flattering words he has turned you to his party. He is indeed a very cunning man.'

'No,' said Olwen, 'he is not cunning, that is for other people, he says. He is simple and open-hearted, and God will witness that he speaks only the truth. He would not mock the truth, he says, for to him it is sacred, more sacred than holy writ, and he would sooner die than be a deceiver.'

'Well,' said Father, 'tell me now, was it simplicity of heart when he and his company roamed round these halls in the night? Was it innocents that hid in the forest all day and watched who might come and go here? Does a simple man set to spy on his host?'

'If his host is a wicked man then he is right to do so, of course. You will not deny that you have been a very wicked man. You have told us yourself of some of the terrible things you have done, nor do you repent any of your sins.'

'Child, I do not deny it. I am what I am nor can I change my nature. Yet I have never deceived anyone or claimed to be the same as human kind. I have kept myself apart from mankind as far as possible so as to do as little harm as possible. There is much about me that you do no know, nor do I wish you to, but I ask you to believe me that my life is nothing but a source of pain to me. I could never deceive a man even if I wished to, for everyone knows who I am the first time they see me.

'But I tell you, this bold man conceals his ill-nature behind a handsome face. He does not want you as a bride — it is myself he seeks, for by destroying me he will get himself a name that will strike fear into all that hear it. He has no kindred, but if he kills me he will become known as the mightiest warrior in the world. You do not matter to him.'

'You must not judge his actions as your own. He is pure in heart, and that is why he will prevail against you if you challenge him. He knows this because he has been told it in a dream.'

Father shook his head and said, 'Go with your man if you must, and be happy with him if you can, but do not let his speech deafen you. Do not let his beauty blind you so that you can see only with his eyes.'

I have an inkling who this Culhuch might be. I recall that I heard a story about such a man in Hefresham.

'I will leave here tomorrow when Culhuch comes for me.' said Olwen, cold as ice, 'I will go to my room now and wait there, nor will I eat any food in this hall, for you may try to give me poison to kill me or make me sleep till Culhuch has left again.'

With these words she left us, and we were bitter to think that our sister could think so ill of us. The words of this man had been enough to turn her against the people she had known for generations.

For generations? How many?

The next morning most of us hid in our hall, but I went up the the gate house to see what would happen. Before the sun had travelled far across the sky I saw the troop ride out of the forest and across the plain, their toes pointing ahead of them and their long shields on their arms. My father had been warned of their arrival, and he stood at the door of his hall with his great battle-axe held across his body. He ordered the gate to open as the men rode up to it, and it made them pause when they saw it swing wide. Slowly they rode into the yard and saw the giant barring their way.

'Where is Olwen the White?' shouted Culhuch, 'Bring her out so that we can take her to her own land.'

'I will not,' said Father, 'I have spent the night meditating on what she said, and I have decided to stop you from taking her away.'

'Do you hear that, men?' cried Culhuch, 'The monster is forsworn, as I promised you he would be. Olwen is eager to come with me, and her father told us that he would let her go if she chose to, yet now he says he will keep her.'

'True, I am what you would call a monster, but one such as you has no right to call me evil. If I have done anything to be ashamed of, it was raising a child who will let other people put visions in her heart and words in her mouth without measuring them first.

'True, I let my daughters go if they freely will it, but she has not consented freely. She has been trained to it as a hawk is manned, till it will not move its head without the consent of its master. That is not free will, nor will I let her go. Leave my land now, and be grateful that I have not whipped you like the dog you are.'

'Monster and demon,' shrieked Culhuch, 'is there no end to your word spells? Your daughter chose me as her destined husband, and you cannot alter that, though you speak all day. Forward, men! We must fight the creature for our rightful property. Forward and show him what real men can do.'

At this his companions pressed their horses toward my father and he raised his battle-axe. When they stood in front of him, they stopped, for suddenly they saw that though they stood taller than other men on their horses, the giant on foot was taller still.

Culhuch, in his place at the gate cried out, 'Why are you stopping. Wretches, where is your faith? You know you only have to strike the miserable demon once and he is bound to fall under honest men's weapons.'

This is just. The giant treated Marighal and her husband in the same way.

Free will — is the monster mocking me? For days as I walked I have meditated on this and now he brings me another notion — education. Is it intended to remove the will or to curb it so that it seeks only the good?

They raised their long spears again, but the horses
had been unsettled by the halt, and they began to caper
and jostle. All at once the men struck out at Father, with
no thought for the careful practice of the drill yard, and
they jabbed at him randomly. It was no effort for Father
to swing his axe and knock two of them to the ground
with one blow so that blood ran out from under their
helmets. The horses cavorted and backed away from the
swinging axe, trampling the fallen men underfoot. The
riderless horses hampered the men even more. Then
one companion threw aside the spear which was too
long to be useful in that turmoil and, drawing his sword,
he flung himself at Father. The mighty axe came down
on the side of his neck, split the rider to the groin and
cut through the horse's backbone. Horse and rider fell
to the ground, almost in two pieces. The company drew
off in different directions and looked down at the red
ruin of their friend. Culhuch gave a shout of rage as the
rank opened and he saw Father standing triumphant.

I smile as I am reading this. Dear God help me. Men are dying and I can smile!

'This is the weapon that will finish you, devil,' he
cried, brandishing a short, black spear. 'This has been
a sacred relic in my mother's family since time began.
Feel its terrible bite now, and die!'

So saying he rose to his full height in the saddle
and flung the spear across the yard. It rushed singing
to the door and sank halfway down the shaft in my
father's gut. Father pulled the spear out and looked at
it, amazed.

'I made this spear myself,' he said, 'and it has returned
to its maker like a child to its mother. Welcome home,
little one. Your journey is over.'

Every creature makes its own bane.

At that moment Olwen appeared at the door of the
hall. My father turned to her.

'Well, daughter,' he said, 'it seems I must let you go
at last. Farewell and may your God go with you, though
I fear you will find little happiness. The man you are
going with has a soul like the bit in a horse's mouth —
it will force you to its will, cruelly. He judges what he
does not understand, and does not value the demands
of simple affection. But my curse lies on his sons and all
the generations to come. He thinks that he can make the
law with his own hands, but that will be his destruction.
The only pity is that many, many more than he will suffer for his error.'

God alone makes the law. Man's duty is to find it, not to

156

make it. Thus far the demon is right.

Olwen walked past him without a word and fetched her tall white horse from the stable. The companions lifted up their wounded and threw them over their saddles, and then the whole troop departed. As she passed under the gate Olwen looked up and saw me standing in the turret, but she did not even nod to me. And then they were gone.

Father still stood in the doorway, the spear in one hand and his axe in the other, and a little of his blood stained the ground. He gave orders for his servants to destroy the dead horse and rider, and retired to his bed. I came down from the turret, and the thought of Olwen was a sourness in my heart.

We did not see Father for two days, but we thought nothing of it. He knew more about healing than any of us, and he hated to be disturbed. We were sure that if we went in to him now his rage would be terrible, and so we all walked past the bolted door. At his order the fires were built up in his hall, and we thought this was a little strange because the leaves were only newly turned, but we knew how much he hated the cold, so we did nothing.

Then Marighal came home and she had heard rumours about the young man's challenge. She understood what had happened and we went to hammer on the door to father's bed but there was no reply. At last we saw there was nothing else to do but break the door in and we found him lying, as cold as ice. The wound in his stomach which he seemed to have taken so lightly had become a vast black hole, and all the flesh for two hands' spans around it was yellow and rotten. The smell was an abomination, and only Mari could bring herself to touch father and prepare him for his departure. She alone of all of us is able to bear the ills of this world, and I wish more of us were like her. Perhaps if we were, my father would still be with us.

Thank God they were not! There is hope for salvation in the meek. The bold are unregenerate.

Selyf takes up the story.

At these words the lady Evabyth was stricken by her grief and the bloody tears of her kind ran down her face. She could not speak for sobbing.

Marighal tried to comfort her, saying, 'Do not weep so sorely, Evabyth. Our father knew his death was written somewhere, and he had been waiting for its arrival for many years. Often before when young men had come to claim his daughters he had been compelled to test them to the death, and only two had suceeded. He told me himself that he was weary of the trials and of the wasting of young life, and he looked with hope for the coming of the appointed one so that he could find peace at last. Each year was longer for him than the one before, and more filled with pain, and with none left to share his past there was not even pleasure in his memories.'

'That is true, Mari,' said Evabyth, 'my father is glad to be gone, but I am also weeping for myself and my sisters. We are left here with no protection, nor have we any hope for the future. I am weeping for the end of our lives.'

'Well now,' spoke Kynan, 'here is myself. Though I am no longer young I am still strong, and I will keep you from danger in any way I can. Was I not fostered here, and were you not my sisters when we were children? I would be a poor brother to you if I did not offer you my protection.'

'That is most generous of you, Kynan,' said Marighal, 'but I feel that great though our need is of your sword arm, our need of the ministrations of my friend Selyf is more urgent. My sisters are troubled by a great agony of soul and need his counsel to help them to start their new way of life. I do not doubt that eventually most of us will be glad to find the stout walls of your city around us. In the meantime, we need his teaching at once.'

It is clear that these creatures could be ripe for conversion to the true faith.

Are they Jews? If so then their conversion would be the sign of great things soon to come.

The lady Evabyth begged leave to go back to her work, and Kynan and Marighal returned to the matter closer to their hearts.

'Lady,' said the king, 'I have always known you to be honourable even though sometimes your ways have been mystifying. When you tell me that I have not dishonoured you or myself I must believe you, but, before God, please tell me, who is the woman I keep in my hall? She and I have been living as man and wife for many years, and if I have not fouled my own honour by this, I have certainly fouled hers.'

'Not so, Kynan.' said Marighal, 'Do not let this thought trouble you for an instant. The woman in your hall is not dishonoured by your knowing her, for you have taken your oath before all to be her loyal and devoted husband, and to cleave to none other than herself. She is truly your wife, and your hand was bound to hers that night here long ago when we were handfasted. She is none other than myself.'

'This cannot be.' cried the king, 'In youth she was as like you as yourself, but now she is nothing like you.'

'Our lives have been different, Kynan, and this has made the difference in our appearance. I tell you before any God you might name, that flesh is my flesh, and that heart is my heart, and as many times as you have felt it beating beneath you, you have known only me.

'It is true she can recall nothing of the days I spent here nor any of my fostering, nevertheless she is myself, and in her heart she knows that you are her only lord till God's kingdom come.'

'How can this be?' said the king, and I shared his disbelief. 'I left her days ago in my city and she does not travel for it tires her. How can a woman be in two places at once?'

'To help you to understand this I will have to tell you more about the last day of your ordeal. First you must understand that the tall tree you climbed was not a tree at all.'

'That I can believe, for I have seen no tree like it before or since that day, and my heart goes cold when I remember the height of it.'

Marighal resumes her story.

I will tell you now that it was none other than my father in one of his guises. Many of our kind know something of shape-changing, but when my father takes on another shape it can only be an ancient and gigantic form like his own. When you climbed the branches you were in his arms, and when you took the eggs you took his eyes and his soul. If he had been without honour he could have saved himself and killed you with a trifling effort, but he could not be so base. My part in it was to make you a road, for only his own kin could combine with him to make more branches, so I merged my substance with his. Any of my sisters could have done the same, but they were not bound to you and to the world, and the sacrifice would not have been made willingly. Without goodwill the ransom would not have been sufficient, and there would only have been calamity.

I survived the ordeal by a secret of our family. But I had to introduce some changes whose effect I did not know. I reformed my flesh on the bones as you left them

What am I to make of this?

when the light of the setting sun struck them, but then a terrible thing happened. After I had refilled my body with my spirit I went to the river and took down the cloth with the discarded flesh to burn it. When I took it down I found to my dismay that the guts were moving. I laid it down and loosed the cords that tied it, and behold, there lay a double of myself, gazing at me with eyes as empty as a new-born child.

I lifted her up and wrapped her in my cloak, and left her while I made sure you were safe. When I returned to her I found her still lying there — she did not even know how to walk! I was sure no one could know about her. We were safe from my father, for he and his servants were helpless until his soul was restored to him.

I took my other self in my arms and fled with her to the side of the sea, and there I took a night and a day to teach her to walk and speak. There I had to leave her, my child and my self in one flesh. I heard the sound of hunters coming, and though I could not know who they were I had no time to wait and see them for I had to return for my marriage to you or father would have sent to look for me. I left her there to her destiny on the beach, and I prayed, weeping to the merciful God to keep her from danger and defilement. He must have heard this suffering maidservant, for all that I am not baptised, for she was found by that good old man who took her for his daughter.

When you took her as your wife you did no evil, for I or she was yours already. When I followed you to that fair city I found out why you had not returned to me, and I rejoiced, for God had preserved us both. My daughter-self had a fine husband and my father was protected from my betrayal of him. I was free at last, but I lived in your country for a while to make sure your life was pleasant. But I will tell you more about that later.

'Now I wish dearly to walk in the sunlight with you my lord,' and she jumped to her feet like a girl, and led us out of the hall into the yard and beyond to the plain where we found the air clear and light.

The king was silent and shook his head as he reflected on what my lady had told us. I recalled the story of Ezekiel in the scripture and marvelled that God had brought the miracle to pass again. Yet I was troubled

Is this more mockery of our Saviour's sacrifice? Or is it envious emulation? Was that incantation about the purity of woman the spell which worked the change? We must know so much more before we can judge the case. I have never heard of such a thing.

Again she is mocking the Almighty. 'Child and self in one flesh'. This is intolerable.

Q. If God is not flesh but is eternal, immutable and incorporeal how did he claim to be the Son also?

A. As Eiriugena showed us — those things which can be perceived by the senses or the intellect can be said to exist. Those which elude perception are the essences of things and God the Father Himself, who is the essence of all things is also imperceptible.

Q. When the woman died could we not say that her essence was separated from her flesh and bones and was thereafter divided between the two? How then did she mock God since she says she did not control her essence? It seems to me that it was used against her will.

A. There is still a mystery here which may be adverse to God. Remember Ezekiel 8:14 'Then he brought me to the door of the Lord's house which was to the north; and, behold, there sat women weeping for Tammuz. Then he said to me, Hast thou seen this, o son of man? Turn again and thou shalt see greater abominations than these.' You will recall, Tammuz was dismembered according to this mystery.

160

that his name had not been spoken during the renewal of the flesh.

'How are you able to do these things, Marighal, and whose aid did you invoke? Was it the hand of Almighty God that did this, or did you name the name of some evil one?'

'I cannot be sure, Selyf,' replied my lady, and she smiled at me. 'I have often seen this mystery, but I have never heard a spirit named. The only enchantment we make is the one I told my husband that day which names no names. But because the effect is beneficial I had concluded that it was sent to us by the Master of the Heavenly City.'

Then she walked over to the river bank to join Kynan. They began to talk idly as I have seen people do when they are deeply troubled. My heart was heavy and I sighed when suddenly a sweet voice spoke up at my side, saying, 'You surely cannot still believe that there is a demon here?' I looked down to see the dwarf, Grig, addressing me.

'My daughter speaks with ease and cheerfulness of your God the Alfather, yet it was always my understanding that if He is mentioned His enemies will writhe in pain. Surely you do not doubt her goodness.'

God's enemies may have learned to suffer His name in silence. There is danger of error here.

'No, sir, I do not doubt her goodness, for I have seen it for myself.'

Grig watched me from under his brows for a moment then spoke again.

'So, monk, you thought that the stronghold was deserted when you came to it yesterday. What do you think of it now? Is it not a very fine hall and full of kindly people?

'Indeed, I am amazed by the way it has been restored overnight. My first sight of it said that it had been deserted many years ago.'

'It was intended that you should think so,' said the dwarf, and his voice was like the wind in the reeds. 'Since my master died many of those who lived under his protection have left the forest. They were afraid that those nearby had been envious of the master's protection of them, and that without his help they would be made to pay for the trouble-free years. They left the hold and the daughters had to fend for themselves. This is only what you would expect from gossocks. The few who stayed are glad to deny that there ever was a giant living here who took care of them. We were obliged to hide the stronghold in illusion.'

'It seems to me that sisters of Marighal would be well able to care for themselves.'

'Nay, monk, not so. My daughter is wise and strong and cunning in battle, but she is the only one of her sisters of whom I can say this. Barve and Evabyth are eager, and will soon learn all we can show them, but of the rest who are young enough to train for combat none can even lift a sword.'

'I recall the strength of lady Marighal. She carried boulders which even a full-grown man could not lift. Surely the other sisters have their father's strength, like her?'

'Indeed they have, but such strength is not to be used every day. If they were to use such strength often they would die within a short week. They have their father's strength, but it is in their mother's bodies.

'They were all given the chance and they chose to sit within these walls and weave and spin and mill while the generations passed. In their ignorance of the world now they are defenceless. My daughter and myself have done our best to keep them from harm and now men who come here to see the monster's hall see only a ruin and leave before nightfall. They would rather face the wolves than the ghosts of this hall. You and Kynan knew the kinder face of this family and were not afraid to stay.'

'Certainly we were well repaid for our vigil.' I said, 'for I am happy to meet my lady's sisters. Nevertheless I must confess I would like to find out more about the mysteries of this stronghold. What, for instance, has become of the golden globes — the strange machines that the giant used for his trivial business.'

'I am sorry to have to tell you that they died with the giant himself. It was his great spirit that gave them motion, and even though my brothers and I made them we never learned how to give them life. When my master died, they sank to the ground, never to rise again. Come with me now, Selyf, and I will show you some of these wonders you wish to see so that you may sleep tonight. Little demons of curiosity will not hover round your head like troublesome flies. I may not show you everything, but I will be happy to show you what I can.'

162

I thanked him heartily for that and we left Marighal and the king to their talk. We wound our way through the passages and up the many staircases that ran about the giant's stronghold. I did not see all the wonders the king had told me of, but I saw other things that he had not mentioned. The size and number of the rooms and the great height and perfect straightness of the walls was something to wonder at in itself. Grig told me that his family had helped the giant from the first days of the building, and with pride he showed me the marks they had cut in the stone to prove their hand in the work. Not only had they cut the stones, but the iron rivets and bands that held the stones in place had been made by the dwarf smith's family. And more, the timbers for the roof and floors had been cut by them and brought to the castle by their draft animals.

'Yours is a very clever family, Grig, and an old one. How did you first come to this country, for your kind are not often found here?'

'As men reckon time we came here eighteen generations ago. We came with Saxons and other peoples who were in flight from the men from the lands in the east. They were terrible to see, those little dark men, for they sat on their horses and drew their short, hard bows to send arrows into our midst like flies on the moor for number. When we fled we found the giant living here, and he alone of all the people in these islands could see how many and how great were our crafts. He took us into his protection, and gave us many tasks so that we learned more than anyone has ever known before. But we kept ourselves apart, and took very few students for there are dangers in throwing your learning around like the sower his grain — what grows up may not be what you had planned to reap.'

'I see, then, that you had a debt to the giant, and that he could command your love and obedience.'

'Not command, monk,' said the little man. 'We both had much to offer the other. Without us the giant would have had none of his servants, for though he had designed how they must be made, when we found him one of his eyes was dark, and the other was failing. He could hardly see at all when he died. Furthermore, he would not have had the companionship of people with

I know who he means. They are referred to in the histories severally as Huns, Magyars, and Tartars.

memories almost as long as his own to beguile the long winter evenings.'

We had by now reached the highest room in the stronghold. It was a wooden garret on the roof of the great hall, and was built very low so that it could not be seen from the plain below, yet there were casements all along one side, and the panes of glass in some of them were so wondrously clear that it was possible to see right into the forest and the hills beyond. The dwarf told me that it had been built so that the queen and the daughters of the house might gather there out of sight of the giant.

Which queen is this?

Carved lamps hung from the low ceiling and red coloured glass had been put all round the sides so that the room was lit with a red glow. All around us were couches covered with cushions, and the walls were hung with thick, soft hangings which were pictures of strange animals and flowers, and laughing people in brightly coloured clothes. Even the stone floor of that sumptuous room had woven pictures on it so that walking was warm and silent and a delight to the feet. All these pictures had been made by the sisters over the years, and I was filled with wonder to think that these women who had never left their halls could find so much to weave into their pictures. I do not doubt that it was the softness lapping around them that would make them see such wonderful sights and dreams. Truly it was a place to fill and drown the senses, and to tempt the flesh with sensations of delight. To eat that strange fruit and to walk under those sunny skies became all at once the greatest of my heart's desires.

I hurried out of that luxurious room after Grig, and was grateful to be gone. Next he showed me the library of that house. Yes, Father, that man had so many books that like the great abbey in Rome you described to me, there was a room made with shelves especially for them. There were all manner of books, papyrus rolls, codices bound in fine leather decorated with gold and jewels, and tablets of something like papyrus which had been made of linen. They were on all manner of subjects also, as well as psalters and scriptures like our own, and with wonderful illuminations in them, as good and better than the best of our scriptoria. Wonder sealed my mouth as Grig showed me one after another and

It is good that you were able to resist this luxury, Selyf. Your devotion is getting stronger. I pray that your strength will be rewarded.

unfurled scroll after scroll. I could make no sense of the writing in some of them and, almost blinded by the colours, I began to think I would lose my senses altogether.

Grig saw that dumbness had come over me and led me from the hall again, saying, 'I am deeply sorry to have troubled you, great-hearted Selyf. I did not see that my idle bragging would have such a baneful effect. My daughter told me of your great love of learning, and I had hoped to please you.'

'You do me too much honour, Grig,' I said, and as I spoke tears escaped from my eyes, 'it is only that my simple soul is stricken by such riches. I think about those which my ancestors made with long patience, and which the Vikings destroyed.'

Then we returned to the great hall, and found that Kynan and Marighal had seated themselves there to greet the other sisters. There was lively talk and laughter, and I saw that the giant's daughters had found a little joy at last. That night they made a feast to celebrate our arrival, and all manner of meats were put in front of us. Pasties and roasts and stews, and cresses from the lake, and fine white bread all were laid out, and a great white cheese was put in front of me which, I am happy to say, I ate sparingly. Unfortunately I did not stop myself from indulging in the thick red wine that was often passed to me.

I am glad that you did not add gluttony to your offences. This is how it is in the house of the Anti-christ. He will tempt you with your greatest weakness 'Better is pain than the abundance which obtains eternal destruction.'

The little man was seated at my right hand and I turned to him to ask if he had made the fine vessel the wine was served in. I saw that he was not joining the joy of the company that night and I asked him what was troubling him.

He answered in his sweet voice, 'I am always troubled when I recall the men who came for Olwen. Not because they destroyed my loving master and paid no recompense, for that will come. But it is nearly a year since they came and they have not been seen here again, yet to think they are not far away fills me with dismay.'

'Why should they trouble you, Grig? They are only a band of warriors, and we have been in the hands of men like them often. With God's grace we are still alive, and may continue.'

'You must see, Selyf, the men who killed Usbathaden were not like the seamen and warriors that use this land of ours like a storehouse. Though these have sometimes plagued us for many generations they have always been satisfied to take our gold and our food. From time to time they have built settlements on our shores, and sometimes they have conquered deep into the heartland, yet they did so only to win honour and gold for themselves. The new men are different, I know, for I have met them before in Frankland and they troubled me. They have scholars who write down everything said at court and keep the words in an archive. They write down who owns what land and who lives on it, and keep that in an archive also. The customs of our ancestors are taken as laws and if they do not suit their purposes they ignore them.

'They are cruel like their Viking fathers, but the Vikings did not try to eat up the minds of the people with pen and ink. The Saxons burn our lands to curb us, but with the hope of doing well for themselves, as a strong child will seize a toy from the hands of a weaker. But these Northmen from Frankland would suck the eyes from your head to know what you have seen. They even ask my brothers how we temper metal and the secrets of our fluxes so that they may make armour as wonderfully strong as ours, and furnish all their warriors with it. I am afraid that by now one of my brothers has told them, for it is our doom to love gold as much as we love our lives, and there is no end to the Northman's prying.'

'This seems to me to be no bad thing, Grig,' I said. 'Such knowledge spread abroad will be of great benefit to mankind. We have a brother who is an apothecary, and he knows of many plants which have healing powers in them. He has written down his practices so that his student may use his healing arts when he is gone to live with God. Is this a thing to fear?'

'You do not stand where I do, Selyf, and look down a long tunnel of years.'

'I know this, and I venerate you before most for your vast knowledge, but I cannot see why you do not wish to see your learning preserved and given to others.'

I fear the wine had affected me, and I was forgetting our Rule. Grig was not angry with my insolence.

'Perhaps it is this shortness of men's lives that drives them to make these records. There have been many generations of men since my brothers and I were born,

I know what he means. These archivists are trying to make written records in order to dispense justice over the ownership of lands. They say it is necessary, but I do not think it is good, for they act as if this sorry world were going to last forever. The only thing that can be said for the practice is that it keeps contention down to a minimum.

and since that time there have been no others born into our family. It is said that we were not born of woman, but that the earth herself bore us as seeds in her body. Our gestation took many years, nor is there a mention of a father in our begetting. When the time came for us to see the light of day my mother tore herself open in the same way she does in the south. In those places she sometimes twists and writhes and gaping holes appear in her body, and trees fall like blades of wheat. One time we were flung out of her womb, not as infants, but as stones which turned soft over a period of years, and turned into ourselves.

This is a legend I have not heard before. It is true that babies have been found in cracks in the earth, but so far as I know they have always grown to full human size.

'Now men have often grubbed about in my mother's womb in search of precious substances — gold and silver, oil and iron — but they did not know the mystery, so my mother crushed them. Only my brothers and I could enter her safely and she gave us her wealth freely. But there are those who make war without end, and now many men will come to tear out my mother's entrails, and they protect themselves from her anger in timber-lined tunnels. They know and care nothing about her mystery.

There is only one lawful mystery, and that is the sacrifice of the Eucharist. All others are unlawful, of that at least we can be sure.

'Men, mighty only in their ignorance, rape her till she sighs and ceases from her generous fertility. What will they do then, the men of words? Will they eat their archives and melt their swords for porridge?

'No, monk, knowledge without understanding is a great evil, and it will destroy those who seek to hoard it. My family alone are fit to carry on the sacrifice of the earth's great mystery, and so it is with other families who teach their children to love what they do before they teach them how to do it.'

By this time the rich wine had heated my brain, and so, dear Father, I have to confess that I spoke of things which should have stayed as close to me as the breath of my body.

'I am not as ignorant as you think I am. When you speak of those who are born to their work as being those fitted to do it I know better than most what you say. Only those of my Rule understand the mystery of the family of God. Yet now we are ridiculed despite the antiquity of our order, and one of the reasons given for rejecting us is that we produce children of our bodies.'

Take care.

The wine and my rattling tongue were both in their full strength as I wagged my foolish head at him and said, 'But consider now, how much more able is a son of mine, raised since birth in a city of God, to love what he is doing? He has taken our ideas of loving service in with his mother's milk. All through his childhood he has learned to keep the commandments, say the offices and sing the psalms as simply as a bird learns to fly. Now, I believe, he is in Orkney where the lady Eithne Cuaransdottir has sent for him. The young men there had started to invoke the demon Othin again, and were fasting and blinding and mutilating themselves in his name, so that they would not be wounded in battle. Men have come from all over the north to join this band, and all go in fear of them, but my son went to fast against them, and to exorcise the demons. He is in terrible danger, not to his body, but to his soul, because the demon has the power to command men's souls to leave their bodies. But this only happens to men who have been recently baptised. His body may even perish, and that will be the end of my line, for he took a vow of virginity when he was young. But I rejoice for his spirit is as it has been since the day he was born — pure, and loving God.'

And, wretch that I am, after this wicked, idle boasting I began to weep for the son I have vowed to disown.

O, father, I am not, I wish that I were! I always strive to be as you describe me, but you have done ill to speak of me like this. Do not weep for me, I am perplexed, but not in despair.

'Come now, monk,' said the smith, 'this wine we drink is thick and strong and has made a fool of many more used to it than you. Come to my closet where I have potions that will remove these bad effects. Tomorrow, forewarned, you will be less generous to yourself, but tonight you drank it as if it was the thin, sour stuff they serve in your guest houses.'

So saying he picked me up and carried me out like a child in his arms. Everyone there laughed, and I burn with shame at the memory, but it is what I deserve, and truly it was an act of charity, for I doubt if I could have walked through the door. I missed the last office of the day.

The medicine Grig gave me gave me some relief and I woke with a clear head for the midnight office. I read extra psalms in penance for the office I missed, peering at my psalter by the faint light of a candle while the dwarf slept at my back. I had just finished when

The second day in the giant's hall.

Marighal opened the door to our bed. With her finger to her mouth she signed to me to follow her silently and led the way into the heart of the stronghold. As we wound our way through the passages I tried to ask her where we were going, but she shook her head and pointed to the places all around where the others were sleeping.

Finally she stopped and lifted the hanging over a low doorway. I passed inside and found a low, wide room with nothing in it, only a bed at the far side. In the far wall another low door led to a brightly lit room beyond. A woman lay in the bed and her face was almost as pale as the linen sheet which covered her to the chin. Her eyes were sunk in black shadows, and her nose was pinched as fine as a quill. At her neck she wore a wooden cross. Marighal led me to the side of the bed, left me there without a word, and went into the other room.

I spoke to the woman on the bed, saying, 'Woman, if you know of any crimes in your heart you must speak now, for it is clear to me that you are dying.'

'Indeed, sir,' she whispered, 'I know it, and I am glad, for I have nothing in this world to live for. I will be happy to make my confession, and I beg you to hear me and absolve me.'

'It is not within my power to give you penance. I am not a priest. Only God can do that now, but I entreat you to be careful to give a full account of yourself, so that when you come to meet your Judge nothing will have slipped by unnoticed.'

'Can you do nothing for me, sir?' she said, and began to make a coughing sound, for she wanted to weep but had no strength left. 'I have terrible sins in my heart and they weigh heavily there. Already I can see the flames of the eternal fire glowing, and I can smell the hot metal of the instruments of torment. Can you not lift my sins from me, so that when I die my soul will fly free?'

'If you have sinned, woman, and that in spite of God's great gift of life, there is nothing I can do. You have rejected His gift of grace and mercy of your own free will, but let us examine your heart together, for we may find something there which will return you to grace.'

The woman was silent and I began to think she had slipped away. Suddenly she roused herself and with the last of her strength she said, 'I was married to a charcoal burner in the forest. He was kind to me and I bore him sons to help him with his work. One day the giant came by our house and saw my sons playing by the door.

'Those boys are strong and well made,' he said to my husband, 'their mother must be a fine woman.' I was pleased to hear him speak well of me for he had been my father's master also. The giant came back to visit us many times, and sometimes he came when my husband was not at home. I told my husband about this but he said that his master was not to be treated like ordinary men, and that I should be pleasant to him. I was glad to do so, for the giant has a lot of stories to tell about foreign countries, and it lightened my days to have him talking to me as I worked. He told me about his fine great hall that no man had ever entered.'

She closed her eyes and tears ran out of them unheeded. Her voice went on, even quieter.

'I have never known any man but my husband, and I was married in my fourteenth year I did not know a man could look at you and turn your belly to water. But the giant changed that. He was so big and so well made, and when he came close to me I saw that his eyes had green flecks in them. Then one day he came to the house when my husband had taken the boys fishing with him. The master said he wanted me to go and stay with him in the stronghold, and that it would not be a sin to do so because he was the master of all these lands and had a right to lie with me. My legs melted beneath me and I fainted, and he lifted me up and kissed me. I said nothing, but I leaned my head on his shoulder, and he brought me here.'

Even so lust betrays us into sin and shame. It is little wonder to me that she can see the fires of purgation.

The poor creature's voice was so faint that I had to put my ear to her mouth to hear it. From the room beyond I heard the sound of a baby crying, and the woman's eyes opened.

You should not have been so near a woman who has just delivered a child. They are certainly most polluting at that point.

'They will not let me see the baby,' she said, more strongly now, 'I am sure this is part of God's punishment to me already for the sin I committed in having him.'

'Woman,' I said, 'your sins are slight. You must not be afraid. You are a victim of lust, not its agent. The man who took you from your husband's house was a sorcerer, and you could not have stopped him once his desire for

I hope you found some means to cleanse yourself. You may be sure that this is part of the plan to destroy you.

you had been kindled, unless you had gone to a priest for his special help.'

'No, Father, you must see, I wanted him. And when he took me for the first time the pain it caused me pleased me. I was proud because he had chosen me out of all the women in the forest, and I was strong enough to take him. I prayed to God that I would be the one to make him a son at last. I have had many months to weigh this in my heart and I know what I have done.

'I have had to wait longer for this child than for my other sons, and this is part of my punishment. Once the giant had taken me and torn me, and he was sure that I was with child he locked me in this room and has not come near me since. In all that time I have not seen daylight. This is a comfortable prison, and I have had some of the daughters for company, but they would not let me out for fear that I would lose the baby. This is the worst part — the child is born and I am dying and I will never see him. My other children will have learned to curse my name. I am sure only those in Hellfire know what I am suffering.'

'Do not talk of hell and its torments — that is your fate or not as only God wills it. Be sure that He is a loving and a merciful father to His foolish children, and He knows your suffering. Now you must think only of His grace and the wonders of His creation, and be at peace for your last hour.'

Again the child's cry came from the other room, and the woman turned her face towards the sound.

'They will not let me see him,' she said, then her eyes dimmed and she gave her last breath. I anointed her with some of the holy water from my scrip, and raised my hands over her, praying that she would be born again into God's loving kindness.

'Poor creature,' I said, 'your sins are indeed heavy, but there are those whose sins are beyond measure, and who will never rise from the fiery pit, though they wait a thousand years.'

Then I went through to the other room to give the newly-born child a blessing. It lay in Marighal's arms, and Evabyth stood beside her. I saw that it was a girl-child, nor was there anything of the demon in its pretty limbs and body, unless it was that the child was stouter than most of the new babies I have seen. She

The woman is foolish but she has the grace to see that her sin is pride as well as lust.

So this is how the giant begets his children. At least we know that the sisters are not born of an incestuous union.

Selyf, you are God's own optimist! I hope your charity is repaid.

was plump and rosy and white like a child a few weeks old.

'Is the child well?' I asked, 'for she looks healthy, or has the struggle her mother had to bring her into the world damaged her also?'

'She is very well,' said Marighal, 'I kept her from her mother's sight for I did not wish the poor creature to know she had failed to get a boy. We always destroy our mothers when we are born, though we never come to any harm ourselves.'

'Every time one of us is brought back to the light we are so strong and big that the woman who bears us is torn like a tree struck by lightning,' said Evabyth, 'yet there was never any lack of women coming here. They were pleased to try and bear a son for my father, though news was abroad that many women did not survive the first mating.'

I saw that blood was flowing down Marighal's cheeks, but Evabyth was less compassionate.

'It was truly pride that brought them here,' she said, 'each one was sure that she could do what no other women had done, but in all the centuries we have lived here none ever did, and now none ever will.'

'Do not say that it was pride, sister,' said Marighal, 'for I have seen the fear in their faces when they came to the hall, and spoken to them during their confinement, and I am sure that most of them accepted the chance of death with true humility.'

I find it very hard to believe that humility was present in such a situation.

The child in Marighal's arms stirred and opened her eyes, and they were as black as sloes. They looked at me, not as infant's do, with simplicity and ignorance, and soon look away, but with a knowing, fixed stare. And then the creature smiled and I saw that her mouth was full of little sharp white teeth.

I drew away and felt in my wallet for the flask of holy water, and, drawing it out, I said, 'Do you wish me to baptise the infant now?' but my cunning was in vain for Marighal answered, 'You taught me that it was misguided to baptise the newly born, for they are ignorant and therefore cannot be sinful.'

Were you hoping for exorcism?

'This is true,' I said, 'but your family have lived so long out of God's sight that it may be necessary.'

'Indeed, you may have the right of it, Selyf. If you wish to bless our poor sister here I would welcome it.

172

*It does not replace a
mother's love — it exceeds it!*

St Brigid preserve us!

*You forgot that the one who
is the instrument of our rites
must be fitting before they can
be effective.*

*Do not forget, however, that
in the life of our holy St
Nynia there is the story of an
infant who speaks in order to
name his father. By this means
justice was done, so such
a manifestation is not always
evil.*

We all grow up without the joy of a mother's love in this
house, and I know that only God's love can replace it.'
And she held the child towards me.

Then something happened which caused me such
fear I almost let the flask of holy water drop, for the
child opened her mouth and spoke to us.

'Why have you summoned me?' she said, 'I told you
that I was weary of this flesh, and that I would not return
again. Why have I been brought here?'

At that I was sure that at last I had found the evil
spirit of the hall. It was clear to me that the giant's soul
had taken possession of the child, so I at once stepped
forward and sprinkled her with the holy water. In haste
I called on the living God who reigns, Father, Son and
Holy Ghost, and I was sure that would be the end of it,
but nothing happened. I can find no words to tell you
of the dread that filled me then. The demon neither
screamed in agony, nor did it burn, nor fly out of the
window. The unholy child lay on her sister's arm and
smiled at me.

'Look, Mari,' she said, 'it is a Christian man. What
is he doing here? Father says they are all foolish creatures.'

'He is a good man, and a holy man,' said Marighal,
'and he has just baptised you. He is doing it to help you
to be happy, so bear with his actions in patience.'

'But why is he so pale, sister? He lookes as if he had
fever on him, for the sweat shines on his face.'

'He is tired and in a strange place, and he drank too
much wine yesterday. He will be better in the morning.'

Then my courage gave out and I fled from the room
to return, I do not remember how, to where Grig lay.
Yet when I saw that strange little face, neither young
nor old, lying on the pillow, I could not return to the
bed, but lay trembling beside it till dawn. At times I
groaned aloud, for I was in an agony of heart and
soul, and I could find no relief. I was tormented by a
vision of the infant as she spoke to me and of the lady
Marighal, whom I had known to be a woman without
stain, and both seemed to be trying to speak to me in
vain. I struggled to hear them and to understand what
they said, but something deafened me.

Then, terrible to behold, I saw at last the master of
the house, who spoke in foul blasphemy and said, 'Who

is this that darkens counsel by words without knowledge? Gird up your loins now like a man for I will ask you these things and you will answer me.'

But I could by no means answer him, for my tongue had been torn from my mouth. He came up to me again and said, 'Where is the road where light dwells, and where does darkness live? Do you know because you were born then? Or because you have lived a great number of years?' And I still could not speak because my mouth had been filled with wax.

Again he said, 'Behold God exalts by his own power; who teaches like him? Who has enjoined him his way, or who can say to him — you have wrought iniquity?' I even tried to pull my mouth open with my fingers, but I found my hands were too weak to grip.

Then all at once I found myself seated on the floor beside the bed with Grig lying in it, and I wept. I examined my soul, saying, 'I have kept the law and followed it all the days of my life, nor have I ever sought anything beyond the limits of my order; I have not stored up wealth for myself; I did not keep my wife beside me; I have not sought the councils of the powerful to sit puffed up at their side.

'Why has God brought me to this? Better for me by far had been the blows of the warriors, and the pain of my body before death. Beside this agony that would be easy to bear, but God has laid this great task on me. Who are these creatures I have found, and what are they to Him? I have no fear for my body, but my soul itself is in pain. I feel it could be ripped from my body. What will become of me? What am I to do?'

Then, at last, came daylight and the second hour. A merciful calm filled me as I said the words, 'I will sing aloud of your mercy in the morning, for it has been my defence and refuge in the day of my trouble.'

Then there came over me a great longing to see God's light growing in the dawn sky. I found my way to the top of the great hall, and went into the garret of the women so that I could look out to the horizon. A still white sea of mist covered the plain and hid the forest, but sunlight was touching the tops of the mountains with a ruddy glow. I longed to be free of that grim stronghold, and looked down to the yard to see if the rest of the household were stirring.

The demon quotes the Almighty. Adso warns us of such blasphemy. Job XXXVIII. 'Therefore I have uttered that I understood not; things too wonderful for me which I knew not.'

Perhaps you did not keep her by you, but you had dealings with her after you became a presbyter in defiance of our Rule.

174

Below me I saw a car with two white oxen yoked to it. As I watched I saw the women of the house appear carrying a corpse in a winding sheet which they placed carefully on the cart. Over this they draped a mantle of deepest black with heavy gold embroidery at the corners, and in the centre a picture of the sun. I could see that their blood of grief ran down their faces. They stepped back out of sight below me and, without a driver, the ox-cart passed out through the gates of the stronghold, crossed the plain and disappeared into the silent mist.

I returned to my place and as I walked along passages I meditated on my trust in God and said to myself, 'If it is His will that these creatures should be destroyed, then He will give me the means to do so; if not, then I must help them to find their way to the light, for I am sure they are suffering in their ignorance.'

Soon Marighal came to me and asked me kindly how I was faring. 'You were very sickly last night, Selyf,' she said, 'and you ran away from us like a wounded beast. I was afraid that you had taken a fever. Have you any fever now, or are you in pain? Tell me, for my sister Edain is a very skilled apothecary, and she can help you.'

'You are most generous, my lady, but it is nothing. I am sure my sickness was only due to strong drink. I am not accustomed to the rich wine you served, and I greedily gave myself more than my poor stomach could hold. I have paid for my greed with affliction, but if I rest a little now I will soon be fit again.'

'I am glad to hear that, Selyf, and if you have fulfilled your duties for now, will you come and break your fast?'

I went with her to the kitchen where warmth and light and a little food lifted my spirits. Our beloved St Maelruin was truly enlightened when he said that too much fasting is a wicked indulgence. The news of the wine's assault on me had travelled, and I was left alone for most of the morning. But soon after the middle of the day I looked up from my psalter to see my lady smiling at me, and I trembled to see that she was carrying her baby sister. The infant was smiling at me also, and Mari placed the child in my arms.

'This is my sister Essyllt who was restored to us last night. She is the sister I have always held dearest, and I beg you to tell her of the great wisdom and love of your

Is not this unholy grief evidence that they are outside God's law. Perfect man is perfectly happy; the greater the misery the greater the sin.

In Saxony and Frankland the ox-cart is reserved for those of royal blood.

Fasting is to chasten the flesh in order to enrich the soul, but some do it in order to enjoy visions of the happiness to come before their due time. We follow the path of white martyrdom, not to leave the flesh but to prove how unimportant it is. We are not seeking misery but freedom from the misery the clotted flesh brings us. The sinless fellowship, and show her the ways of a Christian. Since she is new to this life she may grow into your family as her body grows.'

'Truly, my lady,' I replied, 'I do not think I can teach her any wisdom — it is rather that she should teach me, for I have much to learn here. If you urgently wish to leave her in my care for a while I will be glad to talk to her, though my understanding is poor.'

'Your humility is something we must all copy. But you must not deny your skill in comforting others, and showing them the meaning of love. Teach the child and I will send the others to come and hear you also.'

She left us then and the child tried to sit upright. I was happy to see that she was enough like a normal child to be too weak to do so.

Then she spoke to me, saying, 'Where have you come from, and who are your family?'

'My kindred are not important. I am a companion of God, and must serve Him all my days.'

'Who is your god? What does he do that makes you call him god?'

I answered her with what was uppermost in my thoughts, thus, 'It was He that laid the foundation of the earth and laid the measure of it and marked it out with a cord. Then He laid the cornerstone and fastened it to the firmament. And He shut up the sea with doors, and the clouds He took for a garment and the night for a swaddling band. He has commanded the morning and caused the dayspring to know his place. He opened the gates of death and saw the doors of the shadow of death.'

'What does he look like, this god of yours?' the child asked eagerly, 'Does he have sons and daughters?'

'He has a Son who is yet as old as He is and is like him in all ways.'

'Is he immortal also — the son of God?'

'The Son is not younger than the Father, nor the Father older than the Son.'

'Has he been fostered by many?'

'The Father, Son and Spirit are not divided.'

'Where may I find him, this God who will not let his son be fostered?'

man is truly happy.

Job once again.

Was it your intention to use St Padraig's catechism or did the unholy child abuse you with it?

'He is everywhere, from the springs of the sea to the highest rocks of the mountains and even in the firmament above them. And He sent His Son to be fostered once, by a mortal family. But while He lived on earth as a man He was taken prisoner and put to death by the foul Jews who lived near Him.'

'Oh, indeed,' said the infant, 'and I was hoping he might be kindred to us, for I have not heard of another family who could open the gates of death before today.'

'Why do you say 'another' family that could open the gates of death?' I asked, and my heart began to leap within me, 'It is not fitting to claim kinship with God.'

'Why should that be? Once in the forest I heard Christians talking, and they all spoke of themselves as the children of God, and Mari said you do so, too.'

'But that is not the same as calling God kindred, as if He were king of a country two day's walk away.'

'But you and your kind always talk about the kingdom of God. Where is it, then, if not nearby?'

'Truly it is nearby, but it can only be reached by the death of the body. Now tell me, who in your family has opened the gates of death in the same way that God our Father did when he ransomed his only Son?'

'Why all of us!' cried the child, and when I started, she went on, 'did you not know we are all immortal?'

Abomination! St Brigid and St Thenew pray for us. These creatures are truly vile. Why did you stay there, Selyf?

There was no guile in her face as she said it so I shook my head. Happily she explained, 'We daughters of the giant have lived many times and our spirits are many centuries old. The bodies we inhabit are mortal and we generally must leave them long before the natural death of the human overtakes them. If we do not, the decay of the body may decay our soul also so that it is scattered through the firmament at death and we cannot become alive again.

'The last time I died I did not wish to return at last and so I stayed in the body. I felt the old age settling on my bones and bending them, sucking the blood out of my muscles and weakening them and driving furrows across my face. I lived on with all that pain and the misery of knowing that I could no longer dance and leap and run, for the old body hung on to life by a thread of steel. It is indeed a very terrible thing to be human and to endure all that misery in such a short lifetime. Humans are very courageous.'

'We are consoled everywhere that though our life may be full of misery, when we pass through the gates of death we will live forever in a blissful state.'

'How can this be so?' said the child, amazed. 'I have stood at the doors of death's hall many times and I have never seen a blissful city.'

'Ah, my poor child, I fear that since you are a child of God's adversary the sight of the celestial city will be denied to you for ever. But do not despair, for if you will accept baptism and die at last into God, you may be reborn into His grace. God's mercy is infinite, and He will accept the return of any sinner to His fold, if he repents.'

'I did not know that my father had any adversary,' said the child frowning, 'apart from the humans who tried to attack now and then. Evabyth told me that father was killed by some strangers, but I cannot believe that, for I can feel his presence close to me in the stronghold. Nor did I meet him at deathgate when I last waited there. No, truly he has not gone down to death's hall, but is waiting for his destiny close at hand even now.'

'Child,' I begged her, 'be sure of what you say, for your chance of eternal bliss may hang upon your words.'

Suddenly the terrible child sat upright and said, 'Do not you be foolish! You tell me to be careful, and I am already like one who is walking on dewdrops!

'I am newly reborn, and have not had time to learn everything my family has done since I left them, but I am certain that strange things are afoot. I wished to be free of human flesh for all time, and before, such wishes have always been respected, yet I am recalled. Our father, whom we always knew to be invincible has been destroyed with scarcely a struggle. Worst of all, Marighal has committed the appalling crime of using our death-trance for an alien purpose. In the course of that dreadful act she has created another being whose nature we cannot begin to know. Mari assures us that she acted in good faith and that her creation is benign, but her likeness goes about the earth uncontrolled by her. Nor is that the end of Mari's plans to make new things happen, I am sure of that, and that is all I am sure of.

What have you said? An abomination like this and a female child, yet you talk to her of salvation!

Be on your guard, Sebyf!

The woman Marighal has other plans. We must know what they are.

178

'Even my father's spirit is confounded and is waiting to see what will happen. And you tell me to be sure of my words. I tell you truly, it would be easier to be sure of the very hour the harvest will be brought in, or the number of salmon who will run up the river this year!'

I could not deny that she had some wisdom, this child of terrible knowledge. She asked me many more questions about our faith, and while there were times her innocent blasphemy chilled my blood, I found no more malice in her than in any other pagan I have led along the hard road. I became sure that if any baneful thing lived in that hall it was not in the heart of the infant. To my very great joy the other women of the stronghold came to the corner of the hall we sat in, and stopped to listen. They, too, asked questions and seemed to find comfort in the answers, but it seemed to me that they were not as knowing as the infant.

Ah, you have been seduced by the attentions of these women and the devices of their father.

At the meal that night I sat beside the smith again, and he smiled to see me water my wine liberally.

'Do you think you will be less afflicted by the wine if you water it?' he asked.

'By St Maelruin, I hope so, Grig, for I did not love the sickness that came with strong wine.'

'I can believe that, though that sickness is something my kind have always been spared. But I must warn you that some wines, so far from losing their power when they are mixed, become even quicker to take men's cleverness from them, and turn them into stumbling fools after only a few cups.'

'I have heard something like this, but I wonder how it comes about.'

'I am not sure, monk, but I reflected upon it once and I thought that it might be due to the same process that makes an alloy of metal stronger than its pure form.'

'Your words do not say much to me, for I know nothing of metal working, other than the few lines I heard from Marighal.'

'The argument is made of twisted yarn, but if you will listen to me, I will try and make it unravel.'

'I beg of you to temper the wind for the shorn lamb and keep my slow wits from a tangle,' I said, and he spoke on in his fluting voice.

'It is said by some that the material of all things that grow out of the earth can be found in the earth in the same way that flame, smoke and ashes grow out of wood. But if this were true, when soil is crumbled, finely divided particles of plants and grains and leaves ought to be visible, and they are not; nor, when sticks are broken, do we find in them ashes and smoke and tiny hidden fires. Therefore one sort of thing is not intermingled with another in this way, but in all things there must be a substance which is a mixture of invisible seeds common to many sorts. In wood, therefore, there is a multitude of seeds of heat which start to burn when they are concentrated by rubbing, and not otherwise.

'In the case of wine with water, it must be obvious to you that water has the seeds of wine in it and vice versa so that when they are brought together in a cup sometimes they make each other stronger, depending on the type of wine-seeds there. More than this, there is the evidence of the breeding of animals, although the laws that govern mating are harder to discover.'

'Grig, your mind travels in paths as twisted as a snake, yet I think I follow you. Now tell me, how might this seed-substance of yours affect the breeding of animals more than the seed which is easily seen.'

'The truth of what I say is shown to us clearly by the fact that from the same litter we will get bitches and dogs, nor will their gender determine their temper. I had a bitch once who would outrun any dog in the pack. This was a mystery to me until I saw that each gender, male and female, must carry the seed-substance of the other in it.'

He paused, and I said at once, 'This is not fitting conversation for one of my vocation. Male and female were created separately by the Almighty, nor should we confuse one with the other, for it is a blasphemy against the order He has created.'

'I am truly sorry, Selyf, I had not meant to offend you. I must confess that once my mind starts hunting like this it is hard to beat off the quarry.'

He stopped talking for a long while then and I tried to tell him about my life at home. Suddenly he began again, 'Consider, now, does not a man have paps on his breast, and does that not speak to us of anything but that the woman-seed in him is showing itself?'

'I have no answer for you, Grig. I am not learned, but I do know this — there are some of my calling

Now the dwarf is looking into mysteries which only the wise and the good may fathom.

Surely now he is talking about the essences of things which we know are present but are unchanging and invisible. Combining them in a vessel may change their outward appearances but this is merely contingent — a fact of number. Or is another substance with yet another essence produced by this action? I wish I had had more time to spend on mathematics. Does this explain how it comes about that there are male and female?

180

True, but these are by no means fitting oblations. We should no more accept them than we should accept a blinded child.

who have sought to remove the distraction of fleshly lust from themselves. To further this end they have removed their parts of manhood, and made themselves less than full men. By your argument the woman in them should have broken out at once and breasts and beardless faces should have been the result. Yet their beards have continued and their bodies are still those of men. True, some boys are emasculated by their family before they reach full manhood to make sure the monas-- tery will accept them, and they have indeed grown up beardless and with high voices. Nevertheless, they are by no means women.'

'Your evidence is good, monk, and I do not see how I might answer you. Temptations of that sort do not trouble my kind, and I have not come to any conclusion what my gender means. But consider this — was not the first woman of all made from the body of a man? That is in your scripture.'

'Indeed, she was.' I answered, and I had a moment of enlightenment, 'But it was also she who brought sin into the world, and in both of these she was unique. We must be glad of that, for our afflictions are already hard to bear. But you must see that you are answered, for this woman with man-seed in her was the source of endless grief to her kin. Surely her unlawful nature was the source of all her disobedience.'

Are you criticising the work of the Creator? You must remember that our Remedy and Salvation was also born of a woman. The laws are His to change as he wills.

'Then how is it you people claim that she was free to choose between the good and the evil?'

I had no answer for this, but before I could recall the answers that were given to Godescalc, Grig spoke again.

'Come now, Selyf, I am not trying to tempt you from your faith. Nor would I rest easy with myself if I did. I am only showing you the fruits of my meditation, for I have had many years in which to ripen them, and there have been few to whom they would mean anything before you came. You agree with me at least that, regardless of their gender, offspring will show traces of both their parents in their nature?'

'How can I deny it? All around us we have the daugh- ters of the giant who are women, yet some have their father's strength in them.'

Those mothers were distracted by lust and pride.

'That is well said. They have the best of both their parents in their nature. Not only do they have their father's strength, but they have their mothers' fine, self-sacrificing nature. It is a great pity that they must now die and pass from the world.'

'Is it true, then, that their father's death leaves them without their immortality?'

'It is — they will cease with this generation. With the death of their father they are no longer necessary to turn his wrath aside from mortals. Many, many times they have stepped between him and his victims, but that is all over now.'

As he said this he sighed deeply, and to comfort him I said, 'Be sure that this will only be the end of their fleshly life. Now they will be freed by death to take their places in the Holy City.'

'I am a fool to talk of these things.' he said, 'All my studies are over. I am alone in the world now that my master is dead, and I am growing weary. I will not be bearing this life for much longer.'

'That must be as God wills,' I told him, 'You cannot die unless He wills it, or else you will send yourself to the pit for eternity. I am a short-lived human and so spend all my life closer to death than you do, therefore I have the last word on this. You must heed me about this as I have heeded you on dog-breeding.'

He smiled at this and said, 'I do believe you, o monk of little years.' he said, 'So although I may long to return to my mother's body and leave my seed substance in her, I will not take my departure yet, but wait until you give me leave.'

After this we both became very merry. Although the wine had some work to do on me, he did not have to carry me up the stairs that night. I rose at midnight to read the office, and all the while I did so I felt that someone stood at my back. I read the words, 'in God is my salvation and my glory; the rock of my strength and my refuge; trust in him at all times,' and at the sound of my voice they retreated.

Again that night I did not return to the bed in case I slept past the second hour. Instead I sat in the corner, but at once I fell into a sleep, and in that sleep I was carried to a far and terrible place.

In my dream I found myself in a fair, sunny land. Around me there grew trees with great, yellow fruit, such as the women had woven in their pictures. I was

You would reduce all sacrifice to vainglory by this comparison.

I accept that this is true of Marighal, but what of the others? There is no evidence of it amongst them.

Tu es, Domine, inhuminater caliginum. What man is there alive who shall not see death?

182

Olives? I saw these growing in the Roman Campagna.

Attis? Is that what he is talking about?

part of a procession winding through a grove of such trees, and on to another where the trees were stunted with pruning, and bore big, green berries. We passed through this grove also and I saw that we were going towards a dark, gloomy forest where pine trees grew tall. I looked at the people in the procession with me and saw that they were all men, for they each had long beards and shaven heads. Yet there was a scandal, for although most of them wore red, monkish robes, some had wigs on their heads, with the hair braided before and behind like the daughters of the giant. They also carried masks with faces painted in white and pink and a sweet smile painted on the full red lips. I turned away with disgust from this sight and saw that we had entered the forest. Now all I could hear was the music of the instruments the men carried — wailing flutes, and pounding drums and the tinny clashing of cymbals. The heat among the trees could smother the breath in your body, yet all around me the men began to dance and to spin like twigs in a whirlpool.

The procession was slowing down and I saw that those ahead of me were stopping in a clearing. The space was nearly full and the music faded away to an unceasing drum beat, and the men kept spinning in time to the sound. When I got into the clearing myself I saw that the men had gathered round a gigantic tree that rose far, far into the air above the rest of the forest. To its smooth trunk they had fixed coloured ribbons, some of which had been wound round the tree's grey sides many times. The steady ceaseless beat of the drum filled the burning air. All around me the men had given themselves up to rapture and their eyes had rolled up into their heads till only the white showed, and foam was speckling their beards with white. Some, mostly those disguised as women, were still dancing and circling round endlessly with their eyes closed and their masks raised to heaven.

I was terrified at this hellish ritual, and tried to run, but my feet had struck roots in the ground. All I could do was stand still and watch all these proceedings with dismay. Then, horror beyond horror — my heart darkens still as I remember it — the men disrobed and some of them went about the crowd with little black axes. I can scarcely bring myself to write about it, for they mutilated

their colleagues with the axes and cut off their manly
parts. Nor did they stop at simple emasculation, but I
cannot write any more. I am distraught to think that the
human heart can conceive the hideous woundings that I
saw that day.

Again all the men took up the beat of the drum and
filled the glade with their grim, wordless chant. I could
see nothing but their swaying backs, and I prayed to
the living God to release me from that place. But there
was more yet to come. The chanting grew louder, and
louder, till all at once a voice rose, louder than the rest,
screaming in terror. I looked to where the voice was
coming from and I saw a monk pointing upwards and
shouting. We all looked to where he pointed.

High above the treetops we saw approaching the form
of a gigantic woman. She was so tall and so massive that
as she walked through the trees they broke against her
knees. With each step she came a hundred paces nearer.
At last she stopped and looked down at the crowd in the
clearing, and though she wore a long red veil over her
face I could see that she was weeping. Truly, tears of
blood ran down her face and rained red on the forest.
She spoke at last, and her voice was like the roar of ten
winds yoked together.

'No, my children, no. Do not afflict yourselves like
this in my name. It does me no honour and it displeases
me greatly. It would be better for you to take my other
lessons and leave your bodies whole.'

With these words she bent over, and, taking the top
of the ribbon-decked pine in one hand, she raised the
other high. In it there was a great, black axe with a
double curved blade. The men around me shrieked in
terror at the sight, and I found myself shrieking also as
the axe swung down. Roaring it descended and it cut off
the mighty tree at the root. Then darkness swallowed
me and the vision was swept away.

Grig was squatting beside me and shaking me.

'Wake up, Selyf! Answer me. What devils have been
visiting you in your sleep? You have been shouting like
a man in torment.'

'Ah, Grig, thank you, thank you. I am happy that
you woke me. That was a terrible sight. Forgive me
for disturbing your sleep. I have just seen things — I
cannot talk about.'

I was reading Catullus in Rome when I learned about such as these. They called themselves the Galli and claimed to come from the shores of the Deucalidon sea. But they were suppressed centuries ago. It is said they worshipped a tree as the god Attis, who, like Tammuz, was dismembered. These are the abominable rites of Cybele Theotokos. I was sure there was pollution here. She of the hair. She of the axe! She demands such mutilations of her followers.

What other lessons? She makes her devotees perform these filthy rites.

184

Indeed it is!

He said nothing more, for my distress was written on my face in tears. He put me in the bed and fetched me a reviving drink. I could not bring myself to read the office at dawn, for I felt myself defiled by that foul vision, and some time would be needed before I would be worthy to approach a holy act.

'Surely this is a punishment,' I said to myself, 'for I have not yet confronted the forces I was sent against,' and I resolved not to let the sun set again until I had found the Adversary.

After I had broken fast I went in search of the king. I hoped he might have some light to shed on my darkness. I found him in the stable attending to the horses there and he was singing like a boy. When he saw me coming he frowned and did not speak.

'Well, my lord,' I began, 'I have not spoken to you since that miraculous morning. What news is there with you?'

'Nothing bad, monk, although my heart is troubled for the woman I left behind me. I am sorry I left her defenceless and I pray she is not ill-used.'

'Then, sir, why do you not return home? I am sure the lady Marighal would not detain you against your wish.'

'Indeed she does not, it is rather that I am not willing to leave her. It has been a long time since I saw her and we have had a lot to talk about. Also the lady wishes to have a child of me.' And so saying he walked round to the other side of the horse. I had to run round the creature to speak to him, and you know how little love I have for them.

This must be prevented. By no means should this tribe go on to another generation.

'A child, sir? By your leave, how is that possible? The lady at your house is barren, and has always been so.'

'Perhaps, but that is not to say that Marighal is also. As for myself, there are no few brats running round to testify to my manliness.' His cheeks were red as he said this, but I had to continue.

'But, sir, my lady Marighal is past the age when most women cease from bearing.'

'She is not yet past bearing and her family has a vigour greater than mere men. If she wishes to bear a child she will do so, in spite of difficulties. They have recalled the sister Essyllt who is wise in matters of childbirth, and with her as midwife I am sure everything will go well.'

'Sir, the lady is your wife, and if you agree she should bear a child, so be it. I only wonder how my lady will bear and suckle a human child when she has never seen a mother's loving skill at work. Some knowledge must be acquired to raise a child properly.'

'This is true,' said the king, 'but I am sure that she has seen enough in her time. Even though she and her sisters have never been cared for by a mother, there are some things the heart knows before it is taught them. You say this is the case with God's love, or have I heard wrong?'

'That is what some of us hold to be true, sir. God's grace will make us know things which no man has taught us, and it may be that a mother's love is similarly known.'

I fell silent, for it was on my tongue to say that if the women were daughters of the Adversary there would be no grace in them. I knew that would not please the king.

'Well, sir,' I began again, 'if you are sharing the lady's bed, that is the end of it.

'What are you saying, monk?' exclaimed the king, his face red now with anger, 'Do you take my lady for a whore? Do you think she takes a man to bed for pleasure? She knows the day and the hour when she will conceive and it will be tonight and only tonight that I will go in to her. And that will be the end of it. I will return and see to my harvest and make sure it is protected from thieves.'

His lust is contained, thanks be to God.

'But, sir, I beg you to consider. Is it a good thing that this family should continue into another generation? You have told me with your own mouth of the abominations the giant committed. It is not fitting his seed should remain on the earth.'

'Whatever my master may have done to others, he was always a loving father to myself. He showed me much good by his example, and if sometimes he treated me harshly it was only because he was teaching me a grim trade. Look at this!'

He does not see the evil. Grace has been withheld from him, and he cannot understand the wickedness around him.

He opened his shirt and showed me a pitiful scar. It ran round the top of his arm as if it had been almost cut off at the shoulder.

Christ have mercy upon him.

'My foster-father did this to me one day in training. After he had done it he bound it himself. No mother's

186

hands could have been more gentle, then he watched beside me for days and nights until I returned from the borders of death. Surely such tenderness is part of God's bounty?'

'I believe all good comes from God,' was my only answer.

'Very well, I hope I do not hear any more of that nonsense. Marighal, on her own merit, is a fine woman, and I love her. But understand that it is only from loyalty to her and her family that I am going to lie with her. The fires of lust died down in me many years ago.'

'And what of your baptismal promises?'

'When I made my vows as a Christian I swore to love God and to keep His commandments, and to love my fellow man. That is all.'

'Did you not swear also to hate God's enemies?'

'I did so, and whenever I have met them I have stood fast against them. But there are no enemies of God in this hall — only those who do not know His laws.'

'The giant described Christianity as foolishness. Surely that is enmity?'

'It is not. I described it so myself until my sweet wife — who is, you recall, of this family — pleaded with me to listen to the bishop and consider his words. I did it for her, and thanks to her my eyes were opened. Yet until that day I wallowed in ignorance. Am I the enemy of God?'

'Truly you are not, sir. But these women return from death in defiance of God's law and in blasphemous emulation of the Anointed One. Surely that is sorcery and wickedness?'

'I was taught by the bishop that human kind must try to conquer death and deny the flesh. It seems to me that Mari and her sisters have merely travelled further along that road. They willingly abandon the flesh and become pure spirit, which is more than any Christian can do.'

'The giant took women and destroyed them at his whim. Is this not a crime against humankind, and therefore against God?'

'He was never known to take a woman who was not eager and happy to be with him. Do you deny him the right to fatherhood when you did not deny it to yourself?'

'Indeed, sir, I have no arguments to stand against yours. It would take one of greater faith and learning

But they did not do it to approach closer to God. They did it in pursuit of fleshly existence. To leave the deceiving world of sense and to free the soul to go and meet her bridegroom is the greatest joy we know this side of death, and very few achieve it. Voluntarily to take foul, clotted flesh is to choose to grovel in the midden when a bed with fresh linen is waiting for you — no!

than I to point out the evil to you, and I am just a simple monk. I am afraid, for these people stand so far beyond the natural order of God's world I am sure they must be His wicked Adversary. I hoped that as my fellow human you might be able to help me get to the heart of the matter.'

'Monk, if their strangeness is the only evidence against these good people, then your argument is in a sorry state. There is nothing I can do to help you, for I see no evil here and have received none at their hands.'

With that he strode out of the stable. I raised my hands in prayer and abased myself even in the straw, saying, 'Almighty Father, Sweet Lord, whose goodness endures eternally, hear now the cries of your most humble servant for I am now beyond all help but Thine. I have searched diligently for the evil I was sent here to combat, and I have found only unstinting generosity and unfailing kindness. I have seen no fault in the actions of these people. Nothing, indeed, speaks but of hearts overflowing with good will toward God and man. I can do nothing more but wait and hope for a clear sign from Your hand. If the task is truly Yours, then You will find the means to let me accomplish it, Who Reigns Forever.'

Deception is the first skill of the Antichrist.

For the rest of the morning I kept myself apart and walked on the plain meditating. After the sixth hour the lady Marighal found me and asked after me kindly.

Omnipotens aeterne deus, qui nobis magnatia fecisti, sexta hora crucem ascendisti et tenebras mundi inluminasti.

'You seem troubled, Selyf,' she said, 'and I am sorry. I have not taken time to talk to you alone since the day of your arrival. I am sure there has been much to cause your honest heart dismay in this stronghold, and I have done nothing to help it. I humbly ask your forgiveness.'

'You do not need it, lady. You have your duties to your family. I have indeed been troubled by what I have seen here, but I have lately resolved some of my perplexity in prayer.'

'I am delighted to hear that, Selyf,' she answered, 'for I know I have neglected you, and I have come, with some temerity, to ask you to help me again.'

'If there is any help I can give you, I am happy to do so. Indeed I could never find it in my heart to deny it to you. What do you want from me?'

'You know my lord Kynan and I exchanged vows of marriage, but it has always been a source of grief to me that our union was not blessed by a Christian. Will you do this for us now?'

'I would be glad to do it for you, lady, if it was our custom to bless marriage. But we only marry for necessity and do not think it is worth a blessing.'

'Please believe that my union with Kynan is not one of the flesh. It was only in obedience to my father's wishes and the demands of fate that I married him, but now it is my intention to bear a child, and so our marriage must at last be consummated. There are dangers in this for all of us, and I thought that a blessing would do something to protect us. But I will not ask you to do something you would consider improper.'

'Ah, lady, I knew it was your intention to have a child. I will confess to you that this has troubled me, the more so since you have not come to me before and spoken with your blessed hunger for the joy of faith.'

'Did you think I was removed from blessedness? You must have been deeply offended.'

'I am by no means offended, only confused. I have lived with destruction and chaos all my life, from the day when the men from Eirinnn destroyed the city I was born in and killed my family. In my wickedness that day I cursed God aloud, but I have not been brought to that evil state since I did penance for it.

'No, my lady, it is only a slight grief to me that since I came here I have found nothing as I anticipated. I must tell you now that the Bishop Cellach sent me to rid the forest of the evil I would find here. But I have not found evil. Though the people here are more wise and skilfull than any I have ever met, and there are great wonders, I have not found any heart laden with malice, nor a body glutted with greed and lust. Your father, the most terrible in his ways, is no longer in the flesh. How am I to render my account to the bishop?'

'You must tell him the truth,' said Marighal, 'that none here wish harm to any creature. If God wills it we will one day come to live in His holy laws.'

'But I fear I have deceived my sweet Abbot, also, for I told him about you. I told him about your great desire to be baptised into our faith, and yet now I see you as serene and joyful as a saint in heaven, although you have received neither instruction nor baptism. It was

Are we to believe this? Even if we do I do not think Cellach will. You must do better than that, Sebyf.

my impression that all your heart and soul were bent on the person of your husband.'

'Selyf, you have been deceived,' she said and led me to sit beside her on the river bank. 'I see that I must tell you some more about my history since I left you so that you may judge correctly.

'I am indeed very happy for I know beyond doubt that God loves me. To describe this knowledge to you I will tell you about another, similar experience. You know that we die and are born again from our father's seed. The time between birth and death seems no more than a night's sleep where sometimes we are troubled by dreams. When we are summoned to the flesh again we come into the light as ignorant as any human baby. It is only when we draw our first breath and smell the air that fills our bodies that we begin to recollect ourselves. Some moments later we open our eyes and see the faces of our sisters above us, and in that instant we feel the most painful joy. All of our past lifetimes are recalled to us in the passing of that instant, and our hearts are flooded with knowledge. This great moment of knowing is one of the few blessings of our state, and although much more time must be spent unravelling the tangled thread of our past into knowledge we can use, in that first, burning instant of revelation we acquire the sensations of a lifetime.

'On the day I left you and your brothers at the monastery I was struck to the heart with grief. In my affliction I wandered among the rocks of the seashore. I had thought that when I joined the family of Christ I would find humans with the charity to accept me. Yet even you, my soul-friend, turned your back on me, and drove me away when you found out about my father's strength. I saw then that humans would never take me to their hearts.'

'Sweet Marighal,' I cried, 'I have never ceased to repent that sad day's work. I was afraid when I saw you lift those rocks, and fear makes fools of the best of us. I beg you to forgive a foolish, weak old man.'

'I forgave you then, Selyf, for I am not so far from my human nature that I do not know fear. Moreover I am grateful to you for that day, for out of that suffering I learned the greatest wisdom I will ever know.

Perhaps it is the case that when she went to the city of St Thenew she was in a previous existence. That was not how she told it, but she was concealing so much at that time! We must search harder.

Lost! Lost! You have surrendered completely to the vile ones.

St Benedict writes of his
own experiences in similar
words. St Augustine, also.

What, then, does she think
God demands of us? Only that
we know and honour him?
If this were the case then why
do we do our service to him?
There would be no purpose in
even the slightest genuflection.
You are too simple and
trusting, Selyf. You have put
yourself into the hands of the
Antichrist.

And yet she is happy to
see her sisters being converted.
I can see again that this
is like the story of the Holy
mother Church who must be
torn apart and destroyed by the
barbarians before she can come
to herself. When she is restored
she has two forms; The
secular who go about in the
world, and do not study the
world of the past masters; the

'As I sat among the rocks in misery, weeping my forbidden tears, calmness came over me at last, like the silence that comes in the middle of a storm. Idly for a moment I watched a sea-urchin moving under the surface of the water, and as I looked a tiny breath of wind blew across the surface and made it shimmer. The shimmering stopped and once again I was looking into the dim water. Again the light came, shivering with delight, and was gone. And all at once the sunlight was a blinding joy to me. I saw that no matter what became of me or my family there would always, somewhere, be light flickering on water, and anyone who saw it with his heart would be blessed by it. Even when no one witnessed it, the light would be there and would be wonderful — one of the blessings God pours out on us when we are too small and selfish to see them.

'That instant was like the instant after birth when all my past flooded into my heart and it seemed that I had known this from the first day of my life. I know that God lives and loves me and that His generous love illuminates all creation, whether we see it or not. Nor will it cease to do so till His kingdom is established on earth and we see the light unclouded.

'Now I will have a child of my own whom I will teach to know God from his very first day, nor will he waste years in ignorance and pain as I did. He will also know another blessing that was denied me, for he will know his mother's care.'

'He will be a most fortunate child, Marighal. I hope that I, too will be here to instruct him.'

'I hope so also, Selyf, for all our sakes. We need your just and courageous heart to counsel us, for my sisters are full of dread since our father died. Now none of us will be born again and although I am happy, the fear of death is a torment to the others. In the dark hours of the night they see the darkness that awaits them for all eternity. In this agony they need you to help them find consolation, and if you can be spared to show them the truth it will be a great blessing.'

I promised at once to do all I could for the sisters, though I was not sure how I could help them. At dinner that evening everyone was silent, meditating on the future that night would bring. Even Grig did not give me his learned discourse, but spoke to me like one whose heart is in a place far off. After the meal Kynan and Marighal retired, and I did pronounce a blessing on their union, not because I wished to sanction marriage, but because it would have been a failure in charity to deny them any help within my power. Marighal thanked me from her heart, and I could see that Kynan was not displeased.

Grig did not join me that night, nor could I find sleep, although I lay in the bed till the first hour. After that I knew I would not be able to rest so I wandered about the stronghold alone.

This night the silence which had always filled the passages was gone. Instead they echoed with whispered portents of the things afoot. Now, for the first time, I felt the touch of malignity spreading from the walls, and as I passed the doors of the many chambers I saw that none of them were closed this night. I summoned up my courage and looked in through some of the doorways, and saw things that made me at last deny the wisdom of my senses. In one room I saw a gigantic worm with scales of red and gold and its tail, the thinnest part, was thicker than my thigh. As I stood at the doorway looking down onto it, it stirred slowly and began to raise its head, and I fled before its fiery eyes should meet mine. I halted at another door, nor did what I saw steady me for there was a vast globe of purest glass, and in it a fine young man, naked and still as death. Yet though he seemed dead there was no sign of corruption about his body.

I moved on and at another door saw a room filled with a shower of golden dust which fell and fell and never ceased, but where it came from and where it went to I could not see for both floor and roof were hidden in distance. It seemed as if the room was higher and deeper than the highest part of the stronghold. Another room was filled with the mirrors I had heard of, and I stood amazed at the image of myself seen clearly for the first time. I resisted this self-regard, and passed on nor did I look through any more doors, for my curiosity was at last exhausted. All around me the walls seemed almost to ring with their silent intimations, and I knew the hour Kynan had spoken of was at hand.

By and by I found myself at the roof of the hall in the Queen's garret. With wonder I found that all the sisters had gathered there before me. They watched my arrival

regular who hold themselves apart and work and pray and study in preparation for God's kingdom.

Am I to be like the accursed Pilate, Selyf? Must I walk away from this baffling problem? No! for that is a temptation in itself. Nevertheless both these wonders and these horrors are near to overwhelming me.

in silence then turned away again to gaze through the window at the place where the sun would rise. The moon had risen late, and her wan light shone on the plain and the wall of the stronghold like silver. I went to the window also and the sisters drew closer to me. Below at the outer gate I saw a shadowy figure moving, and the women around me cried out as they recognised it.

'It cannot be her,' said Eadain, 'for we have not felt her malign power for many months. I was sure that she was dead, yet now, there she stands and I am helpless again.'

All at once the door of the great hall opened. A bright shaft of light fell across the yard and lit the figure. I saw a woman, covered with gold from head to foot, her face as white as bone with eyes of ruby shining in the light from the doorway. On her head was a crown of fine wire, hung with glittering crystals. The shadow of a man appeared in the doorway, and I trembled for it was taller by half than an ordinary man. Beside me Roswitha groaned, 'Father!' and a sigh swept through the others. Even the infant Essyllt sat stiff with terror on her sister's lap.

Then the man stepped out of the doorway and we saw the irony, for it was Grig the dwarf. He ran toward the golden Queen and raised his hand above his head, and we saw that he held his great forehammer. With a mighty swing he struck the Queen's head from her body, yet the monstrous creature moved on across the yard on the wheels beneath her rigid skirt. Grig raised his hammer again, and brought it with terrible force down into the torso. There was a hideous shriek, the machine spun round, smashed into the doorpost and bore Grig to the ground with it. The yard was plunged into darkness.

The echoes of that shriek were cast all round the walls and even the passages around us were filled with them. The sound grew and gathered and hung in the air like swarming bees, and the sisters pressed closer around me. They kept looking fearfully at the door, as if waiting for someone, then the humming in the air grew to a howling, and there was the sound of a mighty wind blowing, pausing, blowing again, like a great breath passing in and out. The stone walls of the stronghold began to glow with a reddish light and this soon turned into a flickering and I knew that the Adversary was at hand. I began to make a prayer for our safety, and the howling grew louder and louder still. As it grew it was joined by other sounds like laughter and weeping and shouting, and it seemed as if the walls were recalling all that had happened over the centuries.

At last the din was so loud that I thought the stones would split. Beside me the women sobbed with fear and some of them had fainted and lay on the stone floor of the garret. More of them sighed and sank under the power of that noise, and I also began to feel pain as the pounding hammered at my feet. Lightning flashed in the sky outside, and I saw that the trees on the edge of the plain had been flattened by a mighty wind. I raised my hands and prayed that God would preserve the women from destruction.

'Merciful Father, spare them so that they may be born again into Your mysteries, for they are without sin.'

How can you say this? Who do you think will hear such a scandalous prayer?

Then I felt that heat striking through the soles of my sandals, and I saw that the stones of the floor had begun to glow also. I bowed my head and gave myself up for dead, saying, 'Almighty God, Sweet Jesus, hear me — if it is Your will that I now enter Your kingdom, take me, but I beg You to spare these women, for they are not ready.'

In the room the hangings on the walls beside me and the rugs on the floor were beginning to smoulder, and smoke drifted around the room.

The noise seemed to get louder and I cried aloud, 'Go, whatever you may be, go far away and leave us in peace. Your place is no longer on the earth and you cannot come back. Go and leave us to find our way to God. And for yourself, go hence and seek Him in His mercy and might. Humble yourself before Him and trust that His grace will find you. Leave us in peace!'

And I took out the flask of holy water and smashed it on the floor.

Then I saw that Roswitha and the infant and all the others lay helpless and unmoving at my feet. Their clothes had taken fire from the stones underneath them and all the women with unbound hair had flames around their heads. I tried to lift them off the ground onto the couches but the furniture was alight and there was nothing to be done, there were so many.

In a bitter rage I shrieked, 'Is this the work of a loving father? Does he burn the hair of his dear children and leave their bodies to be consumed by fire? Go and leave your darlings to one who knows how to care for the helpless. Leave your lambs to a fitting shepherd, and cease from consuming them in your eternal spite. Your time is past and their souls might be free. But you cannot forget that you were once all powerful, and you will destroy them rather than lose them. Yet I tell you now that though you may be damned, your little ones need not be, if only their malicious parent will yield place!'

And with that, everything stopped. A great darkness fell across the world, and the moon, the plain, and the forest disappeared from sight. I thought at once that I was blind, then there came the sound of the rushing wind once more, but only once, and I knew it was a sigh. Then light came back and I looked at the horizon, and there I saw a thin white line of light, for the sun was rising.

In the growing light the garret was revealed to me. All about lay a ruin of ashes where the wooden walls had charred and burnt, and most of the hangings and furniture were damaged beyond repair. The women began to rouse themselves again and stood up slowly feeling their charred hair and clothing. They looked about them and were dismayed at the destruction of their refuge.

'Look, sister, look at this carpet. It took me two lifetimes to make it and now it is lying in ashes under my feet.'

'Here is a cushion I embroidered as a child a century ago — it has fallen to shreds in my hand.'

'This is the hanging I made after Grainne was taken — see how even high upon the wall the smoke has ruined it.'

'Do not grieve for these things, my children,' I said, 'they are only posessions you have made which will shackle your souls. Now you will have better ways to spend your time.'

'Monk, you must not speak slightingly of them,' said Evabyth. 'For a very long time these things were all we had that we could call our own. In our empty lives they were our consolation and our pride. Give us leave to mourn them a while, for the time to make them again

Thanks be to God.

Can it be true that you have prevailed against the adversary, Selyf?

is no longer ours. We will be dead long before we could replace a tenth of what was here.'

I saw the truth of what she said and left them for a while. I made haste to the yard below to see what had become of Grig. In the chilly light of dawn he lay in a mass of jewels and gold cloth and tiny wheels. His forehammer lay beside him and he was dead. The Queen's mask glared balefully at him and I turned it over, for it was not fitting that his artefact should triumph over him.

'Poor creature,' I said, 'his like will not be seen again.'

Marighal and her sisters came out of the hall just then and when they saw that Grig was dead they broke down and wept. I saw that at last, by God's mercy, the copious tears that ran down their faces were purest water.

'Father of my hand and of my mind,' said Marighal, 'I shall revere your memory for as long as I live, nor will it be forgotten that your skill was unsurpassed throughout this nation.'

We took him to the place where his master's body was buried and dug his grave. We laid him in it with his hammer and his burning glass, as was his due as smith and firemaster, and as we covered his body for the last time Marighal said, 'Grig's great knowledge was not merely his way of increasing comfort. It was the very well-spring of his soul. He did not see fit to let his wisdom run like a river that has burst its banks and turn the land into marsh. In a marsh the water is thinly spread and soon becomes a poison so that nothing can grow and foul mists arise to threaten man and beast. Grig kept his knowledge within strong banks so that it ran in a clear, powerful stream along a fitting course, and only those with heart enough to step far into that stream could benefit from it. With God's grace I found the courage to face the strong force of knowledge, and now with His grace I will send the little I have saved towards my son.'

I am sure of this. My own learning is certainly thin and fruitless. I can find nothing more to say.

With this we closed the grave and returned him to his mother. In the days of mourning which followed I had time to meditate on my situation and I have come to a melancholy decision.

I see it as my clear duty, father, to stay with these women. I am sure in my heart that this is the right thing

196

*How could anyone deny
you this, father? Whoever loves
his neighbour will not wrong
him. 'Who is my neighbour?'
'Anyone who needs my care'
said the Lord. Perhaps you
will bring even the daughters
of the adversary to Christ by
a simple act of charity. Only
God knows. To love, then, is
the whole of the Law, and
there is no hope beyond that.*

to do, and that if you were here this would be your advice to me. When the king leaves us tomorrow, he will take this letter and send it on to the city of St Modan for me. I can do no more than hope that it will reach you in time for you to forgive your distant child. Kynan himself will return to his city and build a house there for those sisters who have chosen his protection. I hope and pray that the bishop there will not discover their nature, for if he does I am not confident that he will find the charity to keep them in the populace. I will stay in the stronghold here and work to bring the younger ones closer to God and his holy laws for they most urgently need me.

There is a further reason for my staying here. At times, when I have been reading the office, I have felt a great presence beside me, and sometimes also I hear a footfall, yet when I turn I can see no one. I am afraid there is still a restless soul wandering among us, and I am sure that his power is ready to do us harm. Therefore I will stay and contain this evil, if God grants me the grace to do so.

My dearest friend and Abbot, I shall not look upon your sweet face again, not even in death, but though this is a terrible grief to me I will not be overwhelmed by it, for I know that I shall see you again before long. My only regret is that you are left alone in your finest hour and that your last rite will be administered by those pitiful few who are the young men of our order. It is not fitting that one so great as you should go down to death with no friend of your childhood in attendance. My heart's darling, if there is a breath in your body I beg you to pray for me as I pray for you alone here, with none to guide my faltering steps. And pray also that the women here who have lived so long in darkness will be spared many days yet to journey to the light.

Valete.

POST SCRIPTUM.

I have not lived long in this world yet I have already travelled far and met all manner of people. I have seen my family and friends murdered; I have seen the order I was born into reviled and betrayed; I have seen fire and destruction on all sides until I was sure that these were the last days of man. These terrible things have brought me many painful lessons and each year I found that what I had denied and doubted one year I was forced to accept the next. In all this time, I have never doubted that one day the final and certain truth would be shown to me. Tonight, as I sit in the ruins of the stronghold, I have even come to doubt this.

One day I watched the pupils in my care work over their letters. I realised suddenly that each saw the marks on the page with his own, separate eyes, but that all of them together heard me when I told them the meaning of the marks. But if no-one had read the passage to the boys there was no other way that they could receive the meaning, and the black marks on the vellum would be no more than black marks. Is this what we get from God — some meaning for the scrawl that surrounds us?

Last night I had a terrible dream. Underneath the ruins there is a small chamber and in it there is a great stone table with channels cut in it. It is as long as a man, and I decided to rest there at night for the nights are cold and getting colder. But I will not do so again, for while lying there I dreamt of my father. I begged him with tears in my eyes to come away with me but he smiled and shook his head at me, and said, 'I am sorely needed in this place. Why should I leave when elsewhere there is nothing left for me? Our order is at an end, and must take its place in the memory of man. Here there is hope for the future.'

He vanished from my sight, and at last I saw the woman, and she was carrying a child — a boy of very great beauty.

'This is my son Drustan,' she said, 'and through him our line will continue. He is my offering to the world, and through him mankind will learn a new way of looking at itself.'

And beyond her, then, I saw her father standing, and I was afraid. His stature was great, and his shoulders were wide, but these were nothing. The real terror came from his eyes which seemed to glow with fire.

'You do well to lie on our death-stone, mortal man,' he said, 'for it speaks to you of your corruptibility. I kept my daughters confined here so that they would not change and be perverted into the monsters I had seen out in the world. Yet in spite of my strength and wisdom, I could not sustain my rule forever, and in spite of my wishes, changes have come about. Nevertheless, I am not displeased with my daughters in their new life. I see in them a new truth, that corruption is the risk we must take if we are to approach perfection. My daughter Marighal shows me with her child that there is a possibility of renewal, and therein lies hope. I will pass from men's eyes and let events take their course, as a river flows to the sea.

'But whenever mankind forget my daughters, the clever, the kind and the wise, I will come forth and walk the world again, and I will increase their sorrow a thousandfold.'

Then he vanished, and I woke and fled from that place without hesitation. Now I do not know where I shall go, for it is sure I cannot face those good old men at Brychan.

197

GLOSSARY.

All the places named in this book are real, and the people named in the peripheral action are historical figures. Places outside Britain have been given their modern names, but otherwise I have used the names which would have been current. I did this so that the reader would not be misled by the mention of a familiar name, and his mind would not be filled with associations like motorways, street lighting, multi-storey buildings and the furniture of modern towns. This Glossary is intended to explain some of the basic facts, since I see no point in mystification for its own sake, but if the reader were to read this later rather than sooner he might be better entertained. I note in advance the impatience of historians with my treating as fact that which is only interpretation.

Alclyth. Also known as Alcluith, Alt Clut, etc. Known sometimes as Dun Breatann, now reduced to Dumbarton. The rock of Dumbarton stands on the edge of the Clyde overlooking the Vale of Leven to the north. An impregnable situation for a stronghold, it was the capital of the ancient British kingdom of Strathclyde from the end of the Roman occupation until Strathclyde was absorbed into the kingdom of Scotland in 1034. Cumberland, (see below) with which it shared a constantly varying border, was also a Brythonic kingdom, but both had a precarious independence as kings of England, Scotland and Northumberland invaded throughout the centuries. In the tenth century Strathclyde extended as far south as Stainsmore as the Britons rallied, for the last time. At the time this story is set (985-7) the king of the English was Aethelred, not a king noted for his competence, and Kenneth of Alban, was a powerful leader. He kept the kingdom stable for twenty four years and consolidated his hold on much of the territory of the north. Under him, Domnall and his son Maelcolum held Strathclyde, on the understanding that they would keep the vikings of Jorvik off the Irish Sea coast.

Athcliath. Now known as Dublin, at the time of the story it was a Danish colony held uneasily by Gluniarainn, son of Anlaf Cuaran, half-brother of Eithne (see below). It was also the administrative centre of the Celtic church, since their holdings on Iona had become unsafe and the congregation of monks there seems to have been a mere token.

Beya. St. Beya, (Bega) an anchoress who lived on the island of Little Cumbrae in the firth of Clyde. She seems to have specialised in scourging.

'Bone without flesh' (p. 119). This is a translation of an anonymous Anglo-Norman poem.

Brychan. Brechin. The church of the Holy Trinity there was a College of 'Culdees' who are taken by many to be the last manifestation of the old Celtic church in Scotland. They came from Ireland, called themselves the Companions of God i.e. his personal bodyguard sworn to die for him, and their discipline was considered excessively harsh. The Celtic church in Ireland seems to have undergone a reformation in the ninth century and this was carried over to Scotland in the early tenth where it enjoyed a brief period of popularity. However the Benedictines who had established themselves in the administrative capital of Pictland in the eighth century would not accept them as regular monks because of their alien practices.

Caerluel. Carlisle. As I noted before, our idea of the Anglo-Scottish border is meaningless in this context. Dun Mael, for instance had claimed all the territory from Glasgow to Lancaster in the previous century and various kings, bishops and earls of Northumberland had claimed from Lothian to Derby with impermanent success over the centuries. Carlisle's importance during this period was that it overlooked the main route from York to Ireland, and whoever held it held his northern kingdom secure, be he Viking or Briton.

Candida Casa. The White House — according to tradition the original foundation of St. Nynian on the isle of Whithorn. It is said he was a Roman who first brought the word of Christ to north Britain. The see of Candida Casa was Anglo-Saxon until 803 and until David Canmore came to tidy up the Church in the kingdom of Scotland in the twelfth century the history of the cult of St Ninian is unrecorded.

Cathures. Generally reputed to be the monastery of St. Kentigern in Glasgow, although it, too, had to wait for David Canmore to establish it as the see we know today.

City. The oldest meaning of the word denotes a community of Christians. It would take care of the spiritual needs of the district, and provide education and health care to all who came there. Members of the community, particularly the consecrated bishops also travelled abroad to carry the Word to the pagans and maintain discipline among Christians. It was an enclosure surrounded by a low earth rampart, or a stone wall, or even a hedge. The interior was sacred ground and centred on a cross or the tomb of the founding saint. Depending on the wealth and importance of the foundation there would be a common hall, a guest house, an infirmary, a library, a schoolhouse and the cells of the monks. In some, where there was a constant threat from pirates and slavers, there were watch-towers built with the doors raised above the ground and access by a removable ladder. The most important place would be the oratory or oratories which would contain the relics of the saint(s). This would be in the centre of a burial ground since the devoted would demand to be buried close to their saint to gain his support at the gates of heaven. Marighal would not notice these burials in the City since only kings would have memorials at the time. All the buildings would be made of the commonest local material — stone, wood, or wattle. The layout would have been arbitrary, although it is probable that the Abbot's family house would be nearest the shrine, unless he was an anchorite, in which case he would live in a hut at the farthest edge of the City. There were often several such huts in the City, called 'Dark Houses' and they would be reserved for anchorites and penitents.

Coarb. Senior monks — abbots, and, less frequently, bishops — with an hereditary title to the lands of the City were called coarbs (combairbis — heirs) of the

200

founding Saint. In the early days of the Church a claim could be made up to seven degrees of kinship distance, and after that the Abbacy was elective. Before consecration the heir would be required to marry in a levitical fashion, in order to continue the succession, thereafter to set his wife aside after consecration at age thirty. Latterly the title coarb became a formality as the Abbots took vows of virginity and election became the method of chosing a successor.

Confession. Both public and private, this was not a sacrament in the early Celtic church so a priest was necessary only to select a suitable penance.

Cymri. Not Wales, but the area roughly equivalent to Cumbria of modern times plus or minus bits of Southern Scotland. At that time it would still be known under its Brythonic name by most of the denizens.

Eithne Cuaransdottir. Daughter of Anlaf (Olaf) Cuaran, king of the Irish Vikings. She was the wife of Hlodvir of Orkney and mother of Sigurd the Stout. She was reputed to be a witch and gave her son a magic banner which was supposed to ensure his safety in battle.

Erenach. (Aireinnegh) A layman or junior monk in charge of the monastery lands and of collecting tribute from the outlying farms. Such a post was essential if the abbey's holdings were particularly large or if the Abbot were an anchorite.

Galwythel. Galloway. At one time or another part of Strathclyde, Cumbria, Northumberland etc.

Godescalc. A Benedictine monk of Fulda, who died in 869, in exile and at odds with the authorities. He disagreed with the accepted view of predestination, and said that God had determined everything from the beginning of the world.

Golden City. Girvan on the Carrick coast. If built of the local sandstone it would look golden in its early days.

Gobhan. Govan on the south bank of the Clyde. In recent times it has been absorbed into the city of Glasgow, but previously it was a parish in its own right covering a large territory on both sides of the river. At the time of the story it is possible that it would be a settlement of some significance. The evidence for this is to be seen in the parish church where there is a large stone sarcophagus, said to be the coffin of a Saxon saint called Constantine. The monastery was overrun by Vikings at some point in the ninth century and settled by these invaders who left five fine 'hog-back' gravestones, also in the parish church.

Gorze. Near Metz — the first foundation of reformed Benedictines later known as Clunaics, it was a haven of scholarship and learning. A famous Scot, Macallan trained there and he later went on to become Abbot of Waulsort in Dinant on the Belgian Meuse.

Hours. The canonical hours — times for prayer and religious observance in a monastery - were part of the struggle between the Columbans and the Benedictines. According to the Irish Annals most of the Celtic church had fallen into line with Benedictine practice by the eighth century, but a lot of local differences continued. Hw and Selyf observe eight hours, secunda, terce, sext, none, vespers, nightfall, and midnight matins (because of the northerly latitude the sun sets late and rises early leading to a conflation of the two). At that time the day was thought to end at sunset so that the midnight office was the first of the new day, and the second hour the first of the working day. After the seventh century some monasteries added compline. The prayers were originally psalms read, not recited, but as time went by, antiphonaries were developed with new prayers, and chants of higher complexity.

Hy Columbcille. Iona. The original foundation of the Celtic church in Scotland. In the early ninth century the relics of the founder were transferred to Kells, and in 825 they disappeared but seem to have been returned to Iona because in 850 on the pretext of security they were rapidly removed to Dunkeld. There the bishop of Fortrunn claimed to be coarb of Columbcille and leader of the church in Scotland with the relics to prove it. However in 908 the primacy was transferred to St Andrews. As the power of the kings of Alban grew so did the see of St Andrews so that it did not need the relics of Columbcille as testimony. At this point they seem to have returned to Ireland for good. On the island of Hy there was often a dual Abbacy, presumably to keep the peace between the Celtic monks and the Benedictines, since both orders had claims to the island. Sometimes the Celtic Abbot would be an anchorite or hermit, and the other Abbot would be the administrator. Sometimes the Benedictine Abbot would be ordained as a bishop so that he could perform the rites of the episcopate, but since Columbcille himself was not so consecrated his followers would find this distasteful. Despite upheavals and controversies the sanctity of the island was never in dispute and kings of Ireland and Scotland went to Iona at the end of their reign — voluntarily or otherwise. At the time of the story nothing remained on Hy island. The last Abbot and his fifteen monks who were killed there had been seeking martyrdom, and found it on Christmas day 986. The rest of the congregation and the few books and other items left to them by the Vikings had gone to Ireland.

Inan. St. Inan, (possibly Finan). He is reputed to have travelled to Rome and Jerusalem and settled at Irvine on the coast of Ayrshire where his cell was visited by king Kenneth in 839. Many miracles were performed at his invocation.

Jorvik. York, capital of the Danish kingdom of Northumberland. This see had often included large sections of southern Scotland, and monks of this city would be enthusiastic about reasserting any territorial claims to increase the power of their Danish overlords.

Kyil. Kyle. The area roughly covering what used to be called north west Ayrshire and western Renfrewshire, now called Kyle. The only thing you can be sure of is that things will change.

Kyngaradh. Kingarth. The holy city on the island of Bute.

MacFerdalaig, Cellach. Bishop of Alban, he went to Rome to receive the pall from the pope enhancing both hisown prestige and that of king Kenneth.

Modan, City of. The holy city at Ardchattan on Loch Etive.

Queen of Gold. Charlemagne had a near full-size effigy of the Virgin made in gold. The ambassador to his court from Persia, Haroun al Rashid, gave him a clock with knights driven by the clockwork parading on it. So the technology by which Grig and his brothers could have made such a machine did exist at the time.

Rintsnoc. Portpatrick, a small port on the Rinns of Galloway, and the site of the fictional monastery.

Rosnat. The town of Whithorn, landward of the Isle of Whithorn, it later became the site of David Canmore's monastery of St. Ninian.

Scolog. Also 'ferlane' (ferleighin). His would be the responsibility for the boys sent to the monastery. Not all the boys would be intended for admission to the order, but any man who wished his son to read, write and calculate would send him to the monks for education, and, most probably, to mix with the right sort of people.

Thenew. St Enoch. Mother of St Kentigern (Cunotegernos — hound of God), or Mungo (Munchu — darling dog). She was forced into marriage with Owain ap Urien, king of the Strathclyde Britons. She fled from him, raped and pregnant — some say adulterous and same but he caught up with her. Rather than pollute his hands with her blood, he had her put in a box and pushed out to sea. It is said that either she was rescued by St Serf who pulled her out of the sea at Culross in Fife or that she fled for sanctuary to the old man at his monastery on Loch Leven, where she brought the boy into the world. Serf recognised qualities in the child and gave him the education necessary to be a bishop. He was a credit to his teachers.

Walciodorum, Waulsort. See note on Gorze, above.